S0-AGB-257

PRAISE FOR THE OPEN BOOK MYSTERIES

"You won't want to miss new amateur sleuth Penelope Parish as she travels across the pond to the Open Book bookstore in Merrie Old England. Margaret Loudon has penned an irresistible cozy mystery that will delight your imagination and introduce you to a cast of interesting and quirky characters."

—*New York Times* bestselling author Paige Shelton

"A bookshop, lots of tea, a pub, and an English village filled with quirky characters—Margaret Loudon's *Murder in the Margins* has all the ingredients for a delightful read!"

—Marty Wingate, *USA Today* bestselling author of *The Bodies in the Library*

"Bookstores and tearooms and castles in England. Village fetes, charming police officers, and handsome aristocrats. Tea and Cornish pasties and fairy cakes. A town named Upper Chumley-on-Stoke. Plus, a writer struggling with writer's block. What's not to like in this absolutely delightful new series by Margaret Loudon? I can't wait to see what Pen Parish and her friends at the Open Book get up to next."

—Vicki Delany, author of *Silent Night, Deadly Night*

"Delightfully unpredictable characters, a charming sleuth, and a touch of romance enhance this sophomore entry."

—*Kirkus Reviews*

ALSO BY MARGARET LOUDON

The Open Book Mysteries
MURDER IN THE MARGINS
A FATAL FOOTNOTE
PERIL ON THE PAGE

WRITING AS PEG COCHRAN

Gourmet De-Lite Mysteries
ALLERGIC TO DEATH
STEAMED TO DEATH
ICED TO DEATH

Cranberry Cove Mysteries
BERRIED SECRETS
BERRY THE HATCHET
DEAD AND BERRIED

Farmer's Daughter Mysteries
NO FARM, NO FOUL
SOWED TO DEATH
BOUGHT THE FARM

Murder, She Reported Series
MURDER, SHE REPORTED
MURDER, SHE UNCOVERED
MURDER, SHE ENCOUNTERED

WRITING AS MEG LONDON

Sweet Nothing Lingerie Series
MURDER UNMENTIONABLE
LACED WITH POISON
A FATAL SLIP

A Deadly
Dedication

MARGARET LOUDON

BERKLEY PRIME CRIME
New York

BERKLEY PRIME CRIME
Published by Berkley
An imprint of Penguin Random House LLC
penguinrandomhouse.com

ISBN: 9780593547175

First Edition: August 2023

Printed in the United States of America
1   3   5   7   9   10   8   6   4   2

Book design by Gaelyn Galbreath

To everyone who has encouraged me in my writing for all these years—my hubby, Fletcher Cochran; sister, Chris Knoer; and daughters, Francesca and Annabelle

A Deadly
Dedication

ONE

~⚬~

Penelope "Pen" Parish never thought she'd write one bestseller, let alone two, but unless her editor was lying (and that wouldn't be like Bettina at all—she was usually brutally honest), her latest Gothic novel, *The Woman in the Fog*, had indeed landed on the bestseller list.

After her first hit, *Lady of the Moors*, Pen had come smack up against that wall known as writer's block and had chased her illusive muse all the way to Upper Chumley-on-Stoke, England, where she'd taken a writer-in-residence position at the Open Book bookstore. The grass is always greener on the other side (of the Atlantic, in this case), right?

And, much to her amazement, the change of scenery had worked its magic. Her writer's block had dissolved into thin air, and she'd managed to produce another best-seller by the skin of her teeth. *The Woman in the Fog* was doing quite nicely, and Penelope was settling down in Chum, as it was known to the residents, equally well.

It was late afternoon and dusk was quickly descending. Penelope saw the streetlights winking on along the high street through the diamond-paned windows of the Open Book. She was shelving some books for Mabel Morris, the owner, when the door opened and Gladys Watkins rushed in.

Gladys owned the Pig in a Poke, Chumley's butcher shop, and had dashed across the high street with her coat thrown over her apron. Her blue eyes were even wider than normal and her hair, which was never particularly well-coifed, looked even more disheveled than usual.

"I'm not late, am I?" she called out to no one in particular.

Mabel looked up from the invoices she was thumbing through and glanced at her watch.

"We still have twenty minutes."

Gladys's shoulders sagged in relief.

Pen put down the stack of books she was holding and wandered over to the front counter.

"Not late for what?" she said.

"The nerve of the man." Gladys's chin quivered.

"Indeed!" India Culpepper joined them at the counter.

Thin to the point of being gaunt, India had elbows and knees that stuck out at sharp angles and was to the manor born—a distant cousin of Arthur Worthington, the Duke of Upper Chumley-on-Stoke. Unfortunately, she was also one of any number of England's impoverished nobility who clung to the family silver with its engraved crests even as they darned the holes in their socks and put pots under the leaks in the roof.

"Late for what?" Penelope repeated. "What man?"

Gladys fixed her with a stare. "You've had your nose

stuck in that book you're writing or you would have heard by now. Simeon Foster—what kind of name is that anyway?—plans to open a new shop in town. Some fancy gourmet place. With pastries flown in from France and chocolates from Belgium. Well, la-di-da. And even worse, farm-sourced meats. The nerve of him. Blimey! Don't all meats come from a farm? It's going to put all of us out of business! My shop, the Icing on the Cake, the Sweet Tooth, the Jolly Good Grub." Gladys sputtered to a halt.

"I wouldn't worry too much if I were you," Mabel said, brushing some fuzz off the front of her Shetland sweater.

"That's a fine thing for you to say. He's not going to be selling books, is he now?"

"The people who will patronize Simeon Foster's proposed gourmet shop aren't our customers anyway. They'll be the new money who live in developments like Birnam Wood, where all the houses are fake Tudor or newly built Georgians. They do most of their shopping in London. They only pop into the local Tesco when they suddenly find themselves without milk or something equally mundane."

Gladys didn't look convinced. "I don't know." She shook her head and her chin wobbled.

India fingered the strand of yellowing pearls around her thin neck and said in her reedy voice, "And that's not the worst of it. This Mr. Foster, whoever he is, wants to renovate that vacant building next to the one where those law offices are. He plans to put in a large plate-glass window to display his wares and make it more modern. It will look so dreadfully common." She sniffed.

Upper Chumley-on-Stoke was a medieval village approximately an hour's train ride outside of London. It was proud of its history and the residents had fought long and hard against paving the cobblestoned streets or erecting a stoplight at the lone intersection where more than one accident had occurred in the wee hours as the pubs were closing. The residents had successfully lobbied against the former but had lost the battle when it came to the stoplight, the town council having been more concerned for the lives of its citizens than the aesthetics of the high street.

"I still don't know what you're worried about being late for." Penelope pushed her glasses up her nose with her finger.

Mabel leaned her elbows on the counter. As a former MI6 analyst, she kept her calm in even the most trying circumstances, and this was no exception.

"Mr. Foster has requested a permit for the renovations he plans to undertake. The town council is meeting to hear objections to the proposal and will be voting on it tonight. It should make for a lively discussion," she said wryly.

"I'm certainly going to give them a piece of my mind." Gladys shook her fist in the air, color rising up her neck and turning her cheeks red.

India glanced at Gladys in alarm, a look of disapproval crossing her face. Penelope could imagine what India was thinking. *One doesn't make a scene in public. It's simply not done.*

Just then Figgy wheeled over a cart with a steaming teapot, cups and saucers, and a plate of freshly made shortbread biscuits.

Figgy, who was more formally known as Lady Fiona Innes-Goldthorpe, ran the tea shop inside the Open Book. She reminded Penelope of a sprite, with her short, spiky hair, heart-shaped face, and delicate figure. She was wearing one of her vintage clothing finds—a boho-looking tasseled maxi dress in diaphanous blue fabric. She and Penelope had become instant friends upon Penelope's arrival at the store. Two peas in a pod, Mabel had declared them.

"Does anyone fancy a cuppa?" she said, holding the teapot over one of the cups.

A chorus of yesses greeted her, and she began to pour.

Penelope reached for a shortbread biscuit. Lunch, which had been sketchy at best, was a distant memory nibbled at as she worked on her next book. There was no rest for the wicked as her grandmother Parish used to say, and that was certainly true in publishing. You'd barely turned around after handing in one manuscript before it was time to start another.

Penelope mentally reminded herself of her good fortune in being able to earn her living writing and not at some straitlaced job that required her to dress up every day and spend eight or more hours staring at the three walls of a cubicle.

Mabel glanced at her watch again. "We'll have to make it quick if we want to get to the meeting on time."

Just then the door to the Open Book flew open and a man rushed in.

"Rupert," Mabel said with a frown. "I'm sorry, but we're about to close. The town council meeting will be starting shortly."

Rupert Yardley was short and what might be termed stocky but was, in his case, mostly muscle and very little fat. He played right wing on the Upper Chumley-on-Stoke football team, the Chums. He was a solicitor by trade but was better known as the local historian. He'd been working on a book detailing the history of Upper Chumley-on-Stoke for more years than anyone could remember.

"Are you going to the meeting?" Gladys said, her face and neck still blotched red from her recent outburst.

"Meeting? What meeting?" Rupert looked around him as if the answer could be found written on the walls. "Oh, you mean the town council meeting," he said as the answer dawned on him. "I bloody well am." His face had become nearly as red as Gladys's. "What cheek the man has."

Figgy poured another cup of tea and handed it to Rupert. He smiled briefly. "Lovely, thank you."

Gladys looked at him out of the corner of her eye. "Bollocks! What do you care? It's not as if Foster's new gourmet shop is going to put you out of business."

Rupert looked momentarily startled but then recovered. "I should think not. Plenty of work to go around. Contracts to be negotiated and all that." He took a sip of his tea, then put his teacup down on the saucer with a clang. "I object most strenuously, however, to the renovations Foster plans to make. They will destroy the integrity of the town. Upper Chumley-on-Stoke has a magnificent history that goes back centuries—"

"We should leave shortly," Mabel said, cutting Rupert short before he could truly get off and running. It took little more than a willing or captive audience for him to launch into the history of Chumley.

"Quite." Rupert handed his teacup to Figgy. "Where is this meeting to be held again?"

"At Worthington House." India lifted her chin. "Arthur has graciously allowed us to use the great hall for the meeting, given the number of people that are expected to attend."

Foster had certainly stirred up a hornet's nest when he chose Upper Chumley-on-Stoke for the location of one of his chain gourmet shops, Penelope thought as she slipped on her jacket and wound her scarf around her neck. It promised to be entertaining. She'd never seen everyone so agitated. Hopefully the vote tonight would go in the town's favor.

TWO

❧❧❧

It was a cold night. Penelope tightened her scarf around her neck and pulled her gloves from her jacket pocket while Mabel locked the front door to the Open Book. She glanced up at the sky, which looked like a piece of black velvet cloth sprinkled with stars.

Rupert mounted his bicycle, which he'd left leaning against the outside of the building and with a crisp *cheerio*, pedaled off into the distance, the headlight mounted to the frame of his bike lighting a path in front of him.

All the shops along the high street were closed, their storefronts dark and with shadows pooling by their doors. Candles flickered in the window of Pierre's next door, Chumley's only high-end restaurant, and the faint aroma of garlic, onions and herbs drifted into the night air. Across the street, lights blazed at the Chumley Chippie, which Penelope could swear never closed. It seemed that the residents of Upper Chumley-on-Stoke had an appetite for fish-and-chips at all hours of the day and night.

They waved good-bye to Gladys and India, who headed to Gladys's car behind the Pig in a Poke. After a brief discussion, Pen and Figgy had agreed to go with Mabel. Riding with Figgy was a hair-raising experience and while Pen had acquired a new car, her MINI having been totaled when she was escaping a killer, she still hadn't quite mastered driving on the left side of the street and was prone to wandering over the center line into the wrong lane.

Mabel had suggested Penelope consider a bicycle instead given the number of near misses she'd racked up since arriving in Chumley. But then the thought of Penelope riding through traffic with no metal around her for protection had caused Mabel to swiftly reconsider her suggestion.

"The heat will take a few minutes," Mabel said as she started the car and pulled away from the curb.

Penelope hugged herself against the cold as they made their way down the high street.

"Rupert was certainly full of himself tonight, wasn't he?" Figgy said.

Mabel glanced over at her briefly. "He still hasn't recovered from the drama of the Tesco being built. He was dead set against it. The entire town was as well but, in the end, I think most residents would agree that it's been terribly handy having a large-chain grocery store so close by."

Mabel flicked on her bright lights as they headed away from town and down the high street, where the road dwindled into little more than a country lane with darkened fields on either side.

"Although no existing buildings were renovated to accommodate the Tesco and a brand-new building was constructed on empty land, Rupert still objected on the grounds that it was the first modern building erected in Chumley and might lead to wholesale destruction of the town," Mabel explained.

"Why did the residents object?" Penelope said.

"They were worried that it would cause an increase in traffic, but since it's open for such long hours, there haven't been any problems. Housewives tend to shop in the morning and afternoon, while others pop in after working hours. I've yet to see a huge crowd in there no matter what time I've gone."

They were nearing Worthington House now, which sat on top of a rise and could be seen from all over Chumley. "Worthington House" was something of a misnomer—it was an imposing structure—a medieval castle that reminded Penelope of Windsor Castle.

Cars, lined up one behind the other, waited to pull into the driveway, and Mabel joined them.

"Quite the turnout," she said as they inched forward.

Finally, they reached the parking lot itself, where there were signs directing visitors who were there for tours of the castle. A jitney with *Sunshine Retirement Community* painted on the side was leaving as Mabel pulled into an empty parking spot.

Mabel beeped the car doors locked, and they joined the stream of people headed toward the side door of the castle.

The great hall, true to its name, was a vast space with a massive stone fireplace at one end and heraldic banners hanging from the ceiling. Folding chairs had been arranged in tidy rows, with a long table facing them at the front of the hall. A microphone sat at each place, a tangle of wires trailing off to the side. A standing microphone was in front of the table.

Excited chatter echoed around the room as people

greeted each other. Beryl Kent, Penelope's sister, who was hiding out in England after her husband was convicted of running a massive Ponzi scheme, was already there. She waved them over to the seats she'd saved.

"I got here early," Beryl said, smoothing down her blond bob. "I couldn't believe how many people were already here. I tried to get seats as close to the front as possible."

Penelope, Mabel, and Figgy took the empty seats and slipped off their coats.

Penelope noticed that Beryl's eyes were shining, and she seemed more animated than usual.

She leaned toward her sister and whispered, "What's up? You seem excited about something."

Beryl ducked her head. "I am."

Penelope waited a beat, but Beryl didn't elaborate. "What about?"

"I can't tell you now," Beryl whispered back. "I'll tell you later."

Why was Beryl being so mysterious? Penelope wondered.

Penelope looked around. She had been in the great hall several times before and a chill usually emanated from the stone walls, but tonight the heat of so many bodies had warmed the room. She couldn't believe how many people had turned up for the meeting. It looked as if all of Upper Chumley-on-Stoke was in attendance. Foster's proposed gourmet shop was certainly causing a fuss.

"Look." Mabel poked Penelope. "There's Simeon Foster himself."

Penelope recognized him from his photograph in the paper. He had small eyes rimmed by dark circles, a high forehead made higher by his receding hairline; a mustache; and a small, pointed goatee.

Penelope leaned toward Mabel. "Who is that woman with him? Is that his wife?" The couple appeared to be having an intense conversation.

"No, that's Clementine Harrison. She's the owner of the Icing on the Cake."

Clementine was a tiny woman—Foster had to bend forward to hear her—with a narrow face and a sallow complexion. Her blond hair was streaked with strands of gray and hung rather limply to her shoulders.

Figgy turned toward Penelope and Mabel. "It looks like they're having a bit of a set-to."

"I'll say." Mabel glanced at the couple again. "Clementine appears to be giving Foster a piece of her mind."

Penelope watched as Clementine and Foster continued their discussion. Suddenly Clementine's face went white, and Penelope was afraid she was about to faint.

Foster, on the other hand, had a satisfied look on his face as he turned and walked toward the front of the room.

Someone tapped a microphone and static echoed around the hall. Slowly the chatter died away and the only sound was the occasional scraping of a chair against the stone floor.

The hall was filling up and a number of people had filed in and taken seats at the table in front. Penelope was surprised to see Clementine Harrison joining them.

Mabel touched Penelope's arm. "We should get at least one vote for our side. Clementine surely wouldn't want a shop in Chumley that had pastries flown in from France every day. What would happen to Icing on the Cake?"

The town mayor, who was seated in the middle of the table, tapped the microphone in front of him. A screech reverberated around the room. He cleared his throat. "Welcome, everyone, welcome." He motioned toward some people hovering by the door as if they were prepared to bolt at a moment's notice. "There are still plenty of seats. Come on in."

Once the room was silent, the meeting was called to order and Foster was invited to be the first speaker.

He rose from his seat and approached the microphone. A few moments passed while he fiddled with it, moving it up and down until it was exactly the right height. He smiled at the audience and began to speak.

"Thank you all for coming tonight." His smile was wry. "Although I imagine most of you are here to protest my proposed gourmet shop."

"You're going to put us all out of business," a voice from the crowd shouted.

A consenting murmur swept through the room.

Foster held up a hand and the audience settled down again. "Perhaps I should introduce myself. I'm Simeon Foster, and I'm the owner of the chain of Epicurean Gourmet shops."

Gladys leaned toward Mabel and Penelope. "What on earth's an epicurean?"

"It means . . ." Penelope was at a loss as to how to explain it.

"It means someone who likes fancy foods," Mabel interjected.

"Daft name for a shop, if you ask me." Gladys leaned back in her seat, her brow lowered and her arms crossed over her chest.

Foster continued speaking. "I'd be remiss if I didn't introduce my wife, Eloise." He gestured toward a woman in the audience who stood up with an embarrassed look on her face and then almost immediately sat down again.

Beryl made a sound like a squeak, and Penelope looked at her in alarm. Her mouth was partly open and tears were forming in her eyes.

She stood up abruptly. "I have to go."

Penelope grabbed her hand. "What's the matter?"

"Not now," Beryl said, ending on a sob. She excused herself as she began to make her way down the row of seats to the aisle.

"Do you want me to come with you?" Penelope half rose from her seat.

Beryl held up a hand. "I don't want to talk about it. I need some time alone. I'll tell you about it later."

Penelope stared after her. What on earth was wrong? Beryl had seemed so happy moments ago. She was about to run after her, but she knew from experience that would only upset Beryl more. Surely, she'd be able to pry it out of her once the meeting was over. Still, it didn't keep her from worrying about her sister.

She reminded herself that Beryl was known to get upset over the smallest things—the florist delivering the wrong flowers before a dinner party, the yoga class she wanted to go to being full, or finding a tiny stain on her favorite dress. With any luck, her current upset would be something minor as well.

She tried to turn her attention back to Foster, who was still speaking, extolling the virtues of his shop and all that it would bring to Chumley.

Mabel sniffed. "I didn't realize we were lacking all those things," she whispered.

When he had finished his speech, there was a slight smattering of polite applause. He returned to his seat and the mayor invited comments from the audience.

A man stood up and approached the microphone.

"That's Terry Jones," Mabel whispered to Penelope. "He owns the Sweet Tooth."

He was of average height, with broad shoulders and a face more suited to a pugilist.

Penelope couldn't imagine anyone who looked less like the owner of a candy store than Terry Jones.

He cleared his throat and began to speak. "I don't see why Chumley needs Foster's fancy gourmet store. Chumley has always prided itself on its locally owned shops. Some of us have been here for decades." He swept a hand toward the audience. "It was bad enough when Tesco moved in. We don't need another big chain store in town. We've already got all we need right here. Grant Lewis's shop carries plenty of that high-priced stuff, if that's your fancy."

"Hear! hear!" several people in the audience yelled.

By now Terry's face was red and his fists were clenched. He nodded his head at the audience and made his way back to his seat.

Penelope glanced at Foster. He looked unperturbed by the objections.

Several other people went up to the microphone to speak out against Foster's plans. Penelope glanced at her watch. It had already been more than an hour. She wondered how many more people the mayor would call on.

Just then Daniel Barber stood up. His hair was slicked back, and he had on a dark green crewneck sweater. Penelope recognized him as the owner of the local pub, the Book and Bottle, where the residents of Chumley regularly gathered to raise a pint, throw some darts, and catch up with friends. Arthur Worthington, the Duke of Upper Chumley-on-Stoke, was known to join them on occasion.

He swept a hand through his hair as he approached the microphone. Penelope thought he looked nervous.

His voice cracked a bit as he began speaking. "I know this isn't going to be a popular opinion." He gave a rueful smile. "But I think Foster's new shop could do the town a world of good. There won't be anything like it anywhere near here. The only comparable shops are an hour away in London."

He was greeted by a chorus of boos.

Penelope glanced at Grant, whose shop the residents frequented even though it didn't stock products flown in from Europe or brought straight from the farm. She saw him scowl and uncross and recross his legs as if he was in distress.

Barber went on. "Foster's shop will draw the residents of our own Birnam Wood as well as the developments like it that are springing up everywhere these days." His tone grew more adamant. "And maybe some of those people will start to patronize our own local shops like the Pig in a Poke and the Knit Wit Shop."

"Yeah, and maybe they'll stop in at the Book and Bottle for a pint while they're at it," someone from the audience called out. "Ain't that right?"

Barber looked slightly flustered. He balled his fists at his side. "So? What of it? Maybe they'll stop for some fish-and-chips at the Chumley Chippie or tikka masala at Kebabs and Curries."

"That lot's too posh for the likes of fish-and-chips. They'll want that French food at Pierre's, more like," someone yelled.

Barber hesitated, wiped a hand across his forehead, then, with a nod to the mayor, bolted back to his seat.

Folding chairs squeaked and groaned as the people in the audience began turning to their neighbor, all of them speaking at once and causing a rumble that rose to the rafters.

The mayor tapped his microphone. "Can we have silence? Silence, please."

Slowly the chatter died down and people turned their attention back to the front of the room.

"It's time for a vote," the mayor said decisively, banging his gavel for the first time.

After a brief adjournment to another room, the mayor and the council members returned and took their places.

The mayor looked slightly nervous as he leaned toward his microphone.

He had a brief coughing spell and one of the council members jumped up and returned with a glass of water. The mayor took several sips and his coughing subsided.

He fiddled with his microphone briefly. "The council has voted," he said finally, "and the proposal is approved." He banged his gavel for emphasis.

A roar emerged from the crowd. A handful of people began to leave, but most of the audience stayed in their seats, talking in small clusters.

"Well, well, well," Mabel said as she got to her feet. "That was unexpected."

"With so many people protesting, I can't believe the proposal passed," Penelope said.

Mabel rubbed her fingers together. "I wouldn't be surprised if some money changed hands." She frowned. "Somehow I don't think we've heard the end of this."

THREE

A small group—Penelope, Mabel, Figgy, Grant, Gladys, and Clementine—gathered together outside the castle, pulling up their collars and stamping their feet against the cold. The wind had picked up and had a bitter edge to it.

India lived on the grounds of the Worthington estate and had insisted on walking back to her cottage despite everyone's protestations that it was too dark and too cold.

"I'm not afraid of a bit of cold," India said. "We Englishwomen are made of sterner stuff than that. At least we used to be. I'm not so sure about this younger generation." She lifted her chin. "And besides, I have my torch with me." She reached into her pocket and pulled out a small flashlight.

Penelope watched her go with a certain number of misgivings, but she'd learned there was no arguing with India.

As soon as India had disappeared into the inky darkness,

everyone began to speak at once, causing clouds of vapor to form in the air around them.

"I wonder who the rats were who voted for Foster's proposal," Grant said, his lips set in a thin, bitter line. He fingered his bow tie nervously. "When Foster's shop opens, I shall have to close. I shall be done for. It won't be possible for my modest offerings to compete with the likes of products flown in from around the world. The most international item in the Jolly Good Grub is cheddar cheese from Ireland."

He turned and stared at Clementine. "You must know who voted yay or nay."

An angry flush colored Clementine's cheeks. "Don't look at me. Absolutely not. The vote is secret. There's no telling who voted for Foster's proposal and who didn't."

Pen clapped her hands together, the sound muffled by her gloves. "Maybe we could play up the fact that everything in our stores comes from England." She looked at Grant. "Stress national pride and pride in our community."

It didn't escape Penelope's notice that she'd said *our* community. She felt as if she was truly becoming a part of Chumley despite the occasional person still exclaiming over her American accent.

"What a good idea," Clementine cried. "We can put signs in our windows saying *Shop Local*."

"We could build a marketing campaign around it." Mabel wrapped her arms around herself and shifted from one foot to the other.

"Or what passes for marketing in Chum." Grant pursed his lips. "An ad in the *Chumley Chronicle*." He patted his bow tie. "I'd still like to know who the turncoats were who sold us out." He turned to Clementine. "The only local shop owner on the council is you."

Clementine's eyes widened. "It certainly wasn't me." She pointed an index finger at her chest. "Some of the council members—like Maurice Tompkins—live in Birnam Wood. Maybe they voted for it. If they want all that fancy stuff Foster is talking about, they should move somewhere else. Chumley is not the place for them."

"That's right." Gladys puffed out her chest. "We're simple folk and we're proud of it." Her face darkened. "Worthington's chef buys all his meat from me." She straightened her shoulders. "It's almost like having a Royal Warrant. But what if the duke decides he wants farm-sourced meat?" Gladys said the words as if they left a nasty taste in her mouth. "What'll I do then? I can't afford to lose his custom." She dabbed at her eyes with her sleeve.

"Let's not jump to conclusions," Mabel said in a firm voice. "We need to wait and see what happens. It might all be a nonstarter and we'll have been worried for no reason."

FOUR

The first thing on Penelope's mind when she woke up the next morning was her sister, Beryl. She couldn't imagine what had gotten into her. She'd called Beryl's cell phone as soon as she got home from the town council meeting, but it had immediately gone to voice mail. Something was obviously troubling Beryl—Pen just hoped it wasn't anything too serious.

Penelope dressed quickly and went downstairs. Her cat, Mrs. Danvers, wove in and out between her legs as she made her way to the kitchen.

The kitchen was her second favorite room in the cottage Mabel had loaned her. The steadily burning Aga kept the room warm and cozy no matter how damp it was outside. Penelope filled her kettle with water and plugged it in. She'd developed a fondness for English breakfast tea, although she hadn't completely given up her coffee habit.

While she waited for the water to boil, she filled Mrs. Danvers's food and water bowls and got a grateful meow in return.

She peered through the window, which looked out over the back garden. All the flowers were gone now and what was left of the tiny patch of grass was covered with frost, like icing on a cake.

The tea kettle gave its shrill whistle and Penelope hastened to pour the boiling water over the tea bag in her mug. She'd been surprised to learn that the Brits used tea bags as often as not, although loose tea wasn't quite a thing of the past yet. She grabbed a half-eaten container of blueberry yogurt out of the refrigerator, a spoon from the cutlery drawer, and her mug of tea and carried them into the front room.

The sitting room was definitely her favorite room in the cottage. She had learned how to make a fire in the large stone fireplace and she loved curling up on the sofa, the flames hissing and spitting on the hearth, casting mellow light around the room.

She took her yogurt and tea over to the window seat to eat. She pushed the curtain aside and glanced out the window, which overlooked the high street. She enjoyed watching the pedestrians go by. She recognized some of them now—Mr. Patel, who strolled by with his French bulldog every morning, and Mrs. Butterfield across the street, who opened the door in her bathrobe every day to retrieve the *Daily Telegraph* from the mat.

Penelope's laptop was sitting on the coffee table. She glared at it balefully, a sense of guilt washing over her. She really needed to make progress on her current manuscript even though her deadline was quite far off yet. She knew from experience how quickly it could go from being months away to suddenly being tomorrow.

She'd take her laptop to the Open Book with her, she decided, and hopefully she would have time to get some work done.

Penelope finished her yogurt, threw the container in the trash, and rinsed out her mug. She spent a few minutes playing with Mrs. Danvers, who enjoyed going after the string Penelope was dangling but, ultimately, she became bored with the game and wandered off.

Penelope retrieved her jacket, slipped into it, put her laptop in her tote bag, and left the cottage. It was cold but sunny, with only a few fluffy white clouds scudding across the sky. She decided to walk to the Open Book since it was barely a quarter of a mile away. She enjoyed looking in the shop windows along the high street and stopped for a moment in front of the Icing on the Cake to admire a perfect Victoria sponge that was on display. Whipped cream and raspberry jam oozed out from between the layers and made Penelope's mouth water.

She was about to move on when she heard raised voices. Standing next door in front of the Sweet Tooth was Simeon Foster. He was dressed casually in a wax jacket and had some rolled-up papers tucked under his arm. Plans for his new shop? Penelope wondered.

He appeared to be arguing with his companion. Their strident voices reached Penelope, but she couldn't make out the words. The two seemed oblivious to the fact that they might be overheard by a passerby. Penelope's grandmother Parish had drilled into her at an early age that one simply did not air their grievances in public. Even now she could hear her grandmother's voice in her head.

She knew she ought to move on, but she hovered in the shelter of the Icing on the Cake's doorway, not wanting to embarrass the couple.

The woman looked as if she'd dug her clothes out of someone's dustbin. Her coat was too large, drooping off her shoulders and reaching nearly to her ankles, and her shoes were scuffed with worn-down heels. Her dark hair was in need of a wash, the greasy strands hanging limply on her shoulders. She could have used a good trim as well. Her hair kept falling into her face and she brushed it away impatiently.

She was a bit unsteady on her feet—swaying back and forth as if buffeted by a strong wind. Once she nearly fell, but Foster grabbed her by the elbow and righted her again.

Their discussion was becoming more heated. Their voices were harsher and their hand gestures broader. Was the woman another Chumley resident who didn't approve of Foster's proposed new store and was feeling disgruntled about it?

The couple's voices grew even louder, but Penelope still couldn't quite make out what they were saying and, unfortunately, she couldn't glean much from the occasional word that she did catch. By now she was anxious to be on her way, but if she suddenly appeared from the shadows of the doorway, it would be obvious she'd been loitering there.

She was about to chance it when the woman took several steps away from Foster. It appeared as if their conversation—if you could call it that—was wrapping up.

Finally, the woman turned on her heel and began to walk away although if Penelope was putting the scene in a book, she would describe it as more of a stagger. She got a whiff of alcohol as the woman passed her, and she wrinkled her nose.

Foster walked off in the opposite direction and, relieved, Penelope continued down the high street toward the Open Book.

G ood morning," Mabel called out when Penelope finally arrived at the Open Book.

Penelope noticed Laurence Brimble browsing the history section. He was becoming a fixture at the store. He'd quietly pursued Mabel for several months before Mabel was willing to bury past romantic disappointments and go out with him.

India was sitting in one of the armchairs with a pile of books beside her, contentedly thumbing through them.

"I just saw Simeon Foster arguing with someone on the sidewalk," Penelope said as she hung up her coat.

Mabel raised her eyebrows. "Oh? I would think he'd be in a good mood given that he got what he wanted from the town council."

Penelope frowned. "It was a woman and she appeared to be drunk."

"A bit early for that, but I suppose the sun is over the yardarm somewhere." Mabel straightened a stack of books on the counter. "I don't know Foster personally, but I've heard he's . . . how shall I put this . . . one for the ladies in spite of being married. Maybe she was a woman he dumped for someone new and she wasn't happy about it."

Penelope thought about it. "I don't know. She was at least twenty or thirty years younger than Foster."

Mabel laughed. "Since when has that ever stopped anyone? It's called a May-December romance, in case you didn't know. Or robbing the cradle. It happens all the time."

Penelope leaned her elbows on the counter. "That could be it, but somehow I don't think so. That wasn't the vibe I got from them."

"Some discontented resident grousing about Foster's proposed shop?" Mabel suggested. "Heavens knows, plenty of people in Chumley would love to give Foster a piece of their mind."

B rimble wandered over to the front counter just then. "Tonight's the big night," he said, running his index finger over his bristly mustache.

Their voices must have carried over to where India was sitting because she set aside the book she was looking through and joined them.

"Big night? What big night?" Penelope raised her eyebrows.

India looked startled. "It's Guy Fawkes Day, my dear. November fifth."

Penelope was at a loss. The name Guy Fawkes was vaguely familiar, but it didn't conjure up much of anything at all.

Mabel obviously noticed the confused look on Penelope's face and decided to take pity on her. "Guy Fawkes Day is celebrated with bonfires and fireworks and Guy Fawkes is burned in effigy."

Penelope was appalled. That sounded horrible. "Why on earth do you do that?"

Brimble cleared his throat. "Guy Fawkes Day celebrates the failed Gunpowder Plot of 1605." He took a deep breath. "Guy Fawkes and a band of radical English Catholics tried to assassinate King James I by blowing up Parliament."

India nodded. "Thankfully, they failed."

"But why did they try to kill the king?" Penelope said.

Brimble was in his element. He puffed out his chest and fingered his mustache again. "King James did not tolerate religious freedom for Catholics. Priests were put to death and celebrating Mass was forbidden. Since Guy Fawkes was the ringleader of the group, he became a symbol of the whole dastardly plot."

India got a faraway look in her eyes. "I remember when I was young, we used to take our effigies, or Guys, as we called them, and cart them around and ask for a penny for the Guy. And we'd chant, 'Remember, remember the fifth of November.'"

Just then Figgy bustled over, and everyone's attention turned to the plate of buttered crumpets she was holding out. "Happy Guy Fawkes Day," she said. "Fresh crumpets, anyone?"

Within minutes all the crumpets had been claimed and eaten. Brimble pulled a handkerchief from his pocket and dabbed at his mustache, which was glistening with melted butter.

"Who's going to the bonfire tonight?" Mabel said. "We should get a little party together."

Penelope, who was anxious to try all things British, immediately said yes.

"I've made some parkin," Figgy said.

"Yes, it wouldn't be Guy Fawkes Day without it," India said.

Once again, Penelope found herself at sea—linguistically and gastronomically.

"What on earth is parkin?" She looked from Figgy to India and back again.

"It's a sort of cake," India said.

"Much like your gingerbread." Mabel nodded at Penelope.

"But made with oatmeal," India added. "And black treacle or, in some cases, golden syrup."

"You have to make it at least three days in advance." Figgy picked up the plate that was empty save for a few crumbs from the crumpets. "It's quite hard when it comes out of the oven but keeping it in a tin allows it to soften and mellow."

"It sounds intriguing," Penelope admitted.

"And we'll have some bonfire toffee. I've got that all ready as well," Figgy said.

India made a face and pointed to her mouth. "I'll give that a miss, thank you very much. Not with my dentures."

"Where shall we meet? There's always quite a crowd."

"How about in front of the Jolly Good Grub?" Brimble folded his handkerchief and put it back in his pocket. He brushed some crumbs from the front of his sweater. "We can go on from there. I'll bring a blanket to sit on."

"I'd best bring my shooting stick." India fingered the buttons on her cardigan. "It's terribly handy having that little seat attached. Arthur got it for me for my birthday. If I find I've walked too far on one of my rambles, I can always stop and rest." She laughed. "I'm afraid I can't get down on the ground any longer, though. I'd never get up. Besides, the damp isn't good for my lumbago."

"I'll bring drinks," Mabel said. "Do we want something fizzy?"

"Yes," they chorused.

"I'll bring a bag of potatoes." India rubbed her hands together. "There's nothing like a potato baked over a bonfire to warm you up."

Penelope was at a loss. "What can I bring?"

India put a hand on Penelope's shoulder. "Nothing, dear. You come and enjoy your first Guy Fawkes Day celebration."

The whole concept of Guy Fawkes Day seemed a bit gruesome to Penelope. Hanging the poor man in effigy every fifth of November? But she was willing to give it a try. The fireworks ought to be fun at least. India had promised they would be spectacular.

In the meantime, since the bookstore wasn't busy, she would get some work done. She took her laptop into her reading room—a tiny space devoid of any distractions— and set it up on the table.

She'd check her e-mail first, she decided. It was a task she dreaded and often put off for far too long. There was always the possibility that amidst the spam and coupons from stores she didn't visit and requests for political donations would be an e-mail from her editor, Bettina.

She scrolled through the latest arrivals quickly and was about to breathe a sigh of relief when she noticed the word *manuscript* in the subject line of one of them. She hovered her cursor over it and finally opened the e-mail.

Her first instinct was to close her eyes, but that was ridiculous. She reminded herself that her manuscript deadline was eons off, so surely Bettina couldn't be badgering her for it already.

Darling Pen,

Sales and marketing are positively breathing down my neck asking me what your next manuscript is going to be about. Honestly, sometimes they can be

impossible. Could you work up a teeny, tiny blurb so
I can get them off my back?

Still enjoying England, by the way?

XXX Bettina

Penelope groaned. So far, she had only the haziest idea
for a plot. Despite writing five pages of notes—single-
spaced, mind you—she was no closer to a coherent plot
than she had been when she started.

Bettina would have to wait, she decided. Her editor was
quite formidable and more than capable of handling sales
and marketing. She'd have them running screaming from
her office inside of five minutes. And that would buy Penelope some time.

Penelope considered herself a "pantser" as opposed to
a plotter. It was a word writers used to describe someone
who sits down at the computer to write with only the vagu-
est idea of where the story is going to go. Plotters, on the
other hand, outlined the story in advance. And it was at
times like these that Penelope devoutly wished she was the
latter.

She closed out of her e-mail and opened her word pro-
cessing program. She pulled up a blank document and stared
at it. What she needed was a first line to get her going.
Unfortunately, it was the hardest line of all to come up
with. It needed to be compelling, to draw the reader in and
to set the scene. Sir Edward Bulwer-Lytton's famous opening line came to mind—*It was a dark and stormy night.*

Well, why not, she thought? She'd start with that to get
the ball rolling and then during revision she'd hopefully
come up with something stellar with which to open the book.

She flexed her fingers and put them on the keys. She knew her heroine, Luna, was destined for a job taking care of an elderly rich man and his son who lived in a sprawling mansion with an overgrown garden on the desolate moors somewhere in Scotland.

Whoa, she thought. Did Scotland even *have* moors? Wasn't Heathcliff known for wandering the moors in his blackest moods and wasn't *Wuthering Heights* set in Scotland? Penelope paused with her fingers on the keys. Was *Wuthering Heights* set in Scotland? She brought up her favorite search engine and looked it up.

Hmmm, it seemed that *Wuthering Heights* was set in Yorkshire, England, not Scotland. So much for that. Should she change the location of her story? She did another search and discovered that Scotland did, indeed, have moors. She breathed a sigh of relief and began to type.

She was surprised when she finally checked her watch to see that more than an hour had gone by. She was quite pleased with herself. She'd written five pages and was off to a good start. She saved her document, shut down her computer, and went to see what was happening in the shop.

Mabel was unboxing a carton of books at the front counter and nibbling on a piece of shortbread.

"Help yourself," she said to Penelope. She gestured toward the plate of cookies.

Penelope bit into one and inhaled the heavenly aromas of butter and sugar. She found it amazing how so few ingredients could come together in such a delicious fashion.

Mabel slit the tape along the top of the carton and folded back the flaps. She pulled out a book and groaned.

"What's the matter?" Penelope paused mid-chew.

Mabel sighed. "I hate these die-cut covers." She held the book up for Penelope to see.

Penelope glanced at it. It showed a woman in a red coat from behind, glancing over her shoulder as she hurried toward a waiting subway train. The drops of blood that trailed behind her were die cut so that the red showed through.

"I think it's quite striking." She handed the book back to Mabel. "What don't you like about it?"

"Oh, it's striking all right." Mabel ran a hand through her fluffy gray hair. "But they're miserable to shelve. Inevitably, another book will snag the cutout and rip the cover. Our patrons don't necessarily shelve our books with the same care that we do." She blew a lock of hair off her forehead. "But it's a bestseller, so perhaps they'll go quickly before any of them get damaged."

The door opened and Penelope looked toward it. She was surprised to see it was Clementine.

"Clementine," Mabel said. "How can I help you?"

Clementine's narrow face was pinched and white despite the cold. "I'm looking for a birthday gift for a dear friend. We've known each other since primary school. She always looked out for me. Children can be such bullies, you know."

Penelope and Mabel murmured their assent. Penelope could remember being made fun of when she got her first pair of glasses and being called names like *four-eyes*. Her mother wasn't at all pleased when she got in trouble for smacking a boy who'd been teasing her on the playground.

"Is your friend a *he* or a *she*?" Mabel said. "Do you have a sense of what they like to read?"

"Oh, it's a woman. She's quite fond of mysteries, I believe. But nothing terribly graphic, mind you. She's rather sensitive." Her hands fluttered in the air. "Aren't we all, I suppose? I can barely stand the sight of blood myself. My parents had hoped I'd have a career in nursing like my mother and grandmother, but I'm afraid I didn't have the stomach for it."

"Perhaps a cozy mystery then?" Penelope suggested with a glance at Mabel.

Mabel nodded. "That would be perfect. A nice puzzle but without anything upsetting. Except the murder, of course," she said dryly. She went over to the shelves, pulled out a book, and carried it up to the counter. "How about this? *The Diva Runs Out of Thyme* by Krista Davis. It's terribly charming."

Clementine gave a wan smile. "That's perfect. Thank you."

"Are you going to the bonfire and fireworks tonight?" Mabel said as she rang up the sale.

Clementine made a sad face. "I'm afraid not. I'll be working."

"Don't you normally close by five o'clock?" Penelope said. Whenever she passed the Icing on the Cake on her way home, the lights were always already out.

Clementine gave an enormous sigh. "Yes, but I've decided to stay open later. I'm afraid of what's going to happen when Foster opens his gourmet store with his fancy pastries being flown in from France." She pursed her lips. "I'm going to need all the business I can get. A lot of the people who work in London don't get off the train until six o'clock and by then I'm already closed. I'm hoping if I stay open later, they'll pop in for some impulse purchases. Perhaps a nice lemon drizzle cake to take home for their tea or a dozen shortbread biscuits to share at the office."

"Your window displays would tempt anyone," Penelope said with a smile. "I know I'm always tempted."

Clementine ducked her head. "Thank you. That's most kind of you. But I'm afraid my wares are rather pedestrian when compared to macarons and gâteau St. Honoré."

"I've never been disappointed in anything I've purchased from your shop." Mabel leaned her elbows on the counter. "I'm curious. It's obvious you didn't vote to approve Foster's proposal. I wonder who did?"

Clementine looked slightly taken aback. "Why anyone would want that man's shop in this town, I don't know. It's going to put us all out of business."

"I wonder what it would take to stop him?" Penelope said.

Mabel rolled her eyes. "I know his type. Probably nothing short of murder."

FIVE

❧

I t's five o'clock," Mabel announced as she bustled to the
door, closing it behind the last departing customers, their
chattering voices slowly fading into the night air. She flipped
the sign on the door from Open to Closed and pulled down
the shade.

"I think I've got everything." Figgy put the basket she
was carrying on the counter. "I have the tin of parkin, the
toffee, cups, and a thermos of nice, hot tea."

"Bundle up," Mabel said as she pulled on her coat. "It's
cold out there tonight."

Penelope grabbed her jacket, put it on, and wound her
scarf around her neck. She stuck her hands in her pockets,
reassured to find that she hadn't forgotten her gloves. She
pulled her hat from her tote bag and yanked it on as well,
tucking her hair behind her ears.

Figgy was wearing a purple fake-fur jacket that looked
as if it were on the lam from the nineteen seventies and a

bright red newsboy cap. She circled in front of Penelope and Mabel.

"How do you like my vintage finds? I found them at the church jumble sale."

"They're very . . . you," Mabel said and smiled kindly.

Figgy picked up her basket. "I suppose we should be going. We don't want to keep Laurence and India waiting. It's too cold tonight to stand around outside. There will be fires to keep us warm at the fireworks."

Penelope began to shiver as soon as she stepped out into the brisk night air. Mabel flipped off the lights, locked the door, and together they all headed down the high street.

People streamed down the sidewalk, all going in the same direction. The children ran ahead excitedly and then stopped to wait for their parents to catch up, their animated voices rising and falling as they got closer to their destination.

The bonfires were going to be lit in an empty field just beyond the town center, and Worthington was paying for the fireworks display, which he did every Guy Fawkes Day.

Penelope was grateful that Americans celebrated with fireworks on the Fourth of July, when it was at least warm.

They passed the Icing on the Cake and Pen glanced in the window, but the display was empty and the lights were out.

They were about to cross the street when Penelope caught her toe on an uneven cobblestone and nearly pitched forward but was saved by Mabel grabbing her arm. She would have landed flat on her face if it hadn't been for Mabel's quick response.

"Steady on," Mabel said, making sure Penelope was standing firmly on both her feet before letting go of her arm.

Penelope took a deep breath. Her heart was beating wildly and she could feel the blood pulsing in her temples.

"Are you okay?" Figgy said.

Mabel looked concerned. "Did you hurt yourself?"

"I'm fine," Pen reassured them. "At least physically. My dignity, on the other hand, is a bit bruised." She motioned toward the Jolly Good Grub across the street. "Let's go."

They were about to step off the curb when an Aston Martin came whipping down the road.

Penelope gasped. "Who was that?" she said, turning to watch as the car continued roaring down the high street.

"Our very own Duke of Upper Chumley-on-Stoke. I can see that marriage and a baby haven't completely settled him down." Mabel shook her head. "One of these days he's going to kill himself or someone else. I imagine he's bound for the Book and Bottle. He probably wants to get in a pint or two before the fireworks start."

Penelope's heart was beating rapidly again, and her hands were clammy inside her gloves.

"That was a close call," Mabel said. "If you'd fallen, we would have ended up spending the evening in the A&E instead of at the fireworks."

The road now clear, they crossed over to the other side and the Jolly Good Grub where Brimble was waiting outside, his nose and cheeks red from the cold. He had a blanket tucked under one arm and a metal pail with a grocery bag in it in the other.

"I took the opportunity to pop into the Jolly Good Grub for some meats and cheeses and a box of water biscuits," he said, holding the pail out. "It's what the French call *charcuterie*."

Penelope glanced at it curiously. "What is the pail for?"

Brimble cleared his throat. "To roast the potatoes in. I'll find a bonfire that is dying down and place the pail amidst the embers. Have you ever had a potato roasted over a fire?"

Penelope shook her head. "No."

"There's nothing like it." Brimble put down the pail and stroked his mustache. "We used to go camping in North Yorkshire when I was a young lad. I loved cooking over the campfire—mother would even whip up a full English breakfast in the morning."

Brimble fell silent, his eyes taking on a faraway look.

Mabel smiled and gave him a kiss on the cheek. "Now the only thing is to wait for India to arrive."

Penelope glanced through the window of the Jolly Good Grub. The interior looked warm and cozy, flooded with light and with a colorful display of boxes of Sultan's Turkish Delight near the door. A line of customers snaked back from the cashier's desk, where a clerk with white hair was ringing up their purchases.

A taxi veered toward the curb, and they all took a step back. The door opened and India struggled to get out. Her shooting stick was briefly stuck, but with Brimble's help, it was finally freed, and India was safely ensconced on the sidewalk.

"I hope I'm not late." She looked around her. "I've got the potatoes." She held out a bag. "All nicely wrapped in foil."

She was bundled into a black wool coat that smelled faintly of mothballs and a hand-knitted wool cap with earflaps and strings that hung down on either side of her head like braids.

"Shall we go?" Mabel said. "It looks as if the celebration is starting." She pointed into the distance, where a thin plume of smoke was rising into the sky.

Brimble carried India's shooting stick while Penelope took the bag of potatoes, and they began to walk toward where the crowd had gathered.

As they were approaching the field where the festivities were being held, a young boy with bright red hair rushed past them. He was pushing a straw Guy Fawkes dummy in a rather dilapidated baby stroller.

"A penny for the Guy," he called out as he maneuvered past them.

Brimble reached into his pocket, pulled out a coin, and handed it to him.

"Ta!" the boy said as he scooted away, bumping his stroller over the uneven pavement.

Suddenly Penelope stopped short and Figgy bumped into her.

"Look," she said, pointing toward the field where bright orange flames were shooting into the sky.

"Oooh," Figgy exclaimed. "It looks as if things are starting up."

"Or heating up," Brimble said with a self-deprecating chuckle.

They felt the heat of the bonfires as they got closer to the field. Fortunately, the wind was blowing the smoke away from the crowd, which had increased in size, with people positioning themselves farther and farther back from the flames.

Some of the fires that had been lit earlier were already dying down, their embers glowing brightly in the dark, while others were just beginning to catch, the wood crackling and spitting as the flames leaped higher and higher, orange red against the dark sky.

Penelope noticed Constable Cuthbert and several of his

colleagues circulating among the crowd, keeping order, although so far, everyone was very well-mannered.

Suddenly, India grabbed Penelope's arm. "Look who's here."

Penelope looked in the direction of India's pointing finger and saw Foster making his way through the crowd.

"It's awfully bold of him, showing his face here." Brimble frowned.

India agreed. "The nerve of the man."

"I don't suppose he can hide forever." Penelope tripped over a tuft of grass and Brimble took her arm to steady her. "He's going to be operating a store here, after all."

"I hope we find a good spot," India said, nervously fingering her pearls. "It's getting dreadfully crowded."

"There's still plenty of room," Brimble reassured her. "And we'll be able to see the fireworks from anywhere."

"There's Gladys," Figgy said, waving.

A fair crowd had gathered around the folding table Gladys had set up, waiting to buy one of her famous meat pasties. She was pulling the foil-wrapped hand pies from an insulated cooler as fast as she could and distributing them to the outheld hands. Her forehead was sweaty and there was a strand of hair stuck to it.

Brimble led the way through the mass of people until he found an open spot large enough to spread out their blanket.

They all plopped down on it except for India, who set up her shooting stick and perched on the seat. Figgy pulled the thermos from her bag and handed out hot cups of tea. Penelope wrapped her hands around hers gratefully. Despite the heat emanating from the bonfires, it was still a chilly night.

"A spot of tea is just the ticket," Brimble said as he accepted the cup from Figgy.

Penelope sipped her tea and watched, mesmerized, as the flames of the bonfires reached higher and higher into the sky. A dummy was thrown into one of them, where it immediately caught fire. The dummy looked so real that Penelope looked away. She found the sight rather gruesome.

"I'll go bake the potatoes, shall I?" Brimble said, dumping India's bag of potatoes into the pail. "It looks as if some of the fires that were set earlier are burning down, so now is the perfect time." He got up with a groan and brushed off the seat of his pants. "Not quite as limber as I used to be." He smiled apologetically.

"The fireworks should be starting soon," Mabel said as they waited for Brimble to come back.

He wasn't long and returned shortly with a pail of roasted potatoes.

"That was quick," Mabel said.

Brimble winked at her. "I employed a bit of a trick. I microwaved the potatoes first so all I had to do was crisp them up over the fire. It doesn't take long."

"Very clever of you." Mabel smiled at him.

Penelope reached for a potato and held it in her hand for a few moments, enjoying the warmth. The temperature had dropped further and most of the fires were dying down to glowing embers and ash.

After they had finished their potatoes, Figgy doled out pieces of parkin and toffee.

Penelope finished hers and then gathered the discarded pieces of foil that the potatoes had been wrapped in.

"I'll go throw these away. I thought I saw a garbage can nearby."

She crumpled the pieces of foil into a ball, got to her feet, and headed toward where she'd last seen a trash bin.

As she walked back to the blanket, the fireworks began—thunderous booms that shook the ground, followed by brilliantly colored starbursts streaking across the sky and ending with *ooh*s and *aah*s from the crowd. As soon as the bits of color floated to the ground, there was a whoosh and another firecracker was launched.

Penelope slowly walked backward, staring up at the sky. Suddenly her foot struck something soft and slightly yielding. Had she bumped into someone? She was about to apologize when she looked down.

She gave a sigh of relief. It was only a Guy Fawkes dummy waiting to be thrown on the fire. She was about to walk away when something made her turn around. She bent down to look at the dummy more closely.

And then she began to scream. But her screams were drowned out by the fireworks bursting in the sky above her.

SIX

❧

The man's body was lying partially on its side and he appeared to be dead, but Penelope wasn't sure. Perhaps he was simply drunk and had passed out? She knelt down to feel for a pulse and, as she did so, the body rolled onto its back.

Penelope gasped. It was Simeon Foster and he was definitely dead. She felt his neck and his wrist and could not find a pulse. For a moment she wasn't sure what to do and just knelt there and stared at the body. Finally, she pulled her cell phone from her pocket and dialed 999.

She told the dispatcher, whose voice remained remarkably calm although Penelope's was shaking, about the body and her approximate location in the crowd. He assured her that one of the constables would be there immediately.

Penelope looked around her. Foster's body was lying half on and half off a rough wool blanket. He appeared to have been alone. A thermos was lying on its side with a lone mug next to it. There was a takeaway box from Kebabs and Curries, a packet of chocolate-covered Jaffa cakes, and a small box of candy from the Sweet Tooth with half the chocolates missing. It certainly looked as if Foster had had a sweet tooth, Penelope thought.

She forced herself to look at Foster's body again. Perhaps he'd had a heart attack? She looked around at the people sitting near him but they were all looking up at the sky, oblivious to the body within arm's reach.

Penelope was relieved when she noticed the tall conical hat of a police constable above the heads of the crowd. As Penelope made her way toward him, he continued to speak into his radio. She motioned for him to follow her and when they made it back to Foster's blanket, a wave of relief hit her so hard she sat down with a thump, fighting the tears that were pricking the backs of her eyelids. She didn't know why she felt like crying. She hadn't liked Foster. Not that she'd known him, really, but his demeanor at the town council meeting had put her off—he'd come across as arrogant and self-centered.

Penelope was relieved they hadn't sent Constable Cuthbert, but a younger man with straight dark hair sticking out the back of his hat. Constable Cuthbert and Penelope had met on several occasions before under trying circumstances. She couldn't imagine what he'd think if he found her with yet another dead body.

At least this death looked natural, Penelope thought as she got to her feet.

"What do we have here?" The constable knelt beside the body and checked for a pulse, much as Penelope had done. He shook his head as he stood up. "He's gone, I'm afraid."

He looked around at the crowd. "An ambulance is on the way. So is Detective Maguire."

Penelope's heartbeat sped up a bit at the mention of Maguire's name. They had been going out together for several months and the relationship was blossoming nicely. Penelope had begun to harbor hopes that it would turn into something even more serious.

After what seemed like an eternity, Penelope noticed two men pushing a gurney in their direction. Maguire was right behind the ambulance crew, breaking into a jog to catch up. He overtook them as they bumped the unwieldy gurney over the uneven ground.

"Penelope," Maguire said when he arrived at the scene, slightly breathless. "Are you okay?" He touched her arm lightly.

"I'm fine," Penelope said. And she did feel fine now that Maguire was there. She felt her shoulders drop and her neck relax.

Maguire was a hair taller than Penelope's nearly six feet and, while he wasn't exactly handsome, his face was open and honest and very pleasant. He was wearing jeans and a brown leather jacket with a knitted scarf around his neck.

Maguire held up a hand to stop the ambulance crew as they parked the gurney and moved toward Foster's body. He squatted beside the body and looked it over.

"No sign of any wounds," he murmured to himself. "No blood either." He frowned. "His lips are terribly blue. His hands as well." He stood up. "I've seen that in heart attack victims. Still, we can't be too careful. The medical examiner is on the way.

"Excuse me." Maguire went over to a couple and their

two children whose blanket was a foot or two from Foster's. The woman was clutching the hands of two little boys and looked as if she was trying to shield them from the view of the body while her partner gathered their things together.

She gave the boys a shove and said, "Go help your father pack up."

They both looked reluctant to leave and were staring at the body, wide-eyed. The woman shooed them along with her hands on their backs and turned to face Maguire.

"Are you a policeman?" she said, her arms crossed over her chest.

"DCI Brody Maguire." Maguire pulled out his badge and showed it to her. She grunted in satisfaction.

Maguire pointed toward the body. "Did you happen to notice anything unusual about this man? Did he seem ill?"

"I wouldn't know, would I? Not with two boys to look after and the fireworks going on."

Maguire nodded. "How about your husband. Might he have seen something?"

The woman turned and yelled, "Al, Come here. This policeman wants to talk to you."

The man looked up from the backpack into which he was shoving half-empty packages of Tunnock's Tea Cakes and Mr. Porky Scratchings.

He walked over to Maguire with a bag of Wotsits corn puffs in his hand. "What can I do for you?" He was wearing jeans and a plaid flannel shirt and was in need of a shave.

Maguire pointed toward Foster's body. "Did you happen to notice anything unusual? Did he complain of feeling ill or anything?"

The fellow shrugged. "He didn't say anything in particular. Just asked us to keep the boys away from his blanket. You know how kids are. Curious." He scratched his chin. "He did look kind of pale, come to think of it. And he was staggering a bit. As if he'd had a few too many down at the pub, you know what I mean?"

"Did you see him fall down or clutch his chest or anything like that?"

"Nah. Nothing like that. Sorry, mate."

One of the boys came up to the man and grabbed him around the leg. "I want to go home," he whined.

"Sorry. I gotta go." He tipped an imaginary hat at Maguire. "It's late and the boys are getting tired."

The fireworks being over, people began to leave the area, although a small group had gathered in a ring around Foster's body. More constables had arrived, and they joined hands to push the crowd back from the scene.

Maguire looked at Foster again and then at Penelope. "Looks like you've stumbled over another body," he said with a wry smile.

"I did literally stumble over him," Penelope said.

"Poor guy." Maguire shook his head. "It was a heart attack, I suppose." He pointed at the takeaway container. "Not a very healthy diet." He scratched his head. "Did you happen to notice him before you . . . stumbled over him? Was he alone?"

"I saw him in the crowd earlier but not again until just now. I didn't notice anyone with him."

"I don't suppose you know who he is?"

"I do, actually. He's Simeon Foster."

Maguire's eyebrows shot up. "Isn't he the fellow who wants to put in that fancy new shop? I don't imagine the people of Chum will have much use for it."

"And they're not exactly thrilled about it either, if the

town council meeting was anything to go by. He's certainly made more than his share of enemies."

Maguire glanced at the body again and groaned. He ran a hand through his hair. "Maybe this isn't going to be as simple as it looks. With my luck, it won't have been a heart attack after all."

SEVEN

❧

Penelope was in a daze as she walked back to the spot where she and her friends had set up their picnic. She barely noticed the crowd swirling around her as they hastened to leave now that the show was over. The younger children were beginning to fuss and whine, it being past their accustomed bedtimes. A little girl with blond ringlets was clutching a half-eaten chocolate bar but began to cry when she accidentally dropped it and her mother wouldn't let her pick it up.

What would happen to Foster's gourmet shop now? Penelope wondered. Did he have heirs who would carry out his plans? Partners in his company? If either of those were the case, then murdering him made no sense. The Epicurean Gourmet would soon be opening in Chumley despite Foster's death.

Mabel waved to Penelope and Penelope scurried over to their spot. She helped Mabel and Brimble clean up while Figgy packed up the thermos and cups.

"What happened?" Mabel said. "We saw a number of police rushing toward something. We were worried. Laurence was about to go searching for you."

Penelope took a deep breath. How should she put it? How did you announce that you'd tripped over a dead body? Hey, guess what, I ran into Simeon Foster? That was certainly the truth. Blurting out "Simeon Foster is dead" seemed so blunt. Perhaps she should lead up to it?

"There was an accident," she began. "Well, not exactly an accident. Someone became ill and they . . . died."

"How awful," Figgy said. She froze with the bag of toffee in her hand. "And you were there?"

"Not there when it happened, no. I was passing by on my way to the trash bin and I stumbled on the . . . body."

"Has the person been identified?" Mabel said, handing Figgy the tin with the remains of the parkin. "I know so many people in Chumley, thanks to the store."

"Oh, dear," India said. "It's most likely to be someone I know. People my age feel as if they are living on borrowed time as it is."

Penelope gulped and toed the grass with her shoe. "It's Simeon Foster."

"No!" Brimble exclaimed. It was the most dramatic reaction Penelope had ever seen him display except perhaps for the time Mabel fell off the ladder dusting shelves in the bookstore.

Figgy, Mabel, and India gasped, equally surprised.

"That certainly caught me off guard," Brimble said as if he was embarrassed about his previous outburst.

"Do you think someone did it?" Figgy asked with a shiver. "Killed him, I mean."

"I don't know." Penelope looked around to make sure they hadn't missed anything. "Detective Maguire thinks it might have been a heart attack. It looked like that was possible. His face and hands were blue. Don't heart attacks cause a lack of oxygen?"

"They certainly do," Mabel said.

"Were there no signs of foul play?" India said as she folded up her shooting stick. Penelope knew India was a big fan of police shows and prided herself on knowing what she'd come to calling crime scene lingo.

Brimble stroked his chin. "Simply because the man was disliked is no reason to immediately jump to conclusions and suspect murder, I suppose. But it does make one wonder."

"We'll find out soon enough," Mabel said, shaking out the blanket. "It'll be all over Chumley by the morning."

Penelope had planned to sleep in on Sunday morning, but Mrs. Danvers woke her at the usual time, patting Penelope's face until she finally opened her eyes. She pulled on some clothes and when she got downstairs, she immediately filled Mrs. Danvers's bowl. It wasn't completely devoid of food, but Mrs. Danvers had pushed all of what remained to the sides of the bowl so that the center portion was empty. Clearly, that was not acceptable to her. She stared at the bowl as if to prove her point to Penelope.

Penelope planned to spend a good portion of the day writing, but first she wanted to check in with her sister. She still hadn't been able to reach her. She knew Beryl was busy. She worked for Charlotte, the Duchess of Upper Chumley-on-Stoke, as her personal stylist—a dream job, as far as Beryl was concerned. She'd always been fashion conscious, while Penelope was apt to throw on the first clothes that came to hand.

She'd been especially busy lately. Dresses and gowns were needed for the christening of one of the duke's godchildren, an upcoming ball at Buckingham Palace, Remembrance Day services, and the wedding of a distant cousin of the duke's the day after Christmas.

Beryl was also working on some secret project that was keeping her even busier. When Penelope asked her about it, she said she didn't want to share the details until the plans were signed, sealed, and delivered.

Penelope rang her again while she got eggs, bacon, and sausage from the refrigerator. She was going to make herself a proper English fry-up, or at least part of one. The full Monty was a bit too much for her. She'd have the bacon, eggs, sausage, and fried bread, and she'd use up the half of a tomato that was lingering in the produce drawer.

The phone rang and rang at Beryl's end and Penelope finally clicked off the call. If she couldn't get hold of her sister soon, she was going to start worrying in earnest.

Penelope finished her breakfast, cleaned up the dishes and, with a sense of determination, marched into the sitting room. Her laptop sat waiting on the coffee table. She really had to get some writing done if she was going to keep to her self-imposed schedule. For once she was determined not to find herself scrambling to finish at the last minute.

She powered up her laptop and opened the file. Her

working title for the manuscript was *Lady of the Castle*, but she knew from experience that it was up to her publisher's sales and marketing team whether or not that would actually go on the cover of the book.

She debated whether she should go over what she'd already written and do a bit of tweaking, or forge ahead. She decided to forge ahead.

Her heroine, Luna, was just beginning to suspect that all was not right at Raven's Castle or with the brooding Lord Hawthorne. She'd been hearing strange sounds at night—as if someone was moaning—but she'd convinced herself it was merely the wind whistling through the belfry.

Penelope was about two hundred words in when she hit a snag. What to do next? Should Luna take a flashlight and go investigate the noise or was it too early in the story for that? She rather missed the old days when you could chew on the end of your pencil while you were thinking. There was no doing that with a computer. A major downfall of progress, she decided.

Perhaps if she did something else for a few minutes, the answer would come to her. She brought up the Internet and went to the site of a large online bookseller. She thought she would see how *The Woman in the Fog* was faring. She found the page and scrolled down to the sales numbers. Not bad. Not bad at all. Even Bettina must be pleased.

There were some new reviews as well. As much as Penelope tried not to read the reviews, sometimes she just couldn't help it.

The newest one was lovely. Certain phrases jumped out at Penelope . . . *a fantastic read, a page-turner, my new favorite author.*

She felt a glow of satisfaction. It always made her happy

to know her readers had spent a pleasant few hours with her book.

She glanced at the next review and her eyes immediately lit on the word *sophomoric*. She decided it was best not to read the rest of the review. She exited the page and went back to her manuscript.

She lasted all of ten seconds. She had to find out what that reviewer had said. She suspected it was the same feeling that compelled motorists to rubberneck at accidents even knowing that what they saw was bound to upset them.

As she read, her stomach sank with each word. The reviewer had utterly panned the book. She felt a rush of warmth to her cheeks. Oddly enough, her overwhelming emotion was one of embarrassment. She was clearly a fraud. She couldn't write and it had all been a giant fluke—an enormous cosmic joke. And the joke was on her.

The fact that two of her books had reached the bestseller list didn't reassure her. She looked at her current manuscript and scanned a few lines. It was drivel. All drivel. She should quit while she was ahead and go back to the States and get what her sister and mother referred to as a "real job."

By now she was in a total funk. It was useless trying to write. She was going to doubt every single word she put on the page. She exited her document and shut down her computer.

Penelope moped about the house all afternoon. Mabel had said she didn't need her at the Open Book. She considered going in anyway, but then she heard rain pelting the window and pummeling the roof. She pushed the curtain aside and looked out. It must have been raining for a bit— puddles were already forming on the sidewalk. She thought of the line from a W. C. Fields movie: "It ain't a fit night out for man nor beast." That's certainly what it looked like at the moment.

She sat on the window seat and stared out the window for several minutes. Only one person walked by—a woman in a wax jacket and wellies, carrying a red umbrella. The English certainly knew how to dress for the weather, Penelope thought.

She remembered how miserable it was to be caught in the rain in New York City when you were still several blocks from your destination. More than once, she'd purchased a cheap umbrella from one of the street sellers who popped up on every street corner when the weather turned nasty— like flowers appearing after a spring rain.

Finally, she let the curtain drop back into place. There was really nothing to see on such a gloomy day. She decided that perhaps a fire might cheer her up. Besides, dampness was seeping in from around the windows and the door and the warmth would feel good.

Penelope had saved a stack of the week's *Chumley Chronicles*. She grabbed the issue at the top of the pile, separated the pages, and began to crumple them into balls. She was placing them in the grate when the headline on one of the opinion pieces caught her eye—"Modernization of Chumley Must Be Stopped." It was a letter to the editor by Rupert Yardley.

As Penelope read the letter, she could imagine steam coming out of Rupert's ears while he wrote it. He vehemently opposed Foster's plans for modernization of the building in which he planned to house his gourmet shop.

In his opinion, it would be the ruin of Upper Chumley-on-Stoke. He ended with the line "Foster must be stopped at all costs."

The words sent a shiver through Penelope. Foster had been stopped, but had it been by natural causes or had someone—someone like Rupert—decided to take matters into their own hands?

EIGHT

❧

Penelope finally reached her sister late on Sunday night. Beryl was still being tight-lipped about what had upset her at the town council meeting and Penelope didn't press her. Beryl would tell her when she was ready. It wouldn't be the first time she'd held something back until she was prepared to spill all.

They rarely kept secrets from each other, although that didn't mean they told each other everything right away. It was years before Penelope admitted to Beryl that she'd been the one who had swiped Beryl's driver's license in order to go out drinking with her friends.

Still, it didn't keep Penelope from worrying.

The weather had cleared up somewhat by Monday morning. Weak sunshine made its way through scattered clouds and the puddles on the sidewalk were draining away. Penelope checked Mrs. Danvers's food and water bowls, slipped on her jacket, and headed out the door for the Open Book.

Mr. Patel waved as he passed by, his dog tugging on its leash, anxious to reach the nearest light post. He was later than usual, which was unlike him. Penelope wondered what had held him up.

She walked briskly, enjoying stretching her legs, occasionally stopping to window-shop. A gorgeous biscuit cake in the window of the Icing on the Cake caught her eye and she paused for a minute to admire it before glancing up at the second floor of the building where Beryl had been fortunate enough to score a reasonably priced apartment. The curtains were drawn, and it looked as if the lights were out. Beryl had said she was going to London to pick up some dresses for Charlotte—she must already be on her way.

Penelope paused again in front of the Sweet Tooth, where luscious-looking chocolates were displayed. She had indulged herself in some on more than one occasion. Fortunately for her, she didn't gain weight easily, partly because she often forgot to eat.

It was the morning of her book club at the Open Book. The group had chosen to read *The Regency Rogue*, the newest romance from the Duchess of Upper Chumley-on-Stoke, the former Charlotte Davenport.

People's noses had been put out of joint that Worthington had married an American and not a local girl, but they were slowly coming to know and like Charlotte and her books always sold out as soon as they were delivered.

Brimble, who was a member of the book club, had argued vigorously against the choice, claiming it was a woman's book and suggesting some dreary military tale instead. He was easily outnumbered, so *The Regency Rogue* it was.

Penelope arrived at the Open Book, hung up her jacket,

paused long enough at the front counter to greet Mabel and snitch one of the fresh Chelsea buns Figgy had baked for them, and then got to work setting up for her book club. She arranged the miscellaneous assortment of chairs scattered around the place into a circle at the back of the store.

Figgy wheeled over a cart with a pot of tea that was kept warm in a red-and-white gingham cozy, cups and saucers, and a tray of Hobnobs biscuits. Penelope was still hungry despite the Chelsea bun and swiped one of the cookies from the assortment. She munched on it as she reviewed the first chapter of *A Regency Rogue*. She'd read the book over the course of a weekend—she had to admit it certainly held the reader's interest—and wanted to brush up on some of the characters' names.

She had just gotten to the part where Lord Braebourn first encounters the heroine, who is lost in the woods, when India arrived.

She was wearing her customary twin set, tweed skirt, warm tights, and brogues. She made a beeline for the lone armchair and groaned a bit as she sat down.

"Are you okay?" Pen said, feeling concerned.

"Yes, I'm fine. Thank you for asking, my dear. Yesterday I was deadheading the last of my Wedding Days—chrysanthemums, you know. I planted them in honor of Arthur's engagement. They're quite lovely but I'm afraid all that bending down has tired my back. Such a bother."

"Can I get you a pillow . . . or something?" Penelope said.

"No, thank you. No need to fuss. I've put some liniment on it and took some paracetamol and that should do the trick."

The door to the shop opened and Brimble walked in. He made a beeline for the front counter where Mabel was flipping through the spring book catalogue. He lingered for a few moments, then touched Mabel's hand and headed toward the chairs Penelope had set up.

"Cheerio," he said as he joined them and took a seat.

Penelope was taking a seat herself when Shirley Townsend arrived slightly out of breath. She was wearing bright red slacks and a red-and-white polka-dot blouse.

"Tracy can't make it," she said as she pulled her copy of *The Regency Rogue* from her purse. "Rosie canceled on her. She's down with a virus of some sort."

Clementine Harrison had decided to join the group when she heard that they were going to be discussing Charlotte Davenport's book. Mabel said she suspected it wasn't because of the book but because she thought Penelope, who had become friends with Charlotte, would be willing to share some juicy royal gossip.

Clementine slipped into her seat like a wraith. She looked around the group and smiled, then folded her hands on top of her copy of the paperback.

Penelope decided it was time to start the discussion. She cleared her throat.

"So," she said. "What was your impression of the book?"

"I loved it," Shirley said, holding her paperback to her chest.

"Most interesting," India said, and Penelope noticed she blushed slightly.

Clementine giggled. "I couldn't put it down."

"I'm afraid I discovered there were some inaccuracies." Brimble ran his finger over his mustache. "Historical inaccuracies but also she gets the titles of nobility wrong." He sniffed. "But what can you expect from an American?"

"Let's get back to the story," Penelope said before Brimble could elaborate.

The discussion continued for an hour and then, as everyone got ready to leave, turned to general conversation.

"I mustn't linger," Clementine said as she picked up her purse. "I have someone minding the store while I'm gone." She shook her head. "It's so hard to find competent help these days. All young people want to do is fiddle with those phones of theirs."

"Has there been any news about Foster's death?" Brimble said. "Quite shocking. Must have been a heart attack. People just don't take care of themselves these days." He puffed out his chest.

"Didn't I tell you?" Shirley's eyes grew wider and she put a hand over her mouth. "My cousin Philippa—you know, she's the one who works at the police station—overheard some of the constables talking. She does like to keep her ear to the ground. It seems the talk is they think Foster was murdered. Can you imagine? Another murder in Chumley."

"But there were no visible marks on the body." Brimble looked to Penelope for verification, and she nodded.

Shirley tapped her head with her index finger. "Could have been poison. That doesn't leave a mark."

"Like that notorious murder in Norwich, I think it was, where the wife laced her husband's morning tea with cyanide," Brimble said. He gave a fond smile. "It reminds me of that exchange between Lady Nancy Astor and Winston Churchill, where she said that if he were her husband, she'd put poison in his tea, and he responded that if he was her husband, he'd drink it."

Everyone laughed politely.

Shirley clapped her hands together. "There you go, then," she said as if the matter was settled. "It must have been poison that killed him."

NINE

⟋⟍

Penelope was straightening up after her book group and Figgy was collecting the remainder of the tea things when the door burst open and Gladys rushed in. Her face was bright red and she looked like a horse that had just been spooked. She was wearing her customary apron but had dashed across the street without a coat.

Pen and Figgy rushed over to her.

"What's wrong, Gladys?" Mabel said, coming out from behind the front counter.

Gladys gulped, opened her mouth, but no words came out. She swayed slightly and Penelope rushed to grab a chair. Gladys sank into it, her knuckles white as she gripped the arms.

Mabel gave Gladys an appraising look. "Whatever this is," she said, heading back behind the counter, "it obviously calls for a shot of Jameson." She reached under the counter, pulled out a bottle and a glass, and poured a finger's worth of the golden liquid into it. She handed it to Gladys. "Drink it slowly."

Gladys finally managed to catch her breath and took a cautious sip. Her hands were shaking, and a bit dribbled down her chin. Slowly, the flush began to recede from her face although her hands were still shaking.

She started to open her mouth, but Mabel stopped her, pointing at the glass in Gladys's hand. "Drink up first and then tell us what's happened." She leaned against the counter.

Gladys drained the rest of the glass and handed it to Mabel.

Figgy, meanwhile, had retreated to the tearoom and returned with a steaming cup of tea.

"I've put extra sugar in it," she said, handing it to Gladys.

"Ah, yes, a cup of builder's tea will do you a world of good," Mabel said.

Gladys was prone to hysteria, so Penelope wasn't terribly worried about what was causing her panic. A cup of Figgy's builder's tea—a robust brew with extra sugar—usually set her to rights again. Between that and Mabel's shot of Jameson, she'd be back to normal in no time.

Gladys gulped down the tea and handed the cup back to Figgy. She pulled a handkerchief from the pocket of her apron and dabbed at her lips.

Penelope, Figgy, and Mabel stared at her expectantly.

"Well?" Mabel said finally.

Gladys's words came out in a gasp. "The police are searching my shop."

"Whatever for?" Mabel frowned. "Is this some kind of health inspection?"

Gladys fiddled with the strings on her apron. "No, no. But they wouldn't say. They just showed me the warrant and began poking into all my things. One of the constables, a young fellow who sometimes comes in to buy a roast for his family's Sunday dinner—they must have any number of wee ones, considering the size he orders—told me they're looking for sodium nitrite. I've no idea what for."

Mabel and Penelope exchanged a glance.

Gladys threw her hands in the air. "We cure our own bacon at the Pig in a Poke and have ever since Bruce and I inherited the shop from my father. We get the pork belly directly from Sheffield's Farm outside Lower Chumley. You won't get any better than that. We have our own special blend of seasonings that my great-grandfather passed down to my grandfather, my father, and now me." She paused and looked at Figgy. "I'm feeling a bit peckish. . . ."

"I've got just the ticket," Figgy said as she headed back to the tearoom.

"Anyway," Gladys said as she twisted her apron in her hands, "some of our customers were asking for bacon that would keep longer than five or six days, which is all you can expect with fresh bacon, so we began preserving some batches with sodium nitrite."

Figgy had returned with a plate of jammie dodgers and Gladys's eyes lit up as she took one.

"But why are the police searching for sodium nitrite?" Figgy passed the plate around. "Is it poisonous or something?"

"It can be, if ingested in sufficient quantities." Mabel shook her head when Penelope held the plate out to her. "There have been cases where people have used it to commit suicide."

Penelope shivered. "But why are the police looking for it? Unless . . ."

Mabel nodded. "Unless sodium nitrite was found in Simeon Foster's body."

"That would make it murder," Penelope said, and Mabel nodded.

"I doubt he wanted to commit suicide. He had so much to look forward to." Mabel tucked a wayward strand of hair behind her ear.

Gladys clapped a hand to her forehead. "And here I've been running me mouth all over town about how Foster's shop was going to ruin my business. That's what they call motive isn't it?"

Mabel nodded.

"I may have even said I wished he was dead." Gladys choked back a sob. "And now they're going to find sodium nitrite in my shop. What are they going to think?"

"It's possible they're going to think you committed murder," Mabel said dryly.

Mabel's comment sent Gladys into another round of hysterics but, thanks to another cup of tea from Figgy and several more biscuits, they were able to calm her down.

"I don't think you really have anything to worry about," Mabel said as she plucked a tissue from the box on the counter. "You have a perfectly logical reason for having sodium nitrite in your possession."

"I do, don't I?" Gladys dabbed at her lips with her handkerchief. "And I swear I was selling pasties the whole night," she said between bites of the last jammie dodger. "Anyone can tell you that. I didn't go near Foster."

A movement must have caught her eye because she turned to look out the window of the Open Book. Penelope glanced in that direction as well in time to see several constables standing around the counter of the Pig in a Poke.

The sight sent Gladys into a new wave of hysterics. She grabbed Penelope's hand.

"You'll look into it, won't you? You'll do some investigating like you did last time?" she pleaded.

Several images flashed through Penelope's mind, including being held at knifepoint by a murderer. She was going to say no but somehow it came out as a *yes* instead.

Mabel cleared her throat, but Penelope pretended not to see the warning look Mabel gave her.

TEN

❧

The bookstore was quiet that afternoon although most of the tables in Figgy's tea shop were filled with customers craving their afternoon cuppa and a bite of something sweet to tide them over until dinner.

Penelope decided to seize the moment to do a bit of writing. She hoped she could get past the negative effect that bad review she'd read Sunday morning had created and continue on with her manuscript. She set her laptop up on the desk in her writing room and prepared to settle in.

The quiet of the room was so complete it felt like a thick fog clogging her ears, and Penelope was tempted to hum just to break the silence. She forced herself to open the file with her work in progress and bring up the document.

She was still at an impasse. Should Luna investigate the sounds she was hearing, or should she go back to bed?

Penelope knew what she herself would do—she'd dive under the covers as fast as she could and pull them over her head.

But unfortunately, that wouldn't do for Luna. After thinking for several minutes, she came to a decision. Luna would light a candle, put on her dressing gown, and leave her room. She would go down the stairs to the library, where she might be able to hear the sounds more clearly. On the way, she would meet the housekeeper with the mysterious scar, turn around, and retreat to her bedroom once more. Luna was becoming wary of Lord Hawthorne, but she'd been afraid of the housekeeper since their first meeting.

Satisfied with that decision, Penelope began to write. She was finishing up the scene when her cell phone rang. She recognized the number and felt a twinge of excitement.

"Hello?"

It was Maguire, asking if she was free for an early dinner.

Of course she said yes.

Penelope left the Open Book promptly at five o'clock. Maguire was waiting in his car at the curb. Penelope caught the scent of his aftershave as she opened the door. He leaned toward her, gave her a quick kiss, and then put the car in gear.

The lights in the shops winked out one by one as they made their way down the high street. The parking lot at Tesco was crowded with the cars of people doing their shopping after work, and a group of young men was heading into Kebabs and Curries.

The Book and Bottle turned out to be relatively subdued,

at least compared to its normal bustle, with a few regulars sitting at the bar hoisting tankards of ale and a group of women at a table in the back laughing, talking over each other, and drinking shandies. For once, the fruit machine was quiet and no one had started a game of darts yet.

Maguire looked around the room. "It's strange to find the Book and Bottle so quiet." He looked at his watch. "But it is early."

"I was thinking the same thing." Penelope pushed her glasses up her nose with her index finger and stared at the menu scrawled on the blackboard.

"That's new," Penelope said, pointing at the menu. "Maple-glazed pork belly." She frowned. "I hope the Book and Bottle isn't going to turn into one of those gastropubs my sister's been telling me about."

"Not a chance." Maguire laughed. "That's for the tourists. I doubt a single local resident will ever order that dish." He rubbed his chin as he glanced at the blackboard one more time. "Have you decided?"

Penelope hesitated. She'd come to love all the dishes the Book and Bottle offered even if she hadn't recognized half of them when she'd first arrived in Upper Chumley-on-Stoke. "I'll have the shepherd's pie," she said finally. "And a cider."

"Coming right up." Maguire slid out of his seat and made his way to the bar.

Penelope's phone buzzed and she rummaged around in her tote bag until she found it. Not for the first time, she resolved to clean the bag out.

She looked at the screen. It was a text from Beryl asking if Penelope wanted to have dinner.

Penelope texted her back and suggested they meet after dinner instead.

Beryl had just replied that that was fine when Maguire returned to their table with a tray laden with frosty glasses and dishes wreathed in steam.

Penelope stared at the tray. There was her shepherd's pie and cider, ale for Maguire, and two other plates—one Welsh rarebit and one bangers and mash.

"You must be starving," she said as Maguire placed her order in front of her.

"I'm ravenous. All I had for lunch was a handful of crisps I stole from a bag on the secretary's desk. There wasn't time to grab anything else. My governor is pushing hard for a resolution to the Foster case."

"So Foster's death is being considered a case," Pen said around a mouthful of shepherd's pie.

Maguire nodded. "According to the autopsy and toxicology reports, he ingested a large amount of sodium nitrite. The remains of the food we found with him are being tested."

Penelope pictured the scene of Foster's death in her mind. She was quite sure the image would be etched in her memory forever. There had been a container of take-out food on his blanket, some Jaffa cakes, and a box of chocolates. The poison had to have been put in one or the other of those.

"So, you think it was murder?"

Maguire gave a smile that lifted only one side of his mouth. "We don't think it was suicide, let's put it that way."

"Is that why you searched Gladys Watkins's shop?"

Maguire poked at his mashed potatoes before answering. "Let's say we're keeping an open mind," he said finally. He looked up from his plate. "Let's face it. Half the town had a motive for murdering him."

That was one way of putting it, Penelope thought. And it was clear that that was all she was going to get out of him.

Maguire pulled up to the curb outside Pen's cottage. He left the car running as he walked her to her front door.

Pen put her key in the lock and turned to thank Maguire for dinner but before she could speak, his lips were on hers, kissing her gently. He pulled away and put a hand on her cheek.

"I wish I didn't have to go back to work."

Pen was thinking the exact same thing. They reluctantly said goodnight and Penelope opened her front door.

Mrs. Danvers was there to greet her, rubbing against her leg as she hung up her jacket. Pen bent down to pet her, but Mrs. Danvers had other plans and bolted for the kitchen.

Penelope spent a few minutes tidying up her sitting room—plumping the pillows, straightening her to-be-read pile of books, and kicking her slippers under the sofa where Beryl wouldn't be able to see them.

She thought she had a bottle of chardonnay in the refrigerator. She hoped it wouldn't be too oaky for Beryl's taste. Beryl fancied herself a connoisseur of fine wine while Penelope identified a good bottle of wine by whether it had a cork or a screw top.

She was headed toward the kitchen when the doorbell rang.

"I thought I saw a few flakes of snow," Beryl said as she stepped into the cottage. "It's freezing out there."

She was wearing a matching coat and dress—very Kate

Middleton, Penelope thought. It was an elegant outfit, although she couldn't picture herself in anything like it. Her clothes consisted of a collection of leggings, baggy sweaters, and a pantsuit for the rare occasions when she had to dress up.

Beryl had an Hermès scarf around her neck and a Louis Vuitton bag on her arm—the last vestiges of her life as the wife of the notorious perpetrator of a large-scale Ponzi scheme. The subsequent shame and notoriety had been what had sent her fleeing to England to join Penelope.

Beryl glanced at the fireplace with a look of disappointment on her face. "I was hoping you'd have a fire going."

"I would have, but I just got in. I had an early dinner with Maguire."

Beryl raised her eyebrows as she slipped out of her coat. "And he didn't stay? I would have understood if you'd wanted to cancel."

Penelope made a face. "He had to go back to work."

"So he said." Beryl handed her coat to Penelope. "You've been going out how long now?"

Penelope felt herself bristle. She was taking it slow this time around after her disastrous relationship with Miles back in New York. She hadn't known whether to be upset or angry when he'd ditched her to marry someone named Sloan.

To hide her discomfort, she quickly retreated to the kitchen to fetch the wine and get over her irritation at Beryl's insinuation that Maguire was simply passing the time with her. She fussed around, taking the bottle from the refrigerator and dusting off a couple of wineglasses.

She carried everything into the sitting room where Beryl was relaxing on the sofa, leafing through one of Penelope's books. There was an air of excitement about her that had replaced the distress she'd exhibited at the town council meeting and which she'd never explained to Pen. Penelope had to admit her curiosity was aroused.

She poured the wine and handed a glass to Beryl.

"You seem to have gotten over whatever it was that upset you at the town council meeting."

Beryl looked down at her lap. "I was rather upset, wasn't I. I'm afraid it's complicated." She spread out her fingers, the nails polished a glossy crimson. "I met this man on the train. I quite liked him. He was intelligent, sharp, funny. His name was Sam Frost. Or so he said. We had lunch in London a few times. He took me to dinner at Hawksmoor Wood Wharf. It's a steak place that's actually floating on the river." Her mouth twisted into an ironic smile. "We really hit it off."

"You never told me about him." Penelope felt slightly indignant.

Beryl held out her hands. "I didn't want to jinx it. I know that sounds silly but . . ."

"I understand," Pen said soothingly. She had her share of superstitions, too. She remembered the time when she was a kid when she really thought that if she stepped on a crack, she'd break her mother's back.

"Anyway," Beryl exhaled loudly. "It turns out Sam Frost wasn't his real name. Go figure, right?" She clenched her fists.

Pen cocked her head. "Oh?" She couldn't imagine what sort of person would give out a false name.

Beryl ran a hand through her blond bob. "His real name was Simeon Foster. Sound familiar? And he was married. I recognized him at the town council meeting. Sitting with his wife. That's why I got so upset." She gave a bark of laughter. "And now he's dead, so it no longer matters." She looked down at her hands.

Penelope had a horrible thought. What if Beryl became a suspect in Foster's murder? Surely no one would think her sister capable of murder!

"Still. It smarts—to be fooled like that." She brightened. "But something has come along to cheer me up. . . ."

"Another man?" Penelope said. She hoped it was something else. Beryl needed to give herself time to process what had happened with Magnus. The whole affair had been a traumatic experience.

"No. Frankly, something better." Beryl put her wineglass down on the coffee table with a soft clink.

"Don't keep me in suspense."

Beryl looked like the proverbial cat that swallowed the canary. Penelope stared at her expectantly.

"I told you. I don't want to jinx it," Beryl said finally.

ELEVEN

⁓◦⁓

Penelope woke up the next morning with a feeling of excitement. Her writing group was meeting in the afternoon to celebrate one of its members—Davina Parker—who had completed her manuscript and was beginning to submit to agents.

Writing a book was difficult, and Penelope felt it was important to celebrate each step to give the writer a feeling of accomplishment. Having a book published was a long and arduous process and it was too easy to become discouraged and quit.

Figgy was supplying her usual delicious array of pastries, but Penelope wanted to do something more, so she popped into the Jolly Good Grub for some cheese and crackers before heading to the Open Book.

Grant was arranging a pyramid of cans of Baxters Favourites Royal Game soup when Penelope pushed open the door to the shop. She noticed his hands were shaking slightly as he placed the cans in a pyramid.

He twisted around as Penelope grabbed a shopping basket from the stack by the door. "Good morning, Penelope."

"Good morning, Grant," Penelope responded.

"It's looking like rain today, isn't it? Masses of dark clouds moving in, I see."

"I thought I felt a few drops," Pen said. She held out her umbrella. "Fortunately, I came prepared."

"Jolly good show," Grant said, reaching into the carton for another can.

"I've never heard of Royal Game soup before." Penelope picked up a can and examined the label.

"It was created by Ethel Baxter in nineteen twenty-nine. It's quite good—venison and pheasant in a lovely rich broth. The queen bestowed the Royal Warrant of Appointment on it."

"I'll have to try some." Penelope dropped the can she was holding into her basket.

She held her breath as Grant placed the final can on the pyramid. His hands were still shaking and the structure wobbled precariously before settling down.

"Is everything okay?" Pen said.

Grant scrubbed his hands over his face. "No. I'm afraid it isn't. The police were in yesterday searching the store. 'Whatever are you looking for?' I asked them. The young constable took me aside and explained that they were inspecting the shop to see if I had any sodium nitrite in my possession. As if I would even know what to do with it." Grant flapped his hands around his face.

"It's not just you," Penelope said reassuringly. "They searched Gladys's shop as well."

Grant's face brightened slightly. "They did?"

Penelope nodded.

"Is that what killed that dreadful man?" Grant's hand flew to his mouth. "I shouldn't say things like that, should I? Someone might be listening. The police will think I'm guilty."

"But you have an alibi," Penelope reassured him. "You were here at the shop all night, weren't you?"

"Yes," Grant said a little too brightly and she noticed his eyes dart to the right.

Was he lying? Penelope wondered as she picked out some Double Gloucester and a piece of West Country Farmhouse Cheddar. He probably had more to lose than anyone else in Chumley if Foster had opened his proposed gourmet shop.

But why would he be worried—he had been in the shop all evening and surely plenty of people had seen him. Perhaps something else was bothering him. She supposed having the police search your property would rattle anyone.

She was probably reading too much into his reaction. She picked up a box of Jacob's Cream Crackers, added them to her basket, and took everything to the counter for Grant to ring up.

We have a problem," Mabel whispered to Penelope when she returned to the Open Book. She jerked a thumb toward a chair where a rather disheveled woman was sitting. Her eyes were closed and she appeared to be sleeping. She had no books in her lap or on the small table next to her.

"She's been here for an hour," Mabel said. "Do you know who she is?"

Penelope shook her head. "No, but I saw her arguing with Simeon Foster the day after the town council meeting. I thought it was curious."

Mabel arched an eyebrow. "Indeed. With Foster? I can't imagine how their paths would have ever crossed, much less what they would have to argue about."

"She appeared to have been a bit worse for wear at the time."

"Maybe she was asking him for money. You see a lot of that these days—everyone with their hand out. I was shocked the last time I was in Kensington, of all places."

As they were speaking, the woman woke up with a snort and looked around her as if she was surprised to find herself sitting in a chair at the Open Book. She glanced at the tea shop where two women in boiled wool jackets were seated. They hadn't finished their pastries—a Chelsea bun and a cream scone—but had left a bite of each on their plates, which they'd pushed to the center of the table.

The woman who had been sleeping in the chair watched intently as the two women got up, dropped some coins on the table for a tip, and left. She looked around her as if to see if anyone was watching, then slipped on her coat and stood up.

She made her way, somewhat unsteadily, toward the tea shop and the table the women had just vacated, occasionally glancing around the shop to see if anyone had noticed her.

Penelope and Mabel watched in astonishment as the woman reached out a hand and snatched the leftover bits of pastry from the abandoned plates. Her movements were sharp and furtive, like an animal stealing vegetables from a garden.

She stuffed the morsels in her mouth greedily and chewed them quickly. She glanced at the plate as if disappointed that it was now empty. She paused and looked around again before snaking out a hand and sliding the coins off the table. With a lightning-like movement, she stuffed them into the pocket of her coat.

Penelope and Mabel both gasped and looked at each other, their mouths open in astonishment.

Mabel frowned. "The poor woman must be starving."

"I'm going to take her to the Chumley Chippie for something to eat," Pen said.

"How kind of you." Mabel put an arm around Pen's shoulders and squeezed.

Penelope felt slightly guilty since she had an ulterior motive in making the offer. It would give her a chance to talk to the woman—to find out who she was and perhaps why she was arguing with Foster after the town council meeting.

"Let me chip in," Mabel said. She pulled some pound notes from her pocket and handed them to Penelope.

"Thanks." Penelope held up her crossed fingers. "Wish me luck."

The woman spun around as Penelope approached her. Penelope couldn't interpret the look in her eyes. Was it fear? Annoyance?

The woman backed away as Penelope got closer until she came up against one of the tables that forced her to stop.

"What do you want?" she demanded.

"You're obviously hungry," Pen said in a soft voice.

"Yeah? So, what of it?"

"I'd like to take you to get something to eat."

A sly expression came across the woman's face. "I could fancy a bit of fish-and-chips, now that you mention it."

"I'll get my jacket," Penelope said as they walked toward the front door.

She grabbed her jacket off the coat tree and slipped into it.

Penelope noticed the woman was a bit wobbly as they crossed the street to the Chippie. At one point she stumbled and Penelope put out a hand to steady her, but she shook it off with a grunt.

The woman licked her lips as Penelope opened the door to the Chippie and the scents of frying fish-and-chips drifted toward them.

Stan was behind the counter while his brother, Mick, was handling the frying.

"Howdy," Stan said in what Penelope assumed he thought was an American accent.

They'd long since stopped exclaiming over her nationality. Penelope had been something of a rarity when she arrived in Chumley. Most of the residents hadn't been farther than London, an hour's train ride away, and some of them hadn't even ventured that far.

Stan, however, still thought it was a real knee-slapper to greet Penelope with an accent he must have picked up watching American cowboy movies.

The woman was hovering next to Penelope, and Penelope noticed Stan seemed to be startled when he saw her. His expression turned to one of suspicion and he glanced at Penelope with a quizzical look on his face. For a moment, she was afraid he was going to ask them to leave, but instead he said, "What can I get you?"

"We'll have the pollock," Pen said. "Two orders." She held up two fingers.

"Coming right up." Stan turned toward Mick, but Mick was already lowering fish-and-chips into the hot, rippling oil in the fryer.

Within minutes, Mick handed them their order and Penelope led the way to a table. The Chippie hadn't been crowded when they arrived, but she noticed a line had formed at the counter while they were waiting for their food.

Pen carried their tray over to an empty table and sat down. She put one of the plates in front of the woman, who was eyeing it hungrily.

Penelope shook malt vinegar on her chips. "What's your name?" she said, looking down so she didn't appear confrontational.

Pen glanced at the woman from under her lids. She looked suspicious and had crossed her arms over her chest.

"It's Courtney. Courtney Brown," she said finally.

Pen cut a piece of her fish and put it in her mouth. She hadn't realized she was hungry until right now, but suddenly she was ravenous. They ate in silence until they were both nearly done.

"I saw you arguing with Simeon Foster after the town council meeting," Pen said in what she hoped was an off-handed manner.

Courtney's head shot up. "That pillock."

"How did you know him?" Pen toyed with her fork, hoping to look nonchalant.

"He is a right so-and-so, he is. Thinks he's a real toff now that's he got money."

Penelope tried again. "What did the two of you argue about?" She pretended to be busy chasing the last bite of fish around her plate.

"Him and those shops of his. Epicurean Gourmet indeed!"

"Were you opposed to his proposal to open a shop in Chumley?"

Courtney looked at Penelope as if she had two heads, and Penelope didn't blame her. It seemed fairly obvious that Foster's gourmet shop would have no effect on Courtney one way or the other.

Penelope tried again. "Were you friends with Foster? Neighbors? Acquaintances?"

Penelope was beginning to feel frustrated. So far, Courtney had done nothing but deflect her questions. Was that on purpose or because she was still a bit the worse for wear?

Courtney's face had become blotched with red spots. She looked around the restaurant.

"I don't suppose there's any way I could get a wee drop of something to tide me over?" Her tone was wheedling, like a child asking for a cookie before dinner.

"I'm afraid not," Pen said, trying to keep the astonishment out of her voice.

Courtney fixed Penelope with a stare. Her eyes, which were drooping half closed, were bloodshot.

"If I were you," she said, stabbing a finger, into the air, the nail broken and ragged and the cuticle red and inflamed, "I'd stay away from Simeon Foster."

Penelope was taken aback. Was it possible Courtney didn't know? She supposed it was possible. Courtney probably didn't have access to a television or even the local newspaper.

Penelope cleared her throat. "I'm sorry, but Simeon Foster is dead."

Courtney's eyes widened and her mouth formed a small round *o*. She then began to laugh—a high-pitched cackle that had her rocking back and forth in her chair. Several of the other diners turned and looked in their direction.

That was curious, Penelope thought. Did she really not know that Foster was dead? Or, was she trying to cover up the fact that she was the one who had killed him?

TWELVE

~◦¡◦~

Penelope stood back and admired the arrangement of cheese and crackers she'd made. She had found a wooden tray in the stock room of the Open Book, and it had served admirably to hold the Gloucester and cheddar cheeses and the cream crackers she'd purchased from the Jolly Good Grub.

She carried the tray into the shop and set it on the table along with some cocktail napkins and a pitcher of ice water. She straightened the chairs and then sat down to wait.

She heard a loud squeak as Figgy wheeled over the tea cart. There was a pot of tea in a blue-flowered cozy, cups and saucers, and an array of goodies—slices of Madeira cake, shortbread cookies, and a plate of parlies—a buttery cookie flavored with ginger and black treacle or golden syrup.

Even though Penelope had had plenty to eat at the

Chumley Chippie, she was tempted to snatch a piece of the Madeira cake. The crackled sugar topping was so enticing.

Figgy's face was flushed from the hot oven, and she fanned herself with her hand.

"I must look a sight," she said, brushing back the hair that had stuck to her damp forehead. "Fortunately, I'll have an hour to change before Derek gets here. He's taking me to dinner at a place in Lower Chumley-on-Stoke."

Derek was Figgy's fiancé. They would probably have been married by now if she and her mother hadn't been haggling over the type of ceremony they would have. Lady Isobel Innes-Goldthorpe wanted something befitting the daughter of an earl, while Figgy was inclined toward something more casual that would incorporate some of the Pakistani traditions of Derek's family.

"Good luck with your book group," Figgy said over her shoulder as she returned to the tea shop, where three women had taken seats.

"Thanks," Pen called after her.

She was surveying the table and making sure everything was in place when Davina Parker arrived. She'd brought a bottle of sparkling wine along with some plastic glasses. Together, she and Penelope arranged them alongside the tray of cheese and crackers.

Violet Thatcher, who was the wife of the vicar of St. Andrew's Anglican Church in Chumley, drifted in shortly after Davina. She was a spindly woman with fuzzy white hair and a timid manner.

"It's bitter out today," she said as she hung her coat over the back of her chair. "It's the kind of cold that gets into your bones." She wrapped her arms around herself and shivered.

"Cheerio," Brimble called out as he headed toward

them. History, especially military history, was his passion and he'd joined Penelope's writing group to work on a historical novel set during World War I.

Two more people rushed in and took chairs around the table. One of them, Sophie Tuttle, was a student at the Oakwood School for Girls, where Penelope had recently taught a seminar on Gothic literature. She'd been in Penelope's writing group there and had received permission from the head to join this one. Penelope thought she was quite talented and wanted to encourage her in any way she could.

"How is Robert?" Davina said, turning toward Violet.

"He's on a retreat at the moment," Violet said, picking at a frayed spot on her coat. "He spends so much time helping others—our phone never stops ringing, even during the night—that he was wearing himself out and needed some silence and time for prayer."

"How long will he be gone?"

"Not long. Only three days. I don't fancy being alone for longer than that. You never know what might happen." Her glance darted from side to side as if she expected to encounter danger in the middle of the Open Book.

"Quite a shock about that fellow Foster." Davina picked up the bottle of wine and began to fill the glasses. She handed them around to everyone except Sophie, who was too young to drink. "All the shopkeepers here in Chumley were up in arms. I was talking to Terry Jones the other day." She turned to Penelope. "He owns the Sweet Tooth candy shop on the high street. He was beside himself. Chocolates flown in from Belgium indeed! As if English chocolates aren't good enough." She puffed out her chest. "And Terry makes his own truffles. They're fresh every day and they taste divine."

Violet nodded. "They are special, aren't they? Particularly the sticky toffee ones and the eggnog-flavored ones he makes during the holidays."

Davina was nodding as she put down her glass of wine. "You have to get to the shop early in the morning to snag any of those. By teatime, they're all gone."

"I always put in an order at the beginning of the season," Violet said with a smug look on her face. "Robert particularly fancies the sticky toffee truffles." She shrugged. "I prefer the eggnog myself."

"Still," Davina said, helping herself to a bit of Gloucester and a cream cracker. "Terry seemed quite concerned about the competition from Foster's Epicurean Gourmet."

"Concerned enough to . . ." Brimble ran a finger across his throat dramatically.

Davina looked startled. "I don't know. There is something . . . savage about the man. As if he's simmering with barely controlled rage."

Brimble put his hands on the table. "He's a former military man. It affects people in different ways." He brushed a finger over his mustache. "Some of them have a hard time letting go of that state of readiness and the feeling that danger constantly lurks around every corner."

Davina looked skeptical. "All I can say is, I wouldn't be surprised if he'd taken matters into his own hands."

"What about the others?" Violet said in her tremulous voice. "All the shop owners would have been affected by Foster's gourmet store."

"Oh, pooh," Davina said. "I can't picture Gladys Watkins killing anyone, can you? She's way too scatterbrained to pull it off. Or Clementine Harrison, for that matter? She can barely work up the courage to say *boo*."

"What about Grant then?" Violet said. "He certainly wouldn't have wanted another gourmet shop in town."

"Oh, Grant," Davina said dismissively. She held out an arm and waved her hand. "I can't imagine him hurting a fly."

Penelope was about to mention her encounter with Courtney but decided it was time to get things back on track. Besides, there was no point in adding to the gossip that was already swirling around Chum. Instead, she offered up a toast to Davina, who glowed with pride.

Davina wagged a finger at Penelope. "I'm not there yet, mind you," she said, coloring slightly. "There's a long road to publication ahead. But I can tell you there is a certain satisfaction in finishing something. So even if nothing ever comes of it, I'm proud that I stuck it out until I could type *the end*."

After that, and after everyone had helped themselves to some treats from Figgy's cart, Penelope decided they needed to get down to business or they'd never be done.

She cleared her throat and waited until the chatter died down.

"Let's discuss how important it is to give your protagonist a flaw," she began.

But she had to admit that even while she was talking about character flaws, her mind was elsewhere. Davina had made it quite clear that she considered Terry Jones a prime suspect in Foster's murder. She was going to have to check it out for herself, Penelope decided.

Penelope cleaned up the table after the group left, throwing out the used and crumpled napkins and picking at the bits of cheese that were left. Figgy's cart was nearly empty, but she snagged the last piece of Madeira cake and one of the parlies.

Mabel walked by with an armload of books to reshelve. She eyed the cookie in Penelope's hand.

"You're so lucky to have such a youthful metabolism. If I ate as many sweets as you do, I'd put on a stone overnight."

It was true, Penelope thought. She rarely gained weight no matter how much she ate but perhaps it was because she could easily forget to eat altogether. The British, on the other hand, ate often, having elevenses and afternoon tea along with the usual breakfast, lunch, and dinner.

Mabel stopped by on her way back from shelving the books. "India called while you were hosting your writing group," she said, leaning against the table. "The poor thing slipped and fell while hosting a tour of Worthington House. It seems she's sprained her ankle and is hobbling around using a cane."

Penelope's eyes opened wide and she put a hand to her mouth. "Oh, no."

"She insists she's going to be absolutely fine, but you know India. Stiff upper lip and all that."

Penelope smiled. India had more backbone than most of the people she knew.

"A book she was hoping to find used—one of Louise Penny's latest—was just brought in by Olive Payne. She's a teacher at the Chumley Comprehensive. A lovely lady." Mabel brushed a piece of lint off her sweater. "Poor India can't come in to get the book and it would be the perfect thing to cheer her up while she's laid up. I thought you might possibly run it over to her since we're about to close? India said she would leave the door off the latch." Mabel raised her eyebrows. "If you don't mind, that is."

"Of course. I'd be glad to."

"Let me get the book."

Penelope followed Mabel to the front counter. She slipped into her jacket and took the package Mabel handed her.

"Off you go then," Mabel said with a smile. "India will surely be chuffed to see you."

P enelope was on her way home to collect her car when she passed the Sweet Tooth. Perhaps a box of chocolates might perk India up as well. Penelope knew she liked sweets and was particularly fond of the Sweet Tooth's chocolate caramel truffles.

She pushed open the door and stepped over the threshold, pausing momentarily to take in all the delicious smells. It was intoxicating—notes of chocolate and vanilla mingled with those of sugar and fruit.

In many small English towns, the post office was not housed in a separate building but rather inside a store. Chumley's post office was no exception and was located at the back of the Sweet Tooth. It was run with military precision by Mrs. Nutter, the postmistress. She was behind the grill today, stamping and sorting mail with frightening efficiency.

Penelope waved to her, and she smiled and waved back. Even though her face was set in almost-permanent lines of disapproval, Penelope had found her to be quite warm and friendly.

A woman was standing at the counter, handing over a letter, and when she turned, Penelope realized it was Clementine Harrison. She smiled when she saw Penelope.

"I so enjoyed your book group the other day," she said as she approached Penelope. "I loved Charlotte Davenport's book." She giggled. "Or, perhaps I should say the Duchess of Upper Chumley-on-Stoke." She cocked her head to the side. "Does anyone know what they've named their baby? I'm terribly curious." She giggled again.

She had an expectant look on her face as if she was confident that Penelope was privy to that information.

"I certainly don't know," Penelope said, even though Beryl had already told her the baby was named Grace. "But I imagine there will be some news when she's baptized."

Clementine looked at Penelope as if she knew Penelope was holding something back but then she smiled, said good afternoon, and headed toward the door.

Penelope turned to the truffle counter, where luscious-looking chocolates were displayed on trays. She nearly drooled as she read the labels—cappuccino, Black Forest—those had a bright red cherry on top—lemon cream, champagne white chocolate, and, of course, India's favorite—the chocolate caramel.

Terry Jones was behind the counter, filling in the gaps on the tray with fresh truffles. He looked up when Penelope cleared her throat.

"I'll be right with you," he said, turning around.

Penelope noticed he limped as he made his way to the storeroom as if one leg was slightly shorter than the other. She hadn't noticed it at the town council meeting but then she'd been distracted by everything else that was going on.

Within moments Terry was back behind the counter. "What can I do for you?"

He rested his thick, muscular forearms on top of the display case.

"I'll take half a dozen of your chocolate caramel truffles." Penelope pointed to a tray in the case.

"Coming right up." Terry reached for a sheet of glassine from a box behind him.

Once again, Penelope marveled that such a rough-looking man, with his coarse features and slightly flattened nose, made something so delicious and delicate as these exquisite truffles.

Terry was boxing up the truffles when Rupert Yardley approached the counter.

"I'm visiting my mother this weekend and the old girl is quite fond of Terry's lemon cream truffles," he said to Penelope. He peered over the counter. "What's that you're getting?"

"Some chocolate caramel ones for India Culpepper."

"Ah, India. Great old gal. She knows a lot about the history of Chumley. She's been most helpful with my research."

Terry handed Penelope the box of candy. "Half a dozen chocolate caramel truffles," he said.

Penelope took the pink and white box, thanked him, and got out her wallet.

"What can I get you?" Terry turned to Rupert.

"A dozen lemon creams," Rupert said. "Say, that was quite a rousing speech you gave at the town council meeting. Too bad it didn't have any effect on the vote." He laughed. "But I suppose all's well that ends well."

Terry grunted as he reached into the case.

"Did I tell you," Rupert said to Penelope, "Laurence Brimble and I are thinking about collaborating on a book of military history?" He turned to Terry. "Was that limp of yours a war injury? I'm afraid I've forgotten."

"You can't have forgotten." Terry looked up at him from under thunderous brows. "Because I've never said."

That was odd, Penelope thought as she left the shop. Maybe Terry just didn't want to talk about his injury or maybe he was tired of answering people's questions about it.

Or, maybe he had something to hide.

THIRTEEN

❧

Penelope dashed into her cottage to grab her car keys. Mrs. Danvers was not pleased by her brief appearance and let it be known by refusing to allow herself to be petted as Penelope went back out the front door.

Penelope smiled as she got into her new MINI. New to her, at least. It was cold and she was grateful the heat was in perfect working order. It felt heavenly when it kicked in. It took all her concentration to stay on the correct side of the road as she made her way down the high street. The road soon narrowed into barely more than one lane, bordered by hedgerows and with open fields on either side.

India and Arthur Worthington, the Duke of Upper Chumley-on-Stoke, were distantly related and India's cottage was on the grounds of the Worthington estate.

Penelope parked the car and got out. The wind blew her hair across her face as she walked toward India's door. The wild roses on the fence bordering the stone path had become dormant, the blossoms long gone, leaving the gnarly stalks bare. Penelope knocked on the door briefly and then opened it, stepping into the tiny foyer. A tole-painted metal umbrella stand stood in the corner with the wooden handle of a black umbrella along with several carved walking sticks protruding from the top.

"India?" Pen called out.

"In here, dear. Come through."

India was sitting in an armchair pulled up to the stone fireplace, her bandaged foot resting on a cracked leather hassock and a cane with a carved head hooked over the arm of the chair. A steady fire was burning in the grate, the flickering light reflecting on the low, beamed ceiling.

India was wearing her customary plaid wool skirt and sweater and had a hand-knitted throw over her legs. Her face lit up when Penelope walked into the room.

"So good to see you, dear."

Penelope handed her the package from the Open Book. "This should cheer you up."

India removed the book from the bag, stared for a moment at the cover, then held it to her chest.

"I am so looking forward to this." She smiled up at Penelope.

"I also brought you these," Penelope said, handing over the box of chocolates from the Sweet Tooth.

"My favorites. Chocolate caramel truffles. That's most thoughtful of you, dear."

"How about I make us a cup of tea?" Pen said.

"That would be delightful. I can hobble around a bit, but it isn't easy. Arthur has been so kind, having his chef bring me meals."

"Two cups of tea coming up," Penelope said as she made her way to the kitchen.

India's electric kettle was already plugged in. Penelope

filled it with water and switched it on. She found two mugs in the cupboard—one commemorating Queen Elizabeth II's Silver Jubilee and the other celebrating the marriage of Prince Charles and Lady Diana.

Penelope put a tea bag in each mug—Lapsang souchong, which was one of India's favorite afternoon teas—and added boiling water from the kettle. She carried both out to the sitting room.

A small occasional table was pulled up to India's armchair and Penelope placed her mug on it. She pulled up a chair for herself and sat down.

India gave a rueful smile. "So clumsy of me." She pointed at her ankle. "I tripped on a bit of uneven flooring in the great hall and twisted my ankle. Poor Arthur was in quite a state of worry." Her expression became grave, and she looked down at the mug of tea in her hand. "He thinks I should consider moving to a care home."

Penelope was startled. "Just because you tripped?"

India nodded. "He seems to think I can't do for myself anymore, which everyone knows is ridiculous. Anyone could trip and sprain their ankle, but we don't put all of them in care homes, do we? Goodness, the homes would be filled to the brim." Two indignant patches of red blossomed on her cheeks.

Penelope patted India's hand. "I would imagine the final decision is up to you. If you're comfortable living alone, then why move?"

"Exactly."

Penelope took a sip of her tea. "You know so many people in Chumley. I was wondering if you knew a woman named Courtney Brown?"

India wrinkled her forehead. "Such a common name, Brown. And of course, the name Courtney was popular in the late eighties." Her face brightened. "I did know of a Karen Brown." She winced as she repositioned her foot on the ottoman. "How old is your Courtney Brown?"

Penelope closed her eyes in concentration. She tried to picture Courtney in her mind's eye.

"Perhaps around midthirties?"

India shook her head. "Karen Brown must be in her fifties by now."

"Could she have had a daughter?"

India fiddled with a button on her cardigan. "I suppose she might have had. I only knew her because she worked in the Oxfam shop here in Chumley. She was very kind. If something good was brought in that she thought I'd like, she'd set it aside for me." India's hand dropped into her lap. "The last time I was in the shop, she wasn't there. But I suppose it could have been her day off."

"When was the last time she saved something for you?"

India drummed her fingers on the arm of her chair. "Let me see. I haven't heard from her in ages. The last time she had something for me, it was coming up on Arthur's fortieth birthday and she'd found the perfect dress for me to wear. It was quite lovely—light blue chiffon with just a touch of embroidery and a matching jacket. That was more than a year ago, I'm afraid."

"Did you see her after that?"

India furrowed her brow. "It was around Whitsunday. The same week, I think. That was the Sunday that little Robbie Blake was baptized. That would have been early June." India began smoothing out the pleats in her skirt. "Oh, dear. I do hope Karen didn't lose her job because of the little favors she was doing for me."

Penelope patted India's hand. "I'm sure she was very discreet."

"I do hope you're right." India put her empty teacup down on the side table. "She was a lovely lady and so hard-working. She did have a child, I know. A daughter. It can't have been easy being a single mother."

"What about the father? They were divorced?"

India frowned. "He doesn't seem to have ever been in the picture at all. I got the impression he left when the child was quite young." India sighed. "You see more and more of that these days, don't you?" She folded her hands and put them in her lap. "Is there anything else I can do for you, dear?"

Penelope smiled. "You've been a big help already."

India made a move as if to get up. Penelope shook her head and held out a hand. "No. No need to get up. I can see myself out."

She knew what her next step was going to be, Penelope thought as she closed the door to India's cottage behind her. Perhaps she could interest Figgy in a trip to the local Oxfam. If Karen Brown no longer worked there, perhaps someone would know where she'd gone. And if Karen Brown was Courtney Brown's mother, as Penelope hoped, perhaps she would know what the relationship was between Courtney and Simeon Foster.

She stopped halfway down the slate walk. There was no point in getting excited yet. She was assuming that Karen and Courtney were related. But as India had pointed out, Brown was a very common name and there might not be any relationship at all. She'd let herself get too worked up over the idea and felt slightly let down by the thought.

She'd find out soon enough and perhaps it would turn out that Courtney and Karen were related after all.

FOURTEEN

❧

Pen checked the local Oxfam website as soon as she left India's. According to their site, they were open for another hour. She decided to head there before going home. She was driving down the high street when she noticed Figgy looking in the window of the Knit Wit Shop. She glanced in her rearview mirror quickly—no one was behind her. She stopped and buzzed down her window.

"Hey," she called out, waving.

Figgy spun around and when she saw it was Penelope, said, "Do you want to go for a drink at the Book and Bottle?"

"I'm on my way to Oxfam before they close. Do you want to come? We could get a drink afterward."

"Sure."

Penelope noticed a car coming up behind her, but Figgy jumped into the front seat quickly and she was off again before the driver behind her could lean on his horn.

"Are you shopping for something in particular?" Figgy said, quickly fastening her seat belt.

Pen explained about Courtney Brown and how she was trying to track down her mother.

"I know it's a long shot, but I'm hoping she might be related to this Karen Brown who works at the Oxfam shop."

"Well, I'm always up for a trip to Oxfam." Figgy put her purse on the floor and settled into her seat.

Penelope already knew that most of Figgy's clothes were secondhand and came from Oxfam or various jumble sales. It was ironic, given that she had told Penelope that her dress for the party after her graduation from university was designed for her and her shoes were bespoke from Emmy London.

Oxfam was nearly empty when they got there. Penelope had already decided they should look around the shop first and Figgy was more than happy to comply.

"Look at these," she squealed, pulling a hanger off the rack. Hanging from it was a pair of wide-legged, rainbow-striped pants. "I've got to get these," Figgy said, checking the size on the tag.

"Someone must have been cleaning out their attic," Pen said, pointing to the pants. "I remember finding a stack of old fashion magazines in our basement from the nineteen seventies and looking through them. I'm positive I saw those pants in one of the spreads."

"Maybe you'll find something, too." Figgy said, hugging her find to her chest.

Penelope wasn't much into fashion—it could be hard finding clothes for someone as tall as she was—but when she spotted a plain, black turtleneck sweater in a lovely soft merino wool, she pulled it from the rack.

Figgy made a face. "Don't you already have a black turtleneck?"

"I do. But my mother always says a woman can't have too many. She feels the only appropriate style is a simple one based on classic pieces like"—Penelope waved the garment at Figgy—"black turtlenecks."

Figgy pulled a dress off one of the racks and held it out. It was made of some sort of gauzy material in a small floral print and puffed sleeves. "You would look wonderful in this."

Penelope looked at it in dismay. "I can't begin to picture myself in that." She had to stifle a laugh.

Figgy sighed and put the dress back on the rack. "You need to branch out," she said. "Give something new a try."

Pen ignored her comment. "Are you going to buy those pants?" She pointed at the garment in Figgy's hands.

"Definitely." Figgy marched toward the counter. "They're perfect," she called over her shoulder with a grin.

Penelope trailed behind her. She was glad they'd each found something to buy. It would make her questions for the clerk seem less suspicious.

Figgy paused and waited for Penelope to catch up. "Should I ask the questions?" she whispered, her head bent toward Penelope's. "I've been here a lot so perhaps it will seem less like we're snooping?" She giggled.

"That's a great idea."

The clerk was young. Penelope guessed her to be in her early thirties. She would have been pretty but for rather close-set eyes. She had a scrubbed clean sort of look and smelled like soap.

"I'm so glad you've found something," she said, when they approached the counter. She looked at Figgy. "You've been here before. I remember you."

No wonder, Penelope thought. Figgy wasn't your regular, run-of-the mill customer with her short spiky hair, multiple piercings in each ear, and distinctive fashion choices.

"My good friend used to work here," Figgy said as she dug her wallet out of her purse. "Her name was Karen Brown. I'm afraid we've lost touch with each other. Does she still work here?"

The clerk shook her head. "She retired a couple of months ago. I've taken her place." She rolled her eyes. "I was desperate to get out of the house now that my youngest is finally in school. But I didn't want anything full-time, so this was perfect. I'm working late tonight to cover Georgina's shift—she was feeling unwell this morning. Fortunately, Mrs. Fitzhugh—she's our next-door neighbor—was happy to look after the little ones until I got home."

"You don't happen to know where Karen's gone, do you?"

The clerk's face brightened. "I do, as a matter of fact. She left me her contact information in case I had any questions. So far, so good." A shadow crossed her face. "I don't know if I should be giving out her address though."

Figgy gave the clerk her most winning smile. "I'm sure she wouldn't mind. I imagine she would be thrilled for us to meet up again."

"I don't know." The clerk reached under the counter and pulled out a piece of paper. She kept it clutched in her fist.

"Never mind." Figgy waved a hand. "I suppose I can look her up in the BT residential pages."

The clerk's face cleared. "I imagine that would be for the best."

They paid for their purchases, thanked the clerk, and left.

Penelope got out her phone as soon as they were in the

car. Within moments, she'd found the address. "She's on the Southfield Estate, number fifty-six Churchill Drive."

Penelope stuffed her phone in her pocket. I can look up the directions later."

"I have something to ask you," Figgy said as they were headed back down the high street toward town.

She was braiding the fringe on the end of her scarf. It wasn't like Figgy to be nervous, Pen thought. What was up?

Figgy twisted slightly in her seat so she was facing Penelope. "Will you be my maid of honor?"

Penelope felt tears spring to her eyes. She'd arrived in Upper Chumley-on-Stoke, knowing no one and fearing she'd never make any friends, and here Figgy was asking her to be in her wedding.

Penelope's voice was thick when she replied. "Of course, I would be honored to be in your wedding."

Figgy exhaled in a rush as if she'd been holding her breath. "I'm so glad." She clapped her hands together, the sound muffled by the woolen gloves she was wearing. "The wedding is on the twenty-sixth."

Penelope's eyebrows shot up. "You don't mean this month?" Pen paused. "Do you?" She glanced at Figgy.

Figgy laughed. "Yes, this month. November twenty-sixth."

"So soon?" Pen's voice squeaked. "What about all your mother's plans—the dress, the refreshments, the engraved invitations—" She stopped suddenly. "You're not—"

"No, of course not," Figgy said before Pen could finish the sentence. "Derek and I are tired of waiting. We want to buy a house and start our life together. He's going to sell his condo in the city and commute from Chumley. It's only an hour by train."

"What about Lady Goldthorpe? You said she's been

looking forward to your wedding ever since she found out she was having a girl."

"She's not thrilled about it; I can tell you that." Figgy snorted. "Fortunately, she's found a new project."

"Oh?" Penelope couldn't imagine Lady Goldthorpe abandoning her plans for Figgy's wedding for anything less than a royal wedding.

"My cousin Brenda is getting married next year to this positively dreary fellow named Cecil who's the heir to the Murray tire fortune. Brenda is the daughter of the Duke of Pemberton. Her mother was killed in a riding accident several years ago—her horse balked at a jump, and she was catapulted off and landed on her head. Sadly, she never recovered from her injuries. The duke has asked my mother to step in and help with the planning, and of course she was more than happy to oblige. It's going to be a huge affair and there are rumors the Duke and Duchess of Cambridge might attend since the duke and Fernsby were at uni together."

"Where are you and Derek going to be married?"

"In the chapel at Worthington House. Charlotte has graciously allowed us to use it and has offered us the great room for our reception."

"Your mother must be pleased about that."

Figgy nodded. "It went a long way in smoothing her ruffled feathers." She sighed. "It's going to be a small wedding. And it's going to be just what Derek and I wanted."

Penelope was pulling up to the curb in front of Figgy's apartment when her cell phone rang. She waved goodbye to Figgy and pulled her phone out of her pocket. It was

Maguire asking if she was up for dinner. He sounded dog-tired, so Penelope suggested he come by her place and she'd put something together for them. It would be more relaxing than the hustle and bustle at the Book and Bottle.

But that meant she had to come up with something for dinner. She wasn't a terrible cook, but her repertoire was quite limited—*spag bol*, as the Brits called spaghetti Bolognese—she could make a decent omelet and some pretty good chili. She pushed her glasses up her nose with her index finger and tried to think.

Finally, she settled on an array of appetizers, or what Beryl would call a charcuterie board. The Jolly Good Grub was still open, and she could pick up a selection of cheeses, meats, and other goodies for them to nibble on.

The lights from the Jolly Good Grub were warm and welcoming as Penelope drove around back to the small parking lot that served Grant's shop as well as several others.

As she got out of the car, she paused to look up at the sky, which was liberally sprinkled with stars. She inhaled deeply, taking in the scent of woodsmoke combined with the faintest suggestion of curry, which must have drifted on the current from Kebabs and Curries farther down the street.

A bell jingled as Penelope pushed open the door to the Jolly Good Grub. She felt her face flush as warm air hit it.

Grant was behind the counter talking to someone. The fellow turned his head slightly and Penelope recognized Rupert Yardley. He was leaning his elbows on the counter and was deep in discussion with Grant.

Grant appeared to be very animated, his hands constantly fluttering around his face, and his normally pale complexion was tinged with color.

Penelope grabbed a wire basket and began to traverse the aisles. She picked out a package of smoked salmon, sea salt-and-dill seed crackers, pork liver confit, dried salami, cheddar cheese, a round of Somerset Brie, and a jar of olives. She added a fresh baguette to the mix and surveyed her choices. It ought to be enough.

She grabbed a bottle of white wine that was on sale—she judged wine by the price, not the vintage—and added that to her purchases.

Rupert was turning away from the counter when Penelope began to walk toward it. He nodded at her as he passed her on his way to the door.

"Penelope," Grant gushed. "Lovely to see you again."

"Wasn't that Rupert Yardley?" she said as she lifted her basket onto the counter.

Grant's face turned so red Penelope could almost feel the heat radiating off of it.

"Yes, he came in to pick up a few things. You know, some cheese, a jar of Branston pickle, a bottle of wine . . ." His voice trailed off.

Penelope took her purchases out of the basket one by one and placed them on the counter.

Grant raised his eyebrows. "Having company, are you?" he said as he rang up each item. Pen noticed that his hand was shaking slightly.

"Y-yes," Penelope stuttered. So far, she and Maguire had managed to keep the fact that they were dating relatively quiet. Like most small towns, Chumley thrived on gossip, and neither one of them was anxious to become the subject of wagging tongues.

Grant waved his hand over the items on the counter. "This should make a lovely grazing board."

Penelope paid for her purchase, took the bag Grant handed her, and headed to her car.

Grant had been acting so peculiarly, she thought. She couldn't help but wonder why. He'd seemed almost embarrassed to have been talking to Rupert—like an earnest teenage boy being seen talking to a girl he had a crush on.

Was it possible that Grant had a thing for Rupert? He certainly acted like it. Penelope wondered if it was unrequited love or if it was reciprocated. She knew Rupert was a bachelor but that was all she really knew about him.

Poor Grant. It looked like he had it bad. What if his feelings weren't reciprocated? Penelope hoped he wasn't going to get hurt.

FIFTEEN

❧

Penelope heard Mrs. Danvers meowing as she put her key in the door. She eased it open, not wanting to accidentally hit the cat, but Mrs. Danvers had already scampered away, putting a safe distance between herself and the door.

Penelope put her bag from the Jolly Good Grub down and slipped off her jacket. Mrs. Danvers approached the bag, her tail swishing back and forth with curiosity, and gently sniffed at it. She immediately stalked away as if she found the contents of the bag to be unsatisfactory.

"There's smoked salmon in there," Pen said to Mrs. Danvers. "Aren't cats supposed to like fish?"

Mrs. Danvers gave her a pained look and began to groom her front paws.

Penelope carried the evening's provisions into the kitchen, where the warmth emanating from the Aga felt heavenly after the frigid night air. She warmed her hands for a moment, then popped the bottle of wine into the refrigerator and began looking through the cupboards for something suitable to serve as a tray for her grazing board.

She finally found a wooden bread board that would do nicely. She whistled as she carefully arranged the cheese, meats, and salmon, then tipped the olives into a small bowl and added them to the board.

She stepped back and eyed the finished product. Not bad, she decided.

She carried the board into the sitting room and was lighting a fire when the bell rang.

Her heartbeat quickened slightly as she rushed to the door and opened it.

Maguire did, indeed, look tired, Penelope thought. She was glad she had suggested an evening in. He was clutching a paper-wrapped bouquet of flowers in one hand and a bottle of wine in the other.

He kissed Penelope on the cheek. His lips were cold and a shiver went through her.

"This needs to go on ice"—he held up the bottle of wine—"and these need to go into some water." He handed her the flowers and followed her out to the kitchen.

Mrs. Danvers was right on his heels but when he bent down to pet her, she scooted off to stare balefully at him from her perch on one of the kitchen chairs.

Maguire stuck the bottle of wine in the refrigerator while Penelope hunted down a vase for the flowers. She found one on the top shelf of one of the cupboards and for once was glad she was tall, although her height had plagued her when she was younger, especially during the dance and etiquette classes her mother had insisted she take in middle school.

"There's a bottle of white in the fridge already," Pen said, trimming the stems of the flowers. "We can start with that while we wait for the other bottle to chill."

Penelope finished arranging the flowers and carried the vase into the sitting room while Maguire put the cuttings in the trash. She enjoyed the sense of easy companionship she felt as they worked side by side.

She fetched two glasses and Maguire carried them along with the wine out to the sitting room.

He stood by the fire and held his hands out toward the flames. "This was a great idea," he said, turning toward Penelope. "I can feel myself relaxing already." He moved away from the hearth and joined Penelope on the sofa.

"Have things been difficult at work?" Pen said, as she popped an olive into her mouth.

Maguire sighed and ran his hands through his hair, leaving it slightly disheveled. Penelope thought he looked adorable—like a little boy just waking up.

"It's this Foster murder case." Maguire spread some cheese on a cracker. "I guess the guy was some sort of big shot. He owned a whole chain of these gourmet shops and while the chain wasn't exactly as large as Tesco, for instance, it was big enough to earn him friends in high places." Maguire took a bite of the cracker. "There's a lot of pressure to solve the case and solve it quickly." He gave an ironic smile. "Like yesterday." He sighed. "It's not as if we lack for suspects."

Pen sat up straighter. "That reminds me. This strange woman came into the bookstore. She said her name was Courtney Brown and she seemed quite down and out. When I mentioned Simeon Foster, she became awfully agitated." Penelope searched her memory. "She called him a pillock."

Maguire laughed. "That seems to have been most people's impression of Foster."

"She didn't know he was dead and when I told her, she burst out laughing." Pen shivered. "It was all very odd."

Maguire shook his head. "So far this whole case has been very odd." He cut a piece of the baguette and topped it with some salami. "So far all we know is that Foster was poisoned with sodium nitrite, but the sodium nitrite wasn't in the takeaway food from Kebabs and Curries that he was eating when he died or in the tea in his thermos. The packet of Jaffa cakes hadn't been opened."

Penelope frowned. "What about the chocolates?"

Maguire looked startled. "Chocolates? What chocolates? We didn't find any at the scene."

"There was a box of chocolates from the Sweet Tooth on Foster's blanket along with the Jaffa cakes and the bag from Kebabs and Curries."

Maguire was frowning now. "I didn't find any chocolates when I got to the scene. Are you sure?"

Penelope nodded.

"And you dialed nine-nine-nine as soon as you found the body, right?"

"Yes. Shortly afterward, one of the constables at the celebration arrived."

"Did you leave the scene at any time? After you discovered Foster dead?"

Penelope squeezed the bridge of her nose. "No, not really. Wait." She held up a hand. "I saw the constable coming through the crowd and went to lead him to the scene. I didn't go far, and I wasn't gone long."

"Long enough for someone to steal that box of chocolates?" An alarmed look was spreading across Maguire's face. His shoulders dropped. "Surely if someone had taken the chocolates they would have been noticed."

Pen tilted her head to the side. "I don't know. Everyone was intent on watching the fireworks."

"We'll put out an alert anyway and hopefully someone will come forward."

"I suppose the killer was nearby and wanted to snatch the evidence before the police got there."

"Or someone thought the chocolates looked pretty enticing and decided to help themselves when no one was looking." Maguire inhaled sharply and his eyes widened. "What if the poison *is* in the chocolates—all of them? Because how else could the killer be sure Foster was poisoned? And someone out there has them. How long before they eat them?" Maguire groaned. "We could soon have another death on our hands."

When Penelope woke up the next morning, she heard strange noises in the kitchen. She held her breath. Was there an intruder? She glanced at her nightstand, where she'd left her cell phone the evening before. Should she call the police?

Then the realization washed over her. It *was* the police. It was Maguire. He was probably looking for something for breakfast. Unfortunately, like Mother Hubbard, he was going to find the cupboards nearly bare, Pen thought as she jumped out of bed and headed for the bathroom.

She quickly splashed some water on her face, brushed her teeth, and ran a brush through her hair. She dressed quickly and headed down the stairs.

Maguire was standing in the kitchen scratching his head when Pen walked in.

"I was going to make you a real English fry-up for breakfast, but you don't have any eggs or bacon or . . . or much of anything." He grimaced. "I'm going to run to Tesco and pick up some things. I'll be back in a tick."

Penelope followed him to the front door.

"Oh." He paused with one arm in the sleeve of his jacket. "That container of yogurt is well past its sell-by date. You might want to toss it in the bin."

He kissed Penelope on the cheek and opened the door, letting in a gust of frosty air. Penelope shivered and quickly closed it behind him.

She felt odd—unsettled—and found herself arranging and rearranging the throw pillows on the sofa. She was relieved when her cell phone rang. It was Beryl.

"Have you talked to mother lately?" Beryl said.

Penelope felt guilt wash over her. "Um, that depends on how you define *lately*."

"Did she tell you about Bruno?"

Pen frowned. "Bruno? That sounds like a bouncer."

"A gigolo is more like it. They're swarming all over Palm Beach like those wretched palmetto bugs."

"Well, who is he?" Pen hated when Beryl beat around the bush like this.

"I don't know," Beryl admitted. "But she's mentioned him three times now. And you know she never goes down to Palm Beach until after Christmas and she's there now. And it's not even Thanksgiving yet."

Penelope didn't see any connection between the two.

"Who does she say Bruno is?"

"A friend," Beryl said, and Penelope could imagine her putting air quotes around the word.

"Mother has lots of friends. What's the harm in that?"

"I know that," Beryl snapped. "And does she tend to mention them in every telephone conversation?"

Penelope thought back to the last few times she'd talked to her mother. "Um, no."

"I think Bruno is after her money."

"I don't think mother would do anything foolish, do you?"

"I don't know. You hear stories. . . ."

"What do you think we should do?"

"I don't know," Beryl said. "Let's think on it and touch base later."

"Sounds good. I should go anyway," Penelope said. "Maguire will be back any minute. He's gone to get some things for breakfast."

"Well, well, well," Beryl said. Her tone was smug. "It sounds like things are moving along. Maybe you're not wasting your time after all."

The front door opened and Maguire walked in carrying two grocery bags.

"I've got to go," Pen said, grateful for the excuse to end the call.

"Provisions," Maguire held out one of the bags and smiled.

Penelope followed him into the kitchen, where he pulled eggs, bacon, sausage, a can of beans, a loaf of bread, and a ripe tomato from the bags.

He slung his jacket over one of the kitchen chairs and turned to Penelope with his eyebrows raised.

"Frying pan?"

Ten minutes later, Maguire had whipped up a complete English breakfast. He set the plates on the table and rubbed his hands together.

"I'm starved. How about you?"

Penelope suddenly realized she *was* hungry. She sat down and they both dug in.

Penelope was mopping up the last drops of egg yolk from her plate with a piece of toast when Maguire's cell phone rang.

"At least we got to finish our breakfast," he said as he pulled his phone from his pocket.

"You're kidding me," he said after listening for several minutes. Finally, he ended the call.

"You won't believe this." He ran his hands through his hair. "Someone's reported what sounds like a Secret Santa." He chuckled. "I guess the season is starting early this year."

Penelope had the urge to laugh but she stifled it. "Seriously?"

"Yes. A fellow named Rupert Yardley complained that someone rang his bell but when he opened the door no one was there. Instead, he found a jar of Branston Pickle with a ribbon wrapped around it sitting on the doorstep."

Penelope's eyebrows shot up. "Seriously?" she said again.

"He originally thought it was a one-off, but then it happened again, only that time it was a bar of Cadbury Dairy Milk."

"Why did he report it? It sounds perfectly innocent to me. Maybe it's someone who has a crush on him but they're too shy to ask him out."

Maguire shrugged. "I don't know. He's a bit of a fusspot. He said the ringing doorbell interfered with his concentration." Maguire chased the last bit of his tomato around his plate with his fork. "Who is this Rupert Yardley? Do you know him?"

"I do. Not well though. He plays for the Chums and is

writing a book on the history of Upper Chumley-on-Stoke. He's something of a conservationist."

"Huh. A conservationist?" Maguire stroked his chin. "Meaning he might have objected to Foster's planned renovation of that building for his gourmet shop?"

"He was actually quite incensed at the idea."

Maguire's eyebrows shot up. "Really? Upset enough to murder Foster?"

"I . . . I don't know."

"I think perhaps I'll look into Mr. Yardley a bit more."

P en was walking down the high street, her stomach contentedly full from the breakfast Maguire had prepared, when she noticed a bit of a commotion in the distance. As she got closer, she realized there were two constables standing in front of Icing on the Cake. She pushed her glasses up her nose and squinted. It looked as if Clementine was talking to PC Cuthbert, looking agitated and waving her hands in the air.

Penelope picked up her pace. When she reached Clementine's shop, Clementine grabbed her arm. Her cheeks were stained red with fury and her eyes were blurry with tears.

"Look what they've done." She pointed at the window.

Penelope stared in disbelief. The word *traitor* had been spray-painted on the front window of Icing on the Cake in large red letters.

"Who would do something like this?" Clementine cried.

Pen wrinkled her nose. "What does it even mean?"

"Someone must think I voted for Foster's proposal.

That has to be it." Clementine gulped. "But I didn't. Why would I? His shop would have ruined my business," she said, pointing to the gold lettering at the top of the window that read *Icing on the Cake*.

"Why would someone think that?" Penelope was confused. "Like you said, you had as much to lose as any of the other shopkeepers."

Clementine's face went blank. "I don't know. Maybe they've mistaken me for someone else."

Penelope was about to suggest that Clementine come with her to the Open Book where Figgy would make her a strong cup of tea with plenty of sugar and perhaps a jot of the Jameson Mabel kept under the front counter, when a car pulled up to the curb and Maguire got out.

Cuthbert rushed to Maguire's side, and they appeared to be having a hushed conversation, PC Cuthbert repeatedly pointing at the graffiti on the window of the bakery. Penelope thought she caught the word *ruffians* repeated more than once.

Maguire was beginning to look impatient and finally disentangled himself from Cuthbert and walked over to where Penelope and Clementine were standing.

He nodded at Penelope and introduced himself to Clementine.

"When did you notice someone had spray-painted on your window?" He nodded his head toward the window.

"This morning when I arrived," Clementine said breathlessly. The feverish color was finally beginning to recede from her face. "I saw it the moment I went to open the door."

"One moment." Maguire held up a hand and walked over to the window. He touched the paint with his fingertip then walked back to Penelope and Clementine.

"The paint is still tacky. It takes twenty-four hours for spray paint to dry on glass." He pinched the bridge of his nose. "Assuming that whoever did this waited until they could be reasonably sure the high street was deserted, this puts the time at some point after midnight. I'll have someone look at the CCTV footage. Hopefully, we can catch whoever did it in the act."

Penelope took Clementine by the arm. "Why don't you come down to the Open Book and we'll get you a cup of tea."

Penelope could feel Clementine shaking like the branches of a tree in the wind.

"I really should . . ." Clementine gestured toward her shop.

"Nothing will happen if you open the shop a bit later this morning." Penelope reassured her.

Clementine let out a sigh. "You're right. I really could fancy a cuppa right now."

Penelope led Clementine down the street and into the Open Book. Within minutes, they had her ensconced in an armchair with a steaming cup of tea in front of her dosed with Jameson—Mabel's favorite remedy for anything from heartbreak to bankruptcy.

As Clementine sipped her tea and nibbled on the Chelsea bun Figgy had given her, Mabel took Penelope aside.

"I hope Maguire can find the culprits," she said in a low voice. "But why the word *traitor*, I wonder? It's not as if Clementine would sabotage her own shop by voting for Foster's proposal."

"Maybe it's in reference to something else?" Pen said.

"It's got to be." Mabel raised her eyebrows. "Most curious. I wonder what on earth that is."

SIXTEEN

❧

Pen had blocked out the morning to do some writing and she retreated to her writing room as soon as she'd devoured the scone, still warm from the oven, that Figgy had given her. She was powering on her laptop when she heard her cell phone ding announcing an incoming text.

Pen pulled the phone from her pocket and glanced at the screen. It was a text from Bettina, her editor in New York.

Cheerio—isn't that what the Brits over there say? No matter, marketing has come up with the most brilliant title for your next book. Drum roll please. Lady of the Forest. What do you think?

Pen stared at the text for a moment before responding.

But a forest doesn't figure into the story at all.

Bettina's response was nearly instantaneous.

Can you put one in? Please? Marketing seems to be sold on the title.

Penelope sighed. What marketing wanted, marketing got. And in this case, they wanted a forest. Pen glanced through her notes, wondering where she could add in a forest. Were there even forests on the moors?

She brought up her favorite search engine, entered the word *moor*, and clicked on images. Her screen was immediately populated with pictures of rocky, barren landscapes. In one or two, she spotted some trees in the distance. She supposed she could add a forest in the background, visible from the highest point of Lord Hawthorne's estate.

It might even give Luna a place to hide when Lord Hawthorne's housekeeper pursued her—a sort of cat-and-mouse game among the trees.

Yes, she could make it work, Pen decided as she put her fingers on the keys and began writing her next scene.

An hour later, she raised her arms over her head and stretched. She'd racked up a decent number of words and she could add more when she got home that evening. She powered down her laptop and closed the lid.

The store was quiet when Pen emerged from her writing cave, as she thought of it. A woman was browsing the shelves, running her finger along the spines of the books, while a young boy sat nearby in one of the armchairs with a backpack on his lap. He had dark hair and was wearing round glasses that made him look like Harry Potter.

Pen watched as he unzipped the backpack and reached inside. She was startled when he pulled out a box of chocolates from the Sweet Tooth.

Suddenly, his mother whirled around and grabbed the

box from him. She noticed Penelope watching and gave a rueful smile.

"This little hooligan stole this box of chocolates off someone's blanket at the Guy Fawkes celebration. With all the fireworks and everything, I never even noticed that he'd wandered off." She ruffled his hair affectionately. "He hid the box in the backpack we'd brought along for our things. With kids, you always have so much stuff you have to carry with you—juice boxes, snacks, those hand wipes because they always seem to get sticky somehow. I didn't even notice the chocolates until I got home." She shook her head. "He's always had quite a sweet tooth. He gets it from me, I'm afraid." She laughed.

Penelope didn't know what to do. Could those be the chocolates that had belonged to Simeon Foster? If so, it was possible they'd been contaminated with sodium nitrite. She had to say something.

"The fellow who they found dead at the Guy Fawkes celebration was poisoned. The police think the poison might have been put in a box of chocolates that went missing from his things," she said finally.

The woman gasped and put a hand to her mouth. She whirled around. "Steven! You didn't eat any of those, did you?" She reached out and snatched the box off the boy's lap.

Steven's eyes were wide and round. He shook his head.

"Thank heavens," the woman said, wiping a hand across her forehead. "We're going to take them to the police right this instant." She wagged a finger at Steven. "Perhaps that will teach you to never take someone else's property again. It's stealing and that's a crime."

The boy's eyes filled with tears. "I'm not going to be arrested, am I?" His voice wobbled and he was clearly trying not to cry.

"Don't be daft," his mother said. "I'm sure you'll get off with a stern warning." She shook her finger at him again.

She smiled wanly at Penelope, grabbed Steven's hand, and marched him out of the store.

Mabel walked over to Penelope, a stack of books in her arms. "What was that all about?"

Penelope explained about the chocolates.

Mabel's face went white. "My sainted aunt! There could have been a terrible tragedy. Imagine if the whole family had eaten them." She shuddered. "It doesn't bear thinking about. Thank goodness the mother did the right thing and confiscated them."

An hour later, as Pen was shelving some books, her cell phone rang. She pulled it from her pocket and glanced at the number, which she recognized as Maguire's. She felt herself smiling even before she answered the call.

"You won't believe what just happened," he said. "I can't believe it myself."

Penelope could picture him running his hands through his hair and it made her smile.

"Let me guess." Penelope laughed. "A woman came into the station with a box of chocolates from the Sweet Tooth and her son in tow. She was making him return the candy because the little rascal had most likely snitched it from Simeon Foster."

There was profound silence at the other end. "How did you know?" Maguire said finally.

"The woman was just here at the Open Book, and she told me she was on her way to the police station."

"So, you're not clairvoyant then." Maguire chuckled. "I was beginning to think you might be a witch. We're sending the chocolates to the lab to be tested immediately, but they do look as if they've been tampered with. Although it's not so obvious that Foster would have necessarily noticed anything amiss. Especially not in the dark at the fireworks."

"So, I was probably right then. The killer most likely put the poison in the candies. Especially since you didn't find any sodium nitrite in the other food he had with him."

Maguire sighed. "The killer took quite a chance. What if someone else had helped themselves to a chocolate? They might have killed the wrong person."

The afternoon was slow at the Open Book, with only a few people trickling through the door. Brimble made his daily visit to see Mabel. He'd finally given up the pretense that he was there to buy a book. Penelope had been worried that he was on the verge of bankrupting himself in order to have an excuse to spend time with Mabel, but now that they were officially seeing each other, he no longer felt the need to purchase something.

Brimble had just said good-bye when the door opened and Gladys rushed in. She was still wearing her butcher's apron and her face was flushed. "I've only got a minute," she said. "Ralph is minding the store and he isn't too . . ." She pointed to her head. "But I've finished Charlotte Davenport's latest, *The Regency Rogue*." She clasped her hands to her chest. "It was so romantic." Her face took on a dreamy look. "Of course, romance is nothing like that in real life." She snorted. "I should know—look at my Bruce, may he rest in peace."

She leaned on the counter. "Still, I think it was wrong that Worthington married an American. He is a duke after all. There have to be standards."

Mabel rolled her eyes. "Pretend it's one of those novels you like so much. It's terribly romantic, don't you think? Poor American girl snags a rich duke's hand in marriage." She turned to Penelope and winked. "What shall we call it?"

By now, Penelope was tired of hearing how affronted the residents of Chumley were by Worthington's decision to marry an American—and Charlotte was definitely not poor—but she decided to play along.

"Romance isn't my genre, but how about *True Love*?"

"Bah." Mabel waved a hand in the air. "Much too prosaic. We need something more dramatic, like *Dreams Do Come True*."

"I know!" Pen shouted. "How about *Love Has No Bounds*?"

"Perfect." Mabel clapped her hands together, then laughed. "Maybe *Love Has No Boundaries* might be more appropriate."

Meanwhile, Gladys was looking at the two of them as if they'd gone completely barmy.

"If you two are finished," she said rather huffily, "I am looking for another book to read. Do you have any suggestions?"

"Have you read Julia Quinn's series about the Bridgertons? They're classics." Mabel turned toward the shelf behind her.

Gladys shook her head.

"You can start with *The Duke and I*." She pulled out a volume and handed it to Gladys.

Gladys's mouth hung open a bit as she read the blurb on the back of the book.

"This looks like just the ticket. I'll take it," she said decisively.

Gladys put her hands on her hips. "What a shame about

Clementine's window. What's Chumley coming to?" She blew a lock of hair off her forehead. "What's next?"

"Secret Santas," Penelope said suddenly. "Did I tell you Maguire said that a Secret Santa has been reported in Chumley?"

"Isn't it a bit early for that? We're hardly to mid-November," Mabel said. "It seems as if every year the season starts earlier and earlier."

Gladys's eyes lit up. "A Secret Santa here? In Chum?" She fanned herself with her hand and giggled. "Like in that song 'Santa Baby,' maybe he'll put something from Tiffany under my tree. Something sparkly. I love sparkles."

"So far, all he's left are a jar of Branston Pickle and a Cadbury Dairy Milk bar," Pen said.

Gladys' face fell. "Oh," she said in a small voice. "Well, a girl can dream, can't she?"

Gladys frowned. "I guess I'd better keep the curtains drawn in the lounge. I don't want no one seeing me in my knickers while I'm watching the telly, or, worse yet, completely starkers." She laughed heartily. "And I suppose they wouldn't want to see me either."

"So far, the only person who's complained about the Secret Santa is Rupert Yardley. He said it's happened twice."

"That sounds more like someone has a crush on Rupert," Mabel said, as she hit a few keys on the register and rang up Gladys's purchase. "Here you go. I think you'll enjoy it."

"Ta," Gladys said as she made for the door.

A hush came over the store after Gladys left. Penelope worked on a new display of animal-themed cozy mysteries like Krista Davis's Paws & Claws series and

Miranda James's Cat in the Stacks for the large table in the center of the store. She'd borrowed a darling stuffed dog and cat from Tracy, who said her children had so many stuffed animals that Penelope would be done with them before they were even missed.

Things continued to be quiet and since it was almost closing time, Penelope decided it was the perfect opportunity to drop by Karen Brown's house. But first she would have to run home and get her car. And perhaps grab something to eat. She searched her memory—had she or hadn't she eaten any lunch? Her stomach was feeling a bit hollow and she couldn't remember having anything in particular, so she assumed she mustn't have.

Mrs. Danvers was nowhere to be seen when Penelope opened the front door to her cottage. She felt a moment of panic as she went through the rooms calling for her. Had she been trapped somewhere accidentally?

Finally, she heard an annoyed meow and the throw Penelope had bunched up on the sofa began to move. Mrs. Danvers's head emerged and she stretched luxuriously before glaring at Penelope, presumably for spoiling her afternoon nap.

Pen's heart rate slowed to normal again. As prickly as Mrs. Danvers was, Pen was extremely fond of the cat, who provided her with companionship as well as the occasional laugh.

She headed straight to the kitchen to see what there was to eat. She opened the refrigerator and was reaching for the container of yogurt when she remembered what Maguire had said. She peered at the sell-by date to see just how old the yogurt was. Perhaps Maguire was the sort who threw things out the minute the container told him the product had expired. Penelope's yardstick for deciding when something needed to go in the trash was whether or not there was mold on it or if the substance had begun to turn green.

The yogurt did not look at all healthy. There was something fuzzy growing on top that looked like a science experiment gone awry that Penelope was pretty sure wasn't supposed to be there. She tossed the container in the garbage can under the sink and took another look around, opening and closing the cupboards. She would make a run to Tesco soon, she promised herself. A bag from the Icing on the Cake was sitting on the counter. Pen had nearly forgotten about it, but she opened it and found half a Chelsea bun inside. She quickly gobbled it down, washed her hands, brushed the crumbs off her sweater, and within minutes was headed back out the door.

She got a bit lost on the way to the Southfield Estate where Karen Brown lived, but after several wrong turns, she finally heard the roar of traffic on the A10 in the distance and knew she was getting close.

She slowed as she read the street names. Churchill Drive was on the left. She followed along until she found the two-story brick building that housed number fifty-six. Penelope took note of the bright blue door and the clean and starched café curtains in the window as she followed the concrete path.

She pressed the buzzer and waited. Moments later she heard footsteps inside and the clank of locks turning.

"Karen Brown?" Pen said when the door was opened.

Karen gave a tremulous smile and fiddled with the doorknob. "If you're selling something, I'm afraid—"

Penelope immediately shook her head. "No, I'm not selling

anything. I wondered if I could talk to you for a moment. By any chance, do you have a relative named Courtney?"

Karen's shoulders drooped. "You might as well come in." She held the door wider.

The front door led directly into a small but extremely tidy sitting room. There wasn't a speck of dust anywhere, nor was anything out of place. The furniture was nondescript—the sort that came in a set with a matching sofa, armchair, and ottoman, all covered in a bold floral print.

A three-tiered occasional table held a collection of porcelain figurines displayed on lace doilies.

Karen Brown was equally nondescript. She looked faded, with hair that was dishwater blond with streaks of gray and pale blue eyes. She was wearing a pair of mauve polyester slacks and a mauve-and-white-striped sweater.

"Would you like a cup of tea?" she said, clasping her hands together. "I was just about to make a cup for myself."

"That would be lovely," Pen said.

"Please"—Karen gestured toward the sofa—"have a seat."

She scurried through a door and into a small kitchen with slightly dated appliances.

Pen heard the kettle whistle and, shortly thereafter, Karen returned with a tray set with two mugs, a teapot, and a plate of chocolate digestive biscuits.

Karen poured the tea. "Milk, sugar?"

"Sugar, please."

She stirred a spoon of sugar into Pen's mug and handed it to her. "Is this about Courtney?" Karen said. "Strangers showing up at the door usually means Courtney has been up to something." She held her own mug in her hands but didn't take a drink. "Does my daughter owe you money, by any chance?" she said finally.

Penelope was so startled she nearly dropped her tea. She couldn't believe it—her hunch had paid off. Courtney was Karen Brown's daughter.

Karen visibly relaxed, her shoulders drooping in relief. A puzzled look crossed her face. "How do you know my Courtney?"

"We met at the bookstore where I work and had lunch together." That was fudging it a bit, Penelope thought, but the explanation would have to do.

Karen looked surprised. "Oh." She took a sip of her tea. "Courtney can be . . . difficult at times. I'm glad she's made some friends." Karen played with the locket around her neck. "She hasn't been home in a couple of days. I'm afraid we had a bit of a barney over an . . . issue." Karen looked at Penelope. "How is she doing?"

Penelope didn't know what to say. Courtney was clearly not doing well at all.

"I am a bit worried about her," Pen said as gently as she could. "She seems rather upset about something."

Karen nodded. "I'm afraid it's always something with Courtney. It can be the smallest thing and it sets her off."

"I saw her after the town council meeting. She was arguing with Simeon Foster, the man who was murdered. It seemed quite serious." Pen helped herself to a digestive biscuit.

The color slowly ebbed from Karen's face. "Simeon Foster, you say?"

Karen grasped her hands together and put them in her lap, but Penelope had noticed them tremble and how she was gripping them so hard her knuckles were blanched.

Pen nodded. "Yes, she appeared to be quite angry with him. She was still angry with him when we had lunch together a couple of days later."

"I'm not surprised," Karen said. She was obviously mulling something over in her mind. The silence lengthened and Penelope could hear the ticking of the small enamel clock on the end table.

Karen took a deep breath. "I raised Courtney myself, you know. Nowadays being a single mother isn't all that unusual, but it wasn't as common back then." Karen reached for a digestive biscuit and broke off a piece. "I did the best I could. I kept a roof over our heads and food on the table. We even made a trip to Brighton Beach for the weekend when Courtney was twelve years old."

Karen crumbled the piece of biscuit between her fingers. "It's all because of that DNA kit."

"DNA?" Pen said, confused.

"You know, those kits that tell you where you come from and who your ancestors are." Karen brushed the crumbs from her biscuit off her lap and into her palm and deposited them on the tea tray. "You see, I never told Courtney who her father was. Why should I? He didn't want to have anything to do with me as soon as he found out I was expecting."

The light was beginning to dawn on Penelope. "So, she sent in a DNA swab. . . ."

"I wish she'd never done that," Karen said. "But she was determined to do it."

"And she found out who her father was. Is that right?"

Karen nodded silently. "Yes. And it made her furious that he had made all this money while we were still living in a council flat."

She stared intently at Penelope. "Of course, he denied it," she sneered. "He said you couldn't trust those tests and when she said she was Karen Brown's daughter, he said he'd never known anyone named Karen Brown." Karen swiped a finger under her eyes.

"To be dismissed like that . . ." She rummaged in her pocket and pulled out a tissue. "As if I'd never existed." She dabbed at her nose with the tissue. "And then to deny his own flesh and blood."

"No wonder Courtney was furious."

"You can hardly blame her, can you? She asked him for some money—it wasn't a lot—but he still refused." Karen began shredding the tissue. "He said there had to have been something wrong with the DNA test but I read on the package that it was ninety-nine percent accurate. I know there wasn't nothing wrong with the test she took. I knew perfectly well who her father was, and I was hoping she would never find out that her father was Simeon Foster."

SEVENTEEN

❧

There was certainly no lack of suspects in Foster's murder, Pen thought as she drove down the high street. Most of them seemed unlikely murderers though. Perhaps Foster had made an enemy in the city who had followed him to Chumley in order to kill him?

Rupert was clearly incensed at the idea of changing one of Chumley's oldest buildings, but that didn't seem like much of a motive to Penelope. Although people had certainly killed for less.

All the shop owners had motives. Clementine, Grant, Gladys, and Terry were all alarmed at the prospect of the competition and subsequent loss of business that the Epicurean Gourmet threatened.

Perhaps Terry was the most suspect of all. The poisoned chocolates that had killed Foster had come from his shop.

But Courtney had a strong motive as well—revenge

against the father who had refused to acknowledge her and who was living high on the hog while she was stealing crumbs from the plates at the Open Book.

And as far as that was concerned, what's to say Karen Brown didn't feel the need to exact revenge for Foster's leaving her and the hardships she endured over the years?

She felt sorry for Maguire's having to wade through this morass of suspects and motives. No wonder he was stressed. She wondered if he knew about Courtney Brown and her mother. Pen bit her lip. She didn't want to bother him, but on the other hand, this could be important.

There was a dirt road up ahead that appeared to lead to a farmhouse way in the distance. Pen turned onto it and stopped her car. She dug her cell phone from her purse and dialed Maguire's number.

He sounded pleased to hear from her, but Penelope could detect the tension underlying his voice. She quickly explained about Courtney Brown being Simeon Foster's daughter and he agreed that that gave both Courtney and her mother a motive. He promised to look into it.

She turned her car around and headed back toward Chumley's high street.

She noticed Terry and Grant standing outside Clementine's shop as she passed it, working to remove the graffiti that had been spray-painted on her window while Clementine fluttered around, wringing her hands and no doubt gnashing her teeth. There were still Good Samaritans in the world, Penelope thought, waving as she went by.

Pen rather reluctantly pulled into the parking lot of the local Tesco, its bright red neon sign lighting the darkened sky. She couldn't avoid shopping any longer. She tossed some prepared dinners—a Bisto's frozen cottage pie; a Hungry Joe's lasagna; and a Young's cod, spinach, and cheese gratin—into her cart along with a bottle of white wine and, to assuage her guilt, a head of lettuce and a bottle of salad dressing.

She loaded her purchases into the trunk of her car and pulled out of the parking lot. She had a slightly nerve-racking moment when she momentarily forgot which lane she was supposed to be in, but traffic was sparse and she was able to correct the situation with no harm done.

She had just parked her MINI in front of her cottage when Mr. Patel strolled by with his French bulldog. The dog's name was Gresa, which Mr. Patel said meant *grace* in Gujarati, the language spoken in the area of India where he'd been born.

He smiled at Penelope, and Gresa wandered over to sniff her shoes. He was still in his business suit—the knot in his tie still done and his jacket on as if he was on his way to the office instead of finished for the day.

"Good day to you," Mr. Patel said, giving a slight bow.

If he'd been wearing a hat, Pen suspected he would have tipped it at her. Mr. Patel's manners were slightly old-fashioned, but Penelope found them charming.

Pen bent down and scratched Gresa's neck and Gresa rolled over, inviting Penelope to give her a belly rub.

"Did you enjoy the fireworks on Guy Fawkes Day?" Pen said, giving Gresa a final pat.

Gresa got up with a grunt, wandered over to the gutter, and began sniffing something. Mr. Patel tugged on the leash and pulled her closer to him.

"I did not go to the celebration," he said. "Gresa finds the noise quite disturbing, so I took her on a long walk to distract her." He bent down and patted Gresa's head. "She was a good girl, weren't you, Gresa?" He straightened up and smiled at Penelope. "We went all the way to that cottage by that small pond. Do you know it?"

Penelope tried to picture it in her mind. "I think that's Rupert Yardley's house."

"Ah, yes, the fellow who plays football for the Chums." He smiled again. "I think that would be *soccer* to you Americans."

"Did you notice if there was a light on in his cottage?" Perhaps Mr. Patel had seen Rupert and she could rule him out as a suspect? He couldn't be in two places at once—in his cottage while simultaneously watching the fireworks.

Mr. Patel looked puzzled by the question, but he was too polite to ask Penelope what business it was of hers.

He wrinkled his brow. "Yes, I think a light was on."

"Did it look like Rupert was home?"

Now Mr. Patel looked slightly leery. "I don't know. He might have been. Or, he could have forgotten to turn out the light." He pursed his lips. "I did see something else though. There was a man ringing the doorbell. It looked as if he was delivering something. He left a package on the doorstep and left before anyone answered the door."

Pen shifted from one foot to the other. "Did you happen to recognize him?"

"No, I didn't. He had his back to me. And by then it was getting dark so I doubt I would have been able to see much anyway."

P en was putting away her groceries when there was furious banging on her front door. It was so loud that it even caught Mrs. Danvers's attention. The cat streaked into the living room in a blur of black and white fur to stand sentry in the foyer.

Who on earth is that, Pen wondered. Was someone having an emergency? She mentally went through all the emergency procedures she could think of, which, unfortunately, consisted only of stop, drop, and roll, which her second-grade teacher Mrs. Fischer had drilled into the class and that in the case of fainting, the person's head should be raised above the level of their heart. Or was that their feet? But judging by the knocking on her door, it was doubtful she would be encountering someone swooning at her feet.

Penelope opened the door and Beryl nearly fell across the threshold. Pen could immediately tell something was wrong. Her lipstick had worn off and she hadn't bothered to touch it up. Beryl never went anywhere without dabbing on some lipstick and powdering her nose, even if it was just out to the mailbox to get her mail.

"You look upset," Pen said, mentally kicking herself for stating the obvious.

Beryl was wearing a black coat with large jet buttons over a cowl-necked red dress with an Hermès silk scarf filling in the neckline. Her hands were trembling as she handed Penelope her coat.

"First a glass of wine," Pen said, grateful she'd thought to pick up a bottle of white, "then you can tell me what's happened."

Beryl sniffed loudly. "Okay." She collapsed onto the sofa.

Penelope hurried out to the kitchen. She opened the refrigerator and felt the bottle of white wine. It was barely chilled, but it would have to do. She popped the cork, poured two glasses, and carried them out to the sitting room.

Beryl was sitting on the sofa, slumped over, her elbows on her knees and her face buried in her hands. Her expression brightened when she saw the glass of wine Penelope placed in front of her. She grabbed the glass, took a big sip, and then frowned.

"It's not very chilled, is it?" She looked at Pen.

"Sorry. I just picked it up from Tesco on my way home."

Beryl shrugged. "It's wine, so who cares? That's all that counts."

Pen sat at the other end of the sofa and tucked her legs underneath her.

"Time to spill the beans. What's happened?'

"Oh, Pen," Beryl cried. "It was so awful. I went up to London to pick up some new outfits I'd decided on for Charlotte. With the holiday season almost here, she's going to have a full social calendar. I was walking down Bond Street and these tourists were coming toward me. I could tell they were Americans—he was wearing a New York Yankees baseball cap and they were both wearing sneakers." Beryl shuddered. "Suddenly, out of nowhere, they began screaming at me—thief, crook, things like that. Apparently, they recognized me from all those tabloid articles back home."

Pen reached out and put her hand over her sister's. "That's horrible."

"Obviously, they blamed me for Magnus's Ponzi scheme. But I had nothing to do with it and knew nothing about it." She held her hands out, palms up. "I've lost everything." She plucked at her dress. "This is one of Charlotte's cast-offs. She said she'd been photographed in it too often to continue to wear it." She looked imploringly at Penelope. "Will I ever be able to escape the past?"

Pen put a hand over her sister's. "The public is fickle. They'll soon be on to the next scandal, don't worry."

"I hope so." Beryl's face brightened slightly. "But there is my project to look forward to. I think it has real possibilities and if it takes off . . ."

"Now are you going to tell me what this mysterious project is?" Penelope said. She took a sip of her wine and wrinkled her nose. She supposed that old saying was true—you get what you pay for.

Beryl toyed with the stem of her wineglass. She opened her mouth then closed it again.

"I think I'd rather wait. At least until I'm a little further along in the planning."

Penelope felt a pang of frustration. What on earth was Beryl being so secretive about? But she knew her sister—when she had made up her mind, nothing was going to change it. Her only hope was that Beryl wouldn't be disappointed again.

It was overcast when Penelope left the house the next morning. She glanced up at the dark, heavy-looking clouds that were scudding swiftly across the sky. The wind had a raw, bitter edge to it, and she quickened her step as she made her way down the high street to the Open Book.

Terry Jones was outside the Sweet Tooth sweeping the sidewalk when Penelope passed by.

"Good morning," he called to her, briefly leaning on his broom. "It's beginning to feel like winter's around the corner, isn't it? I wouldn't be surprised if we saw a bit of snow."

"It certainly has gotten colder," Pen said. She waved and continued down the street.

She'd barely arrived at the Open Book when Rupert walked in. He was wearing a wool Harrington jacket with a silk scarf at his neck and had a newspaper tucked under his arm.

"You're looking terribly smart today," Mabel said as he approached the counter.

"Thank you." Rupert briefly bobbed his head. "It's quite brisk out there," he said, motioning toward the window and loosening his scarf. "It almost feels like snow."

"Terry Jones just said the same thing," Penelope said. "Does it snow here often? I don't remember there being much more than a few flurries last year."

"We don't usually see snow until December," Mabel said, joining the conversation. "And then it never amounts to much."

Rupert pulled the newspaper out from under his arm and put it on the counter. He tapped the front page with his finger.

"The *Chumley Chronicle*'s run an obituary on Simeon Foster." He scowled. "It's more of a feature story really. A sort of *This Is Your Life* piece in print." He looked at Mabel. "Do you remember that television show?"

"I do, indeed."

Rupert shook his head. "The man doesn't merit that much ink, in my opinion. Tampering with a listed building." He grunted. "I still can't believe the Chumley town council was willing to give him permission."

"Fortunately, it's not going to happen now," Mabel said. "Chumley is safe from Foster's renovations. I just read in the newspaper that because of all the brouhaha in Chumley, Foster's nephew—he's running the Epicurean Gourmet now—has decided to find another location for his next shop. Apparently, he's looking into Nether Thrompton. It's their problem now, Lord help them. But I suspect he won't exactly get a warm welcome there either."

"Quite," Rupert said. "Thank goodness for that, at least."

Pen heard the door open and glanced in that direction. Brimble strolled in with Gladys right on his heels. She was carrying a paper-wrapped bundle and a brown paper bag. She put both on the counter in front of Mabel.

"Here's a nice top rump roast, just like you ordered," Gladys said.

Mabel looked startled. "You needn't have run over with it. I would have stopped by the shop."

Gladys waved a hand. "It's no bother. I've got Ralph working with me today and he's been talking me ears off. All about some show he watches on the telly—*The Repair Shop*, where they fix broken things like toy cars, violins, clocks, and some toff's leather briefcase. Useless rubbish, if you ask me. Why not just throw it in the tip and save yourself the trouble?" She pulled her sweater around her more closely. "I'd best be going then. It was nice to get out for a bit," Gladys said, but she didn't make a move to leave.

She took a breath and gestured toward the paper bag. "I've thrown in a couple of pasties for all of you, too. You can have them for lunch or save them for your tea."

"Thank you," Pen and Mabel said at the same time.

Brimble gave Gladys a sidelong glance. "I was looking forward to one of your pasties at the Guy Fawkes celebration but when I went by your booth, you weren't there."

Gladys's back stiffened. "I needed a break, didn't I? No harm in that."

"No, indeed," Brimble said.

"So, you don't have an alibi for Foster's death," Rupert said with a cheeky smile.

Gladys rounded on him. "And what about you? Do you have an alibi?" She glared at Rupert.

"I was at home working on my book. I had no interest in attending the Guy Fawkes celebration. All that noise and all those people . . ." He shuddered.

"Not much of an alibi, is it?" Gladys's fists were still clenched and a tide of red had flowed from her neck to her forehead.

"You had a stronger motive," Rupert retorted. "Foster's Epicurean Gourmet could have put the Pig in a Poke out of business."

Mabel cleared her throat. "I think that's enough. I think we can all agree that the murderer isn't one of us."

A sullen look settled on Gladys's face as she crossed her arms over her chest.

"What's this?" Mabel pointed to the *Chumley Chronicle*, which Penelope had spread out on the counter.

She had opened the paper to the page with the piece on Foster. Brimble read over Penelope's shoulder as she scanned the article. He pointed to a sentence with his finger.

"Looks like Foster served in the army. That's one good thing that can be said about him. It says here he fought in the Falklands War. Not a total loss then."

"Oooh," Gladys squealed. "Didn't Prince Andrew go to the Falklands? I wonder if Foster ever met him?"

"I think there were quite a lot of people there," Mabel said. "So I highly doubt it."

"Ah, the Falklands," Brimble said, stroking his mustache. "Fascinating conflict. Country was split over it. That's when they began to call Margaret Thatcher the Iron Lady. Quite an impressive victory by Britain, if I must say so myself."

"Did you know the fellow who owns the Sweet Tooth—Terry Jones—also fought in the Falklands?" Rupert said.

Mabel raised an eyebrow. "I wonder if that's where he got that limp he refuses to talk about."

That was food for thought, Pen decided later. If both Terry and Foster fought in the Falklands, perhaps they'd known each other before Foster moved to Chumley? They'd laughed at Gladys for suggesting that Foster might have met Prince Andrew but perhaps that wasn't so far-fetched after all and there was some shared history between Terry and Foster—and some kind of bad blood as well.

Brimble stayed behind after the others had left. "I'd be glad to lend a hand," he said to Penelope.

That afternoon, the bestselling thriller writer Nathanial West was doing a book signing at the Open Book. The store wasn't normally a destination for authors whose books had sold millions of copies, but West happened to be staying with Worthington, who was an old school chum. Mabel had managed to persuade him to grace the Open Book with his presence.

Cartons of his latest hit, *Turn a Blind Eye*, were stacked in the storeroom alongside a case of Machair mineral water, which came directly from the Isle of Lewis and was the only water West would deign to drink.

Mabel had also ordered several packages of his favorite snack—Marks & Spencer Salt & Vinegar Twists.

Mabel carried several bottles into the store where, with

Brimble's help, Pen had already set up a table at the front and draped a white cloth over it. Mabel set the bottles on top. She tapped one of them.

"This water costs the earth," she said. "We'd better sell lots of books."

Brimble disappeared into the storeroom and came out with an armful of copies of *Turn a Blind Eye*. The cover was very dramatic—all black with a huge eye peering out of the darkness. West's name was in large white letters at the bottom. They arranged the volumes in a pyramid on the table next to the large cardboard poster with the cover of the book on it along with a picture of Nathanial West.

West himself arrived as they were putting the finishing touches on the display. He was tall and slim, with slicked-back silver hair and a thin aristocratic-looking nose. He was dressed in a black turtleneck and black slacks and looked every inch the successful thriller writer.

Penelope looked down at her own clothes—leggings and a tunic-length blue sweater. Did she look like a successful Gothic novel writer? What did a successful Gothic novel writer look like anyway? Maybe it was time to take Beryl up on her offer to help her update her wardrobe.

Penelope was surprised to see that a line had formed inside the bookstore and several people were already waiting outside.

West took his seat and, with a great flourish, pulled out a special ostrich leather case. He opened it and removed the gold pen inside. He smiled at Mabel and Penelope.

"I'm ready now." He reached for the first bottle of Machair water and poured some into the glass Pen had set on the table.

Customers were grabbing copies of *Turn a Blind Eye* as

fast as West could sign them. Penelope was startled to see Maguire in the line.

He grinned sheepishly when he saw Penelope. "I'm a huge fan," he said.

The woman in front of him was taking an inordinately long time chatting with West and dictating the lengthy inscription she wanted in her copy of the book. West was beginning to look irritated and Penelope hoped he wouldn't stalk off—something he'd been known to do when displeased.

Finally, the woman moved on and Maguire stepped up to the table. He picked up a copy of the book and handed it to West.

"I'm really looking forward to reading this," Maguire said. He held out a hand. "DCI Brodie Maguire."

West leaned back in his seat and steepled his fingers. "Worthington's told me about you. I gather you have a murder on your hands right here in Chumley. He's wondering what's taking you lot so long to find the murderer." He gave a grin that reminded Penelope of a shark. "I told Arthur it was too bad you can't call on my hero Clint Robertson. He would have solved the case long before now."

He chuckled, but Maguire looked anything but amused. He practically grabbed the signed book from West's hands as he turned away from the table.

Penelope put a hand on Maguire's arm. He made an attempt at a smile.

"If only solving real-life murders was as easy as solving fictional ones," he said, and Pen could tell he was gritting his teeth. "But West is right. Worthington is putting more and more pressure on us to solve the case and that's making the guv more and more impatient for us to produce a result."

He ran a hand through his hair. "I've questioned Terry Jones and the staff at the Sweet Tooth, and it seems as if everyone in town had purchased a box of chocolates on Guy Fawkes Day." He raised an eyebrow and looked at Penelope. "Including your sister."

Pen put a hand to her chest. "You can't possibly think Beryl . . ."

Maguire looked uncomfortable. He shifted in his seat. "It's a murder case. We have to look at every angle, I'm afraid."

Pen felt color rising to her face. "I know Beryl didn't do it."

Maguire put his hand over hers. "The truth will come out in the end. If your sister didn't do it, she has nothing to worry about." He smiled. "And if you want my unofficial opinion, I don't really think she did it either, but I have to examine all possibilities."

Penelope felt somewhat mollified. She decided it might be best to change the subject. "Did you ever find out who scrawled the graffiti on the Icing on the Cake's window?" Pen said. "Did the CCTV footage show anything?"

"Yes and no." Maguire scratched behind his neck. "We were able to identify the culprit—a young kid named Alfie Watts. I guess he'd never heard of CCTV because he didn't make much of an effort to disguise himself or cover his face. We found him easily enough. Constable Cuthbert recognized him. Let's just say the family isn't exactly strangers to the local constabulary. Alfie's older brother is doing time for nicking a car." He laughed. "I guess Alfie is just getting started—first graffiti and then who knows what? Social services have done their bit trying to help but with a family like that, it's hard to make an impression."

Maguire shifted the book from his right hand to his left.

"It was a young kid?" Penelope frowned. "What would motivate him to write *traitor* on Clementine's window?"

Maguire rubbed two fingers together. "It wasn't his idea. Someone paid him to do it. He said he was hanging out with some blokes behind the Book and Bottle when a man came up to him and asked if he wanted to make some money. Of course he said yes."

"Who was the man?"

Maguire sighed. "That's what we don't know. He didn't recognize him. He said the fellow was wearing a baggy overcoat, a wool hat pulled down low on his forehead, and had a scarf wrapped around his throat, partially hiding his chin and mouth. Obviously, he didn't want to be recognized."

Maguire shifted from one foot to the other. "He paid Alfie and told him what he wanted done—the word *traitor* scrawled on the window of the Icing on the Cake."

"But why *traitor*? I don't get it."

"Perhaps they suspected that Clementine had voted in favor of Foster's proposal and they felt betrayed."

"I wish we knew who that man was." Penelope nearly stamped her foot in frustration.

Maguire shrugged. "Odds are it was a disgruntled shop owner. They were the most up in arms about stopping Foster's plan."

"What's going to happen to Alfie?" Penelope frowned. "The real criminal is the mysterious man who paid him to scrawl graffiti on Clementine's window."

Maguire smiled. "I suspect Alfie is going to lose all the money that man paid him and then some. It's likely he's going to be slapped with a hefty fine. I doubt he'll be getting up to mischief like that again anytime soon."

Penelope was thinking. "Maybe Terry Jones did it? He

fits the description and it would have been easiest for him to have doctored those truffles."

Maguire frowned. "That's true, but we can't find a thing to link him to Foster other than the fact that the Epicurean Gourmet would have cut into his business. But then any number of people were in the same position."

"Did you know that Terry and Foster both fought in the Falklands War? Maybe they met up there and Terry's still carrying a grudge about something."

Maguire raised an eyebrow. "There were about thirty thousand men sent to the Falklands. The two of them running into each other during the conflict is about as likely as me pulling off a shot like Jimmy White did in the Scottish Open."

"The what?"

"Snooker tournament."

"Sure, it's a long shot, but what if the two men *had* known each other back then and something happened?"

Maguire raised an eyebrow. "Something between the two of them, you mean?"

Penelope nodded. "Yes. Something that gave Terry an even stronger motive for wanting Foster dead."

EIGHTEEN

⊷∘⊶

Penelope was standing at the counter talking to Mabel when Figgy joined them. She put a plate of shortbread cookies on the counter.

"I thought you might be in need of a pick-me-up," she said.

Pen's eyes brightened at the sight. She selected a cookie and took a bite. "How are the wedding plans coming along?" she said around a mouthful of shortbread.

"Great." Figgy's face lit up. "Derek has found a wonderful sitarist to perform the recessional."

Pen nearly choked on her cookie. "A sitar player? What on earth is Lady Isobel Innes-Goldthorpe going to think about that?"

"My mother?" Figgy shrugged her shoulders, but Penelope noticed the dark cloud that passed over her face. "It's our wedding, not hers." She grinned. "I'll be sure to have some smelling salts on hand. That will be your job as the maid of honor."

Mabel raised her eyebrows. "Should be interesting. Very interesting indeed." She glanced at the calendar open on her computer screen. "Today is India's birthday."

"We must get her something," Pen said, swallowing the last bite of her cookie. "I doubt she's going to get all that many birthday wishes."

"That's true," Mabel said. "She's often lamented the fact that she's one of the last of her group of friends to still be alive." Mabel turned to the shelf behind her. "I have just the thing for her." She pulled out a book and patted the cover. "This ought to be right up India's alley."

Pen read the title out loud. "*The Palace Papers: Inside the House of Windsor—the Truth and the Turmoil* by Tina Brown."

"India takes no end of delight in following the antics of the royal family. She ought to love it."

"There's certainly a lot to follow," Pen said. "Do you think it's true that Kate and Will are having marital problems?"

Mabel snorted. "Where did you read that?"

"*OK!* magazine."

"That rag?" Mabel cocked her head to one side. "I didn't figure you for the scandal sheet type."

"I'm not. It was the headline on the cover. I happened to glance at it while I was waiting in line at Tesco." Mabel continued to look doubtful. Pen held up a hand. "I swear. You've got to believe me."

Mabel and Figgy laughed.

"There's no harm in it, I suppose," Mabel said. "People need to find amusement somewhere." She frowned. "Although I suspect it does rankle the royal family, poor things."

"I'll have this wrapped in a tick," Mabel said, reaching under the counter for a sheet of wrapping paper and a spool of ribbon.

"I'll put together a plate of her favorite treats," Figgy said. "I have a Madeira cake about to come out of the oven."

A book and a plate of goodies to nibble on—it was the perfect gift, Pen thought. All that was needed was a roaring fire and a cup of tea.

And a vase with flowers, she decided. She would stop at Bloomers down the street and pick up a small bouquet for India.

"There," Mabel said, placing the book on the counter. It was now covered with the Open Book's wrapping paper, which was printed with the covers of classic novels, and a dark blue ribbon with *Open Book* printed on it in gold.

"I can run those over to India," Pen said. "I'm going to pop into Bloomers and get her some flowers."

"Why don't you go get the flowers," Mabel said, sweeping some bits of ribbon off the counter and into her palm, "and we'll all go visit India right after we close? We can make a party of it."

Penelope had just crossed the street when the wind kicked up and blew a bit of dust into her eye. She stopped in front of the Crown Jewels for a moment and blinked rapidly while tears washed the speck away. She glanced in the window of the shop and was surprised to see that they were already anticipating the holiday season, with tiny white lights outlining the window and a display of engagement rings arranged against a black velvet background.

As soon as her eye stopped watering, Penelope continued

down the block to Bloomers and pushed open the door. The air in the shop was perfumed with the scent of flowers and the glass display cases were foggy with condensation.

A man was at the counter and, when he turned his head slightly, Pen realized it was Terry Jones from the Sweet Tooth. The girl behind the counter was taking down an address, so Pen assumed that whatever he'd ordered was being delivered to someone.

The clerk ran his credit card and handed it back to him. She smiled brightly.

"Thank you and I'll see you next year."

Terry looked at Penelope as he passed her, giving her a small nod of acknowledgment.

The clerk leaned on the counter. She had blond hair pulled back in a ponytail and was wearing an apron with a ruffled bodice and *Bloomers* embroidered in flowery script across the front.

"He comes in every year on the same day," she said in low tones, "and always orders flowers to be sent to the same address. I've been told it's been going on for years."

The shop door opened and a young man stuck his head in. Penelope noticed a white delivery van double-parked outside.

"Delivery," he called out.

The clerk held up a finger. "I'll be right with you." She smiled at Penelope. "I apologize. I have to open the back door for him. I promise I'll be right back."

Penelope drummed her fingers on the counter as she waited. She wondered who Terry could be sending flowers to once a year. His mother? A sister? Penelope couldn't contain her curiosity. Her mother used to remind her that curiosity killed the cat, but she didn't believe that for a minute then and she didn't believe it now. Besides, weren't cats supposed to have nine lives?

The clerk had disappeared into the storeroom. Penelope made sure she was out of view before casually turning the order pad around.

The flowers were being sent to a convent—the Sisterhood of the Sacred Cross, to the attention of Sister Rosamund.

Was that a relative of Terry's? Penelope wondered. It was curious, but it was unlikely to mean anything so she put it out of her mind.

She heard a rustling noise coming from the stockroom and quickly turned the order pad back around.

"I'm so sorry to have kept you waiting," the clerk said when she emerged from the stockroom. "How can I help you?"

"I'm looking for a small bouquet to take to a friend," Pen said. She gestured toward the display cases. "I'm afraid I don't know where to begin."

"Oh," the girl said. "You're the American, aren't you?"

Pen somewhat reluctantly agreed that she was, indeed, the American.

"My friend Jade went to New York City last year and when I asked her if she went to Disneyland, she said it would take days and days to drive there. I had no idea the country was so big."

"Yes. From New York to California is nearly three thousand miles."

"I'm reading your book," the girl said, blushing slightly as she reached under the counter and pulled out a copy of *The Woman in the Fog*. "Would you mind signing it for me?" Her blush deepened as she handed Pen the book.

Pen felt a creeping sense of embarrassment as she took the pen the girl gave her. She opened the book and scrawled her name across the page. She was still trying to perfect an authorly looking signature, but she hadn't nailed it yet.

The girl smiled broadly when Pen handed back the book and pen.

"You're looking for a bouquet?" she said, moving out from behind the counter. "What kind of an arrangement were you thinking of? Something elegant? Casual?"

The word that came to Penelope's mind was *cozy*. Was there such a thing as a cozy arrangement of flowers?

"Something . . . something that looks like the flowers were just picked from the garden."

The clerk's face lit up. "I know exactly what you mean." She opened one of the cooler doors and stood for a moment, wrinkling her nose. She studied the selection and then began pulling flowers from the various white enamel buckets.

"How do you like this?" She turned toward Penelope and held out the bunch of blossoms clasped in her hand.

"It's perfect," Pen said, relieved that she didn't have to pick out the flowers herself.

The clerk pulled a length of kraft paper from a roll, lined it with a piece of pink tissue paper, and wrapped it around the flowers. "Do you need a card?" she said as she tied a length of raffia ribbon around the bundle.

"No. Thank you. I'm going to deliver them directly." Penelope reached for her wallet, slotted her credit card into the reader, and picked up the bundle of flowers. She held them to her face and inhaled. She was sure India was going to like them.

Promptly at five o'clock, Mabel switched the Open sign to Closed and reached for her coat and the bag with

India's present. Figgy turned the lights off in the tearoom and joined them, carrying a plate covered in plastic wrap with slices of Madeira cake, chocolate biscuit cake, and a half dozen hobnobs. Pen picked up her bouquet and they headed to Mabel's car.

The sky was still thick with heavy clouds that obscured the moon and made the lane leading to India's cottage even darker. Mabel switched on her high beams, which startled a deer standing by the side of the road. It stared at them for a moment and then bolted into the shadows.

"That was a close call," Mabel said. "I was afraid it was going to run in front of the car."

Fortunately, they reached India's cottage without further mishap.

Mabel knocked on the door and they heard India slowly hobbling to the foyer. She gasped in surprise when she opened the door to see Mabel, Penelope, and Figgy waiting outside.

"What a lovely surprise," she said as she held the door wider.

"Happy birthday," they said together as they walked in.

"We decided to throw you a party," Figgy said, showing India the plate of cake and cookies.

Penelope handed her the bouquet of flowers.

"These are delightful." India's face glowed and her eyes glistened with tears.

She was leaning heavily on a cane and was rather pale. She winced as she stepped away from the foyer. Penelope took her arm. "Let me help you."

"I should make some tea." India turned toward the kitchen, looking slightly flustered.

"I'll do that. You go sit down," Figgy said. "And I'll put the flowers in some water while I'm at it."

"The tea is in the cabinet next to the sink," India called out as Figgy headed into the kitchen.

Once the tea was prepared and poured and everyone was comfortably ensconced in India's sitting room, she opened her present.

"How wonderful!" she exclaimed when she undid the wrapping. She ran a hand over the glossy book cover. "I shall enjoy this immensely. I do love reading about the royal family." She ruffled the pages.

She looked up and lowered her voice. "Did you know that there's a rumor that Kate Middleton, the Princess of Wales, is expecting? Arthur told me that isn't true. He had tea with the queen last week." She beamed like a proud parent. "The queen is quite fond of Arthur, you know. He's one of her favorites."

Figgy held out the plate of cake and cookies. "It's a bit late for tea, but better late than never, right?" she said.

India hesitated, her hand hovering over the dish. "Oh, dear, everything looks so delicious. I don't know how I shall choose." She finally settled on a piece of chocolate biscuit cake. She pointed to her dish. "This is what the queen served at tea, Arthur told me."

Penelope noticed that India's color had improved. Her eyes were shining and there was a pink flush to her cheeks that hadn't been there before.

"Arthur and Charlotte came to wish me a happy birthday," India said. "And they brought little Grace. Such a darling baby."

"Does she resemble Arthur or Charlotte?" Figgy said, nibbling on a cookie.

India frowned. "She has a bit of wispy hair—red, the color of Arthur's. And large blue eyes like Charlotte's." She laughed. "No matter. I am sure she will grow up to be a gorgeous young lady."

"How is Charlotte?" Mabel said. "Recovering nicely, I hope."

"Oh, yes. She's right as rain and so happy." India cocked her head. "She seemed rather excited about something." She waved a hand. "Nothing to do with the baby. Something else. But when I asked her about it, she wouldn't say, only that I'd find out in due course."

That was curious, Pen thought. Beryl was excited about something and wouldn't say what and now Charlotte was as well. The two of them had become quite friendly. Could they be cooking up something together?

Penelope leaned forward and tapped Mabel on the shoulder. "Could you let me out in front of the Chumley Chippie? I want to pick up something for dinner."

"Certainly," Mabel said as they drove down the high street.

Penelope couldn't imagine how she could possibly be hungry after a piece of chocolate biscuit cake and two hobnobs, but there was no denying it. Her stomach was actually rumbling.

A few minutes later, Mabel put on her blinker and pulled up to the curb in front of the Chumley Chippie. Even before Penelope opened her door, she could smell frying fish and potatoes and her mouth began to water.

She said good-bye to Mabel and Figgy and went into the restaurant. It was busy. All the tables were taken and there was a line at the counter. Fortunately, Stan and Mick worked so quickly that Penelope barely had to wait at all before her order was taken, bagged, and she was out the door.

The heavenly aroma emanating from the paper bag surrounded her as she headed home. She crossed the street and passed the window of the Chumley Chemist and the Sweet Tooth. The display window was empty and the lights were off except for one burning way in the back of the store. Pen thought she saw Terry Jones moving about in the shadows.

The trays in the window of Icing on the Cake were also empty, ready to display freshly baked goods the following morning. The Closed sign was on the door, but the light was still on toward the back of the shop.

Clementine was inside, talking to someone. It was easy to tell from her body language that she was upset. As a matter of fact, Penelope thought she looked furious. She peered through the window again, curious to see who Clementine was arguing with. It appeared to be a woman, but she had her back to the window and Pen couldn't identify her.

Pen waited a few minutes, still peering through the glass, the warm bag from the Chippie clutched to her chest. She was beginning to shiver when the woman finally turned and Penelope saw that it was Courtney Brown.

What had gotten the two of them so riled up? Normally, Clementine came across as timid and almost wishy-washy, but she'd looked even more upset than Courtney. Pen wished she knew.

NINETEEN

✦

Pen opened the door to her cottage with a feeling of relief. It was good to be home. Mrs. Danvers seemed mildly excited by her appearance—or was it the smell drifting from the Chumley Chippie bag that had her meowing and weaving in and out between Penelope's legs as she took off her jacket and hung it up.

She opened the Chippie bag and grabbed a french fry as she headed toward the kitchen. There was still the last bit in the bottle of chardonnay in the refrigerator and she poured it into a glass. She took a sip and then dumped the contents of the Chippie bag onto a plate. The fish looked mouthwateringly crispy, and she couldn't wait to dig in.

She was sitting at the kitchen table, picking up her fork, when her cell phone rang. She groaned. Should she ignore it? But what if it was an emergency or even just Beryl needing a ride home from the train station?

Penelope dug her cell out of her purse and glanced at the number. She groaned again. It was her mother.

"Have you heard the news?" her mother said breathlessly as soon as Penelope picked up the call.

"No," Pen said, picking up a fry and nibbling off the end.

What was it this time? she wondered. Was someone in her mother's bridge club caught cheating? Or had her hairdresser confessed to an affair with the shampoo girl? Those were all the sorts of things that passed for drama in her mother's life and that might have prompted a sudden telephone call.

"I haven't heard," Pen said, wiping her mouth with the paper napkin from the Chippie bag. "What's happened?"

There was a dramatic pause and then her mother said, "Miles and Sloan are having a baby!" Her voice vibrated with excitement. "My golf instructor knows Miles and told me all about it."

Penelope was at a loss for words. While her ex-boyfriend's marriage had prompted a few twinges of jealousy at the time, she was well and truly over him by now.

"That's wonderful news," she said finally.

Her mother breathed down the line. "What are you doing with your life, Penelope? That could have been you, you know. I also heard Miles purchased a lovely townhouse on East Seventy-Fourth Street in Manhattan and that Sloan is looking for a place in the Hamptons for their summer getaway."

"Oh," Penelope said with a noticeable lack of enthusiasm.

"And what are you doing—living in a rented cottage and working in a . . . bookstore."

Penelope thought of all the hours spent writing *Lady of the Moors* and *The Woman in the Fog* and the weeks they spent on the bestseller list, which obviously meant nothing to her mother. She felt a sense of dread settle over her like a bloated cloud.

"Of course, Phyllis—she's my bridge partner—was quite excited to hear about your books. She asked me to tell you she's really enjoyed them."

That was a crumb at least, Penelope thought. And probably all she was ever going to get from her mother.

"So, who is Bruno?" Penelope said as casually as she could.

There was a long pause. "Beryl told you?"

"She certainly did. And she's quite worried. She's afraid Bruno is after your money."

Penelope could sense her mother's irritation.

"It's none of her business and it's none of yours either. Just because Magnus turned out to be a crook, Beryl thinks all men are suspicious."

Add Simeon Foster to the list, Pen thought.

"Bruno is a perfectly lovely man. He's a wonderful bridge partner and enjoys the ballet and symphony."

Penelope tried but couldn't quite picture someone named Bruno at a performance of *Swan Lake*.

"Besides," her mother continued, "I hope I'm intelligent enough not to be taken in by a con artist."

Unlike your sister was clearly the subtext, Pen knew.

Her mother changed the subject, and they made idle chitchat for a few more minutes—mostly about things that interested her mother—and finally Penelope clicked off the call.

Talking to her mother had left her feeling out of sorts.

Her fish-and-chips, which had become cold and soggy, no longer looked so appealing and she was finding herself questioning everything in her life.

How long was she going to stay in England? Would her next book sell or be a dud? And what about her relationship with Maguire? Where was that going, assuming it was even going anywhere?

A brisk wind was blowing the next morning, sending large fluffy clouds skittering across the bright blue sky as Penelope walked to the Open Book. She saw Grant across the street opening the door to the Jolly Good Grub and she smiled and waved.

She was nearing the Icing on the Cake when the door to the shop opened and Clementine walked out carrying a sandwich board announcing that the traditional British Christmas cake was now available for purchase.

The board was awkward and as Clementine was trying to maneuver it through the doorway, she caught her toe on the threshold, lost her balance, and went sprawling onto the sidewalk with the sign collapsed beneath her.

The movement stunned Penelope for a moment but she quickly recovered and rushed toward Clementine, who was struggling to get up.

"Are you hurt?" Penelope said as she held out a hand.

Clementine grasped it and after a bit of a struggle, managed to stumble to her feet. She brushed off the front of her dress and looked in dismay at the blood trickling down her shin and the abrasions on her palms.

"You're bleeding," Pen said.

"That's rather obvious, isn't it?" Clementine said, pointing to where the blood was dripping into her shoes.

"Let me help you."

"No need to bother," Clementine said, her face reddening. "I have a first aid kit in the storeroom."

Penelope took the sandwich board from Clementine and set it up on the sidewalk. "At least let me help you inside," she said.

Clementine looked as if she was about to refuse. She took a step forward and winced.

"That would be very kind of you," she said finally, as she took Penelope's proffered arm.

The aroma inside the shop was heavenly, and Penelope took a deep breath as she admired the displays in the bakery case.

Clementine gestured toward the rear of the store and Penelope helped her through the doorway and into the storeroom. There was an old wooden desk chair pushed into the corner and Penelope wheeled it over. Clementine groaned as she sank into it, her injured leg held out in front of her.

The storeroom was lined with metal baker's racks filled with bags of flour, tins of baking powder, and other supplies, and there was an ancient fireplace, its bricks darkened by decades of soot, on one wall. Cobwebs hung across the opening and clung to the fireplace set stored in the firebox. Most of the shops in Chumley had fireplaces, although they were no longer used since radiators had been installed. Penelope couldn't imagine what an incredible hazard they must have been. It was a miracle all of Chumley hadn't burned to the ground long ago.

Beyond the storeroom she could see part of the kitchen and a marble countertop with several stand mixers lined up on it. A man in a white jacket with black buttons up the front was moving about, rather tunelessly whistling an old Beatles song.

"Where's your first aid kit?"

Penelope hoped the first aid course she'd taken the one year she'd spent as a Girl Scout would cover this situation. She still remembered how to bandage a sprained ankle, so that was something. Everything else was bound to come back to her.

Clementine gestured toward a metal cabinet against the wall. The door, which was slightly warped, screeched as Penelope slid it open. There was an assortment of things stored inside—a packet of McVitie's milk chocolate digestive biscuits, a box of Taylors of Harrogate Afternoon Darjeeling Tea, a slightly stained mug honoring the Queen's Jubilee, and stacks of printer paper, invoice pads, and a bunch of pens held together with an elastic band.

"I saw your sandwich board is announcing the sale of a traditional Christmas cake. I've never heard of it."

Clementine looked taken aback. "Christmas cake is like your fruitcake. It began as a sort of plum porridge centuries ago, back when people used to fast on Christmas Eve. In the sixteenth century, butter, wheat, and eggs were added to create a cake. Now it has spices and dried fruits like raisins and currants in it. Some people feed theirs." Clementine smiled when Penelope looked startled. "In other words, they pour a few tablespoons of brandy or sherry over the cake every week until Christmas. That's why they must be made well in advance of the holidays."

"I can't wait to try it," Pen said as she poked through the cabinet. She found a red plastic box with *First Aid Kit* written on it in large letters on the bottom shelf. She blew the dust off the top, undid the latch, and opened it.

She took out several bandages and a half-used tube of antibacterial ointment and set them aside.

The bleeding from Clementine's cuts had slowed to a mere trickle. Penelope found a clean cloth, dampened it, and carefully wiped away the blood and grit on Clementine's leg. Clementine winced as she dabbed on the antibacterial ointment.

"Almost finished," Pen said in a cheerful voice. One thing she'd learned in her first aid course was to always speak to the patient in reassuring tones.

It took several bandages to cover the cuts and scrapes on Clementine's leg. "That should do it," she said when she was finished.

"This is really most terribly kind of you," Clementine said. "Please let me at least make you a cup of tea for your efforts. It's no bother."

"Thank you, but that's not necessary. I'm still not quite the big tea drinker you British are, and I really should get down to the Open Book."

She packed up the first aid kit and replaced it in the cabinet. As she was straightening up, she noticed a small framed black-and-white photograph hanging on the wall above the cabinet. It was a picture of a small shop with a sign over the door that read *Clementine's*. The photograph was rather grainy, but Pen could see several cakes displayed in the large front window.

"Did you have another shop before you opened Icing on the Cake here in Chumley?" Pen said, turning around toward Clementine.

Clementine looked momentarily startled. "Oh," she exclaimed after a pause. "You noticed the photograph." She shook her head. "No, it wasn't my shop, I'm afraid. It was a little bakery I came upon when I was wandering around

Paris. It has my name on it, you see, so I simply had to have a picture of it."

Pen looked at the photo one more time. There was something about it that seemed off somehow, but she couldn't put her finger on what it was.

Clementine followed Pen out into the shop.

"Let me give you a little something," she said, her hand hovering over various items in the bakery case. "A Chelsea bun? Or a scone, perhaps, for your afternoon tea?"

"A scone would be lovely, thank you."

Clementine whisked her apron from a hook, tied it on, and reached for a piece of glassine. She chose a scone, popped it into a white bakery bag, and handed it to Penelope.

Penelope thanked her and headed out the door.

Seeing the picture of that bakery in Paris named Clementine's gave Penelope an idea. She and Beryl ought to plan a trip to Paris for a weekend. With the Chunnel, the train ride was only two hours. They could leave Friday night and be back by Monday morning.

She was thinking about Paris—the Eiffel Tower, the Louvre—as she was passing the estate agent's office when she realized what had seemed off about Clementine's photograph of that bakery.

Clementine had said that the photo had been taken in Paris, but Penelope was quite certain there had been a traditional British postal box just barely visible at the edge of the photo.

Clementine had always seemed a bit wifty to Penelope, so she wasn't entirely surprised that she had forgotten the location of that shop. It made her wonder how Clementine was able to run a successful business, but she supposed everyone occasionally had a lapse in memory.

* * *

Mabel was scribbling on a pad of paper when Penelope opened the door to the Open Book. She looked up, smiled, tore the piece of paper off the pad, and waved it at Penelope.

"We did quite well with Nathanial West's book signing. *Turn a Blind Eye* sold a record number of copies. Looks like we can keep the Open Book afloat for a bit longer."

What did Mabel mean by that? Pen wondered as she headed toward the delicious smells emanating from the tea shop.

Figgy was taking a tray of scones from the oven when Pen stuck her head into the tearoom's kitchen.

"Your eyes are lighting up," Figgy said as she transferred the scones to a rack. "You must be hungry."

Penelope held up the bakery bag from Icing on the Cake. "Clementine gave me a scone."

"Oh, pooh," Figgy said, grabbing a plate. "These are fresh from the oven and still warm."

"You've twisted my arm," Pen said. She gestured to the bag. "I'll save this one for later."

Figgy placed a scone on the plate. "Here you go. Let me get you some butter."

Penelope's mouth watered as she watched the cold butter slowly melting and oozing into the craggy top of the scone. She took a bite and closed her eyes in rapture.

"Mabel said the book signing was a success," Pen said around a mouthful of scone. She frowned. "She said it would help keep the Open Book going. I can't help but wonder if the store is losing money."

Figgy waved a hand dismissively. "Oh, that's a load of codswallop. Mabel comes from a family that's rolling in money. And the whole lot went to her since there were no other heirs. The Open Book is something to keep her busy, although she's quite passionate about it."

"But she used to work for MI6," Pen said, licking her finger and swooping up the remaining crumbs of the scone.

"Mabel isn't the type to simply sit around and count her money." There was a blast of heat as Figgy pulled another tray of scones from the oven.

That was certainly curious about Mabel, Pen thought as she walked toward the front of the store. She was so unpretentious—living in a small cottage when she could apparently afford a house in one of the fancy developments and wearing clothes that obviously had some age on them. She supposed that's what happened when you had real money and didn't feel the need to flaunt it. Beryl's husband suddenly came to mind. He hadn't been shy about spending other people's money, with that huge home in Connecticut, his bespoke suits, and expensive cars.

Penelope was still thinking of everything that Magnus had put Beryl through when the door opened and Beryl herself walked in. She was wearing an elegant plum-colored trouser suit with a silk blouse and black suede heels.

She greeted Penelope with a kiss on each cheek.

"Did you come to visit?" Pen said.

Beryl ran a hand over her blond bob. "Not exactly." She gestured toward the shelves. "I'm looking for a book on business. Something basic, like business for dummies."

Pen raised her eyebrows. What on earth did Beryl want with a book like that? So far, as a stylist, Charlotte was her only client and certainly that didn't require much more business acumen than balancing a checkbook.

"Let's see what we have," Pen said as she led her sister over to one of the shelves. She ran her finger down the spines of the books. "This should do it." She pulled a volume from the shelf and tapped the cover. "*Basic Business Skills*," she said, reading the title. She handed it to her sister.

Penelope pushed her glasses up her nose with her index finger.

"I'm curious. Are you going to expand your business?"

Beryl looked like the proverbial cat that had swallowed the canary.

"I suppose I can tell you about my project now. Things are far enough along that I actually believe in it myself."

Pen cocked her head. This was curious indeed. She motioned toward two overstuffed armchairs. "Why don't we sit down?"

Beryl chose a chair and sank into it, crossing one leg over the other.

"Sam Frost, or rather Simeon Foster," Beryl said, scowling, "was going to back me in my new venture but we know how that turned out." Her lips snapped shut in a bitter line.

"Whoa." Penelope held up a hand. "Start at the beginning."

Beryl sighed and fiddled with the bow on her blouse.

"I told you I met Simeon on the train and we went out a couple of times. When I told him I wanted to open my own boutique, he offered to loan me the money to get started." Beryl gave a sharp laugh. "Like Grandmother Parish used to say, 'If it sounds too good to be true, then you're probably right.'" She sighed.

"But—"

Beryl held up a hand. "Simeon's death was certainly a setback but I wasn't ready to give up. I talked to Charlotte about it and we cooked up another idea together. It won't require as much start-up financing and she's agreed to loan me whatever money I do need."

"So not a boutique . . ." Pen couldn't imagine what else would interest Beryl.

Beryl gave a triumphant smile. "No, not an actual boutique—an online styling service."

Penelope wrinkled her forehead. "What exactly is an online styling service?"

"It will be unique," Beryl said, her face flushing with excitement. "It will all be done online. People will send me a picture of themselves and a description of the event they are dressing for. I'll research suitable options and send them back pictures and a link to a store where they can buy the items."

"And people will pay for this?"

"Yes. And I've already contracted with several large department stores that have promised to pay me a small commission on all sales of the items I recommend."

So, this was what Beryl had been so excited about. Penelope felt her head spinning. As someone who pulled things randomly from her closet every morning, more mindful of comfort than fashion, it was hard to fathom someone paying for a service like Beryl's. But, undoubtedly, there were plenty of people who would. Besides, she was pleased to see Beryl so happy. It had been a long time since Penelope had seen her be so positive—since before the debacle with Magnus. And if she thought back, Beryl had never seemed very happy even then.

TWENTY

❧

"Would you mind if I took some time off this afternoon?" Penelope asked Mabel.

Mabel smiled. "Of course not. Do you have something exciting planned?"

Pen pursed her lips. "I'm not sure you'd call it exciting, but I've got a few ideas I'd like to pursue. I'm hoping something will lead to some clues to Simeon Foster's murder."

Mabel lowered her brows. "Do be careful. You gave us all a right scare the last time you got yourself involved in a murder."

"I don't think there's anything dangerous about this." Penelope explained about Terry Jones and the annual bouquet he sent to Sister Rosamund. "She might know something that will tie Terry to Simeon."

"You should be safe enough in a convent at least," Mabel said, wiping a smudge off the counter with the edge of her sweater. "You think Terry Jones had something to do with

Foster's murder because of an event that happened in the past?"

"It's possible. Both Terry and Foster served in the Falklands War so it's possible they knew each other from back then and there's bad blood between them."

"That last seems a bit of a leap," Mabel said.

"I suppose it does," Pen said. "But Maguire said you have to consider everything in a murder case so . . ." She fiddled with a piece of her hair. "Besides, I've hit a brick wall with everything else so I might as well give it a shot."

Mabel slapped her hands down on the counter. "Off you go then! Be careful and remember we drive on the left side of the street here." She gave Penelope a look that was half bemused and half concerned.

It didn't take Penelope long to walk home and get her car, and in half an hour she was on her way to the convent where Sister Rosamund lived. There were few clouds in the sky and the sun shone through the windshield of Penelope's MINI. She squinted as she flipped down the visor and headed down the high street and into the countryside.

Everything was going smoothly until she forgot where she was and drifted across the road onto the other side. She had no idea how long she'd been driving in the right lane, but the blare of a horn from an oncoming blue van with *Ellison's Electric* written on the side in white letters brought her to her senses and she quickly moved back into the correct lane.

A bead of sweat trickled down her back and her palms were damp on the steering wheel. She could do with a drop of Mabel's Jameson right now. Or a couple of drops. Maybe

Mabel was right and she'd be better off without a car, but she didn't want to part with her MINI—she'd become quite fond of it. It was only a matter of concentrating, she told herself, as she turned onto a narrow lane that led to the convent of the Sisterhood of the Sacred Cross.

The convent was a formidable-looking redbrick building. Pen shivered as she followed the signs to the parking lot. In the distance, she noticed a large plot of land with stakes planted in tidy rows, the strips of fabric tied to them flapping in the wind. The vegetables that Penelope assumed had been grown there had obviously long since been harvested.

She beeped her car locked and followed the path to the large front door. She rang the bell with a sense of trepidation, but the kind, smiling face of the sister who answered it immediately put her at ease.

"I'm Sister Joan. How can I help you?" Her voice was soft and melodic.

"I'd like to see Sister Rosamund, if possible."

"Is she expecting you?"

"Not exactly," Penelope hedged. "I'm a friend of Terry Jones's." Penelope fiddled with the buttons on her jacket. "Sort of a friend of a friend."

A shadow crossed Sister Joan's face, but she promised to see if Sister Rosamund was available and scurried down a corridor, her rubber-soled shoes making no sound on the marble floor.

Pen looked around her. There was a simple wood table in the middle of the foyer. On top of it sat a vase with a beautiful bouquet of flowers. Was this Terry's bouquet? The garden was in hibernation for the winter, and she doubted the nuns would spend the money on a floral arrangement.

It was eerily quiet and, although Penelope strained her

ears, there was nothing to hear—no animated chatter, no clack of computer keys, no doors opening and closing.

A movement caught her eye and she noticed a nun coming down the corridor toward her, like Sister Joan had, making no noise despite the marble floor.

She was wearing a plain blue dress that reached nearly to her ankles. It had a high, round neckline and long sleeves, which she had pushed up to her elbows. She had on a white apron and a short veil was pinned to her hair. Although there were gray strands woven through her blond hair, her fair skin was smooth and unwrinkled as if living in a convent had somehow kept the ravages of age at bay.

When she spoke, her voice was soft. "I'm Sister Rosamund. Sister Joan told me you're a friend of Terry's." She smiled at Penelope. "Let's go into the parlor."

She began to lead Penelope down the corridor. Penelope was horrified by the clatter of her shoes against the floor and tiptoed the remainder of the way.

Sister Rosamund opened a door and they entered a small parlor containing two unyielding sofas and little else in the way of décor save a large wooden cross on the wall.

Sister Rosamund sat on one sofa and Penelope the other. She clasped her hands in her lap and leaned toward Penelope slightly.

"How do you know Terry?" Sister Rosamund tilted her head and gave the impression that she had all day to wait for Penelope's answer.

"I'm working at the Open Book in Upper Chumley-on-Stoke and Terry owns a store there—the Sweet Tooth."

"I see." She stared at Penelope expectantly.

"There's been a murder in Chumley, I'm afraid," Pen said. "And I'm sorry to say that Terry is being considered as a suspect."

Sister Rosamund's placid demeanor was momentarily rocked, and Pen heard her indrawn breath.

Penelope was waiting for lightning to strike her. It was bad enough to lie, but it must be considered doubly sinful to lie in a convent and to a nun.

"I thought you might be able to tell me something about Terry. Maybe something to persuade the police that he wouldn't commit murder."

Sister Rosamund's eyes took on a faraway look. "I knew him forty years ago. I'm not sure what I can tell you. The young man I knew then certainly didn't appear to be capable of murder."

"How did you meet?"

"It was during the war in the Falklands. I was a rehabilitation worker at the facility where Terry was sent to recover from injuries he received during combat. He was there for several months, and we became . . . friends."

Penelope noticed how Sister Rosamund had hesitated over the word *friend*.

"I worked with Terry every day and eventually I came to care for him deeply." Sister Rosamund's pale skin turned pink. "He felt the same way and one day he proposed." Her blush deepened. "We went so far as to set a date and plan a small wedding with our families and a few close friends." She fingered the cross around her neck, twisting the silk cord it was hanging from. "I felt more and more conflicted the closer we got to the date we'd selected. I'd suspected for some time that I had a calling but I wasn't entirely sure. I was waiting for a sign." She looked down at her hands. "But when I contemplated married life—a husband, family, and all that goes with it—I realized that wasn't the life I was meant to live."

"You got cold feet?"

Sister Rosamund gave a small smile. "I suppose you could put it that way. I joined the Sisterhood of the Sacred Cross as a novitiate the day we were to have been married. Terry was devastated, of course, and I felt terrible, but I couldn't ignore my calling any longer."

"And the flowers?" Penelope asked, although she suspected she already knew the answer.

Sister Rosamund smiled again. "He sends them every year on the anniversary of the day we were to have been married." She waved a hand toward the hall. "It would be too selfish of me to keep them for myself, so I put them in a vase on the table in the foyer for everyone to enjoy."

Terry certainly seemed like a decent guy, Pen thought, remembering Sister Rosamund even after all these years. But sometimes even normally decent people were moved to do terrible things.

Sister Rosamund folded her hands in her lap. "The Terry I knew would never have committed murder. What makes the police suspect him?"

Penelope explained about Simeon Foster and the Epicurean Gourmet and the competition it was going to give to the other stores in town.

Sister Rosamund suddenly became very still. The blush had disappeared from her face and it was blanched.

"What did you say the man's name was?"

"Foster. Simeon Foster," Penelope repeated. "Do you know him?"

"I didn't know him, but Terry did. They fought in the Falklands together." Her voice shook.

The feeling that she was about to hear something important had Penelope nearly holding her breath.

"Terry blamed Simeon for something that happened

during combat. Something Simeon did." Sister Rosamund
fingered the folds of her dress.

"What was that? Do you know?" Penelope realized she
was clenching the arm of the sofa.

"Terry and Simeon were facing enemy fire. Terry was
shot." Her voice caught slightly. "Simeon fled—he . . . he
left Terry behind."

Even so many years later, the pain was evident on Sister
Rosamund's face.

"Terry never would have done that to Simeon. Or to any
of the men, for that matter. He was a kind, caring soul."

"What happened?"

"Fortunately, Terry managed to crawl to safety, but his
leg was injured. He was in a horrible way. He was in hos-
pital for weeks and then he was sent to the rehabilitation
center."

So that's how he got that limp, Penelope thought. No
wonder he didn't want to talk about it. What terrible mem-
ories he must have.

Unfortunately, it also gave Terry a really good reason to
want to see Foster dead. Penelope thought of the proverb
"Revenge is a dish best served cold." Had Terry waited all
these years to make Foster pay for what he'd done?

Penelope was starved by the time she got home but when
she looked in the refrigerator, the light shone on nearly
empty shelves. She had some leftover takeout but when
she opened the container, she realized she wasn't that desperate. It was definitely past its "best-by" date, and she reluctantly chucked it in the garbage can.

She was going to have to go out and buy something unless she wanted to make a meal out of some kalamata olives, a stick of butter, and a bottle of malt vinegar.

Her near miss on the way to the Sisterhood of the Sacred Cross had scared her to the point where she'd driven home, her hands white-knuckled on the steering wheel and the constant refrain in her head of *drive left, drive left* set to the tune of the theme song from the movie *Frozen*. She decided her safest bet was to walk into town and she retrieved her jacket from the closet and headed out the door.

Penelope passed under the light from a streetlamp and glanced at her watch. She was going to have to hurry if she wanted to make it to Grant's shop before he closed. She knew she could find something there that didn't require much more effort than microwaving or heating in the oven. She didn't want to waste time cooking. She'd had some ideas for her manuscript on her way back from the convent and she was itching to implement them.

She groaned when she saw the light wink out in the Jolly Good Grub as she approached. She'd either have to walk all the way back to Tesco or settle for fish-and-chips from the Chippie again.

Penelope watched while Grant came out of the shop and stood in the shadows as he locked the front door. He tested the handle and, satisfied that the door was locked, he turned toward the sidewalk. As he crossed the street, he continually looked behind him. Why was he being so furtive?

Penelope's curiosity was piqued, and she melted into the pool of blackness in the doorway of the Icing on the Cake, which was already shuttered and dark.

Grant made his way down the street, looking all around him as he walked. Why on earth was he being so stealthy?

Penelope wondered. He clearly didn't want anyone to see where he was going. What could he possibly be doing?

On impulse, she decided to follow him. He was clearly up to something that he didn't want anyone else to know about.

She kept some distance between them, wishing she'd thought to wear her scarf. The night air was nipping the end of her nose and sending icy fingers down the back of her neck. She stuffed her hands in her pockets and hunched her shoulders as she followed the bobbing red blur of Grant's hat down the high street.

Penelope's feet were numb by the time Grant turned down a small road barely wider than a lane. She noticed a light in the window of a cottage in the distance. Was Grant visiting someone? But why the secrecy then?

Grant turned around and looked behind him and Penelope quickly stepped behind some pine trees that were by the side of the lane. She gave a sigh of relief when Grant seemed satisfied that he wasn't being followed and continued on toward the cottage.

The moon was partially covered by clouds and the lane was unlit. Penelope cursed when she stubbed her toe on a rock and she made a squeak, which she quickly stifled, when a branch from an overgrown bush brushed against her face.

Grant was still ahead of her, blissfully unaware of her presence. Penelope suddenly began to feel silly. What was she doing spying on him like this? Did this visit have anything to do with Foster's death? Probably not, and she was going to feel even more foolish if Grant simply went to the front door of the cottage and rang the bell. But if that was the case, why was he acting so peculiar?

Penelope stepped back into the shadows when Grant reached the cottage. He bent down and placed a gift-wrapped parcel on the doorstep before ringing the bell and taking off at a trot.

Penelope inhaled sharply. Grant was Chumley's Secret Santa!

She ducked out of sight as Grant ran past her, back toward the road. Fortunately, he was so intent on getting away that he hadn't noticed her lurking in the shrubbery. Her hands were freezing, and she was about to head back herself when the door to the cottage opened and a man emerged. He looked right and left before bending down to pick up the package.

The clouds parted suddenly and light from the moon shone down, partially illuminating the landscape. Penelope had to stifle a gasp when she realized it was Rupert Yardley standing on the steps to the cottage.

She'd gotten the impression that Grant had a crush on Rupert, but did he have it that bad?

She remembered the boy she'd had a crush on in seventh grade—his name was Barry and he'd had light blond hair, a chip in his front tooth, and wore white Levi's jeans to school. She'd done some things that made her cringe now, like retrieving a piece of paper he'd thrown in the trash because he'd touched it and keeping it tucked under her pillow as if it had the magic power to make him notice her. But as intense as her infatuation had been, she'd never thought to leave gifts on his doorstep.

It looked as if she'd at least solved one mystery for Maguire, she thought as she retraced her steps back down the lane.

TWENTY-ONE

❧

By the time Penelope got back to her cottage, the persistent buzz of hunger that had sprouted in her stomach had turned into a dull roar that was impossible to ignore. She'd stopped in at Tesco and picked up several of their ready-made meals to put in her freezer.

She shrugged off her coat and emptied her grocery bag onto the counter. What to have for dinner? She went through her selection—toad-in-the-hole, cottage pie, chicken tikka masala. She settled on the tikka masala, which could be cooked in the microwave and would be ready in less time. She put the other containers in the freezer.

She carried her plate out to the sitting room and set it on the coffee table. Mrs. Danvers leaped onto the table with the grace of a ballet dancer and stood a safe distance away, sniffing the dish. Penelope shooed her off and turned on her laptop. She was itching to get back to her manuscript, but she found her mind constantly wandering back to her evening. She still couldn't fathom why Grant was leaving packages on Rupert's doorstep.

She was going over what she'd written previously when the doorbell rang.

That was odd. She wasn't expecting anyone. Perhaps Beryl was having another crisis and needed a shoulder to cry on?

She pulled open the door just as Figgy raised her hand to knock again.

"Surprise," she said as she walked into Pen's sitting room. She was carrying a plastic container, which she handed to Penelope.

"What's this?" Pen said, peering through the clear top.

"I had the urge to bake some fairy cakes and I thought I'd better bring you some before I eat them all myself." She patted her stomach. "I have to fit into my wedding dress."

Figgy had chosen to wear a Pakistani wedding dress given to her by her fiancé's mother—a vibrantly colored and beautifully embroidered lehenga and choli—a long skirt with a short, cropped top.

"These look delicious." Pen swiped a bit of frosting from one of the cupcakes. "I just have to finish my dinner," she said, wrinkling her nose. "Microwaved chicken tikka masala, and then I'll make us a cup of tea."

Penelope forked down the rest of her dinner with an eye on Figgy's cupcakes, then carried her plate into the kitchen and made them both cups of tea. She carried them out to the sitting room and handed one to Figgy.

Figgy shivered and wrapped her hands around the steaming mug. "There's frost on the windows tonight." Penelope reached for the container of cupcakes and studied them before choosing one with a swirl of vanilla frosting on top.

She held the container out to Figgy, but Figgy shook her head. "I've already had more than my share."

Penelope sat on the sofa, her legs tucked up under her, and took a bite of the cupcake. She closed her eyes in ecstasy. "Delicious," she murmured.

"You won't believe what happened tonight," she said, licking some frosting off her lip.

Figgy raised her eyebrows. "With you? Nothing would surprise me."

Penelope gave a fake scowl. She couldn't be annoyed because she knew what Figgy had said was perfectly true.

"I was headed to Grant's shop to buy something for dinner, but I was too late—he was already closing up. He began walking down the street, but he was acting so weird—looking around as if he was afraid he was being followed."

"Was he being followed?" Figgy took a sip of her tea.

Penelope felt the heat rise from her neck to her face. "Sort of. *I* followed him."

Figgy started and some tea splashed out of her cup. "Where did he go?"

"You won't believe it. Grant is playing Secret Santa!"

"No!" Figgy's mouth dropped open. "Who was he leaving presents for? Certainly not me." Figgy pretended to pout.

Penelope started to laugh but then began to choke on a crumb. Figgy jumped up, ran over to her, and patted her on the back.

"But seriously," Pen said when her coughing fit subsided, "what on earth has gotten into Grant?"

Figgy shook her head. "You never know about people. Did you see who he was leaving the presents for?"

"Rupert Yardley, of all people." It now seemed more

obvious than ever, Penelope thought. "Obviously, Grant has an old-fashioned crush on Rupert!"

The next morning was damp and chilly with heavy clouds hanging low in the sky. Penelope thought about Grant and Rupert as she walked to the Open Book. She still could barely believe what she'd seen.

Did Rupert know Grant had a crush on him? She hoped Grant wasn't going to have his heart broken.

Mr. Patel had said that while walking his dog, he had seen someone outside Rupert's cottage the night of the Guy Fawkes celebration. It had to have been Grant. And that meant he had an alibi for Foster's murder.

It also meant that Rupert most likely had an alibi as well. Mr. Patel had said there had been lights on in the cottage.

As far as Penelope was concerned, Terry Jones still had the most compelling motive for murdering Foster, although resentment might have driven Courtney Brown or her mother to do the deed. Penelope couldn't imagine what it must have felt like to find out that while you and your mother struggled, living in council housing, your father had become highly successful and was worth a lot of money.

Penelope inhaled deeply as she passed the Icing on the Cake. The scent of freshly baked goods drifted out as a customer opened the door, a bulging white bakery bag in her hands. Pen hoped Figgy would have something to treat them with that morning—perhaps one of her Chelsea buns. Pen's mouth watered at the thought.

She was nearing the Chumley Chemist when her cell

phone buzzed. She pulled it from her pocket and saw that it was a text from Beryl. Penelope was so busy responding that she didn't notice the commotion down the street until she'd hit Send and put her phone away. A group of people were clustered in front of the alley between Pierre's restaurant and the building next door. That was curious. What was going on? She began to walk faster.

As she got closer, she noticed several constables among the crowd. They appeared to be trying to hold the onlookers back. Back from what? Penelope wondered. She noticed that Gladys, still in her butcher's apron, along with Brimble and Violet, the vicar's wife, were among those straining to see what was happening.

A man emerged from the alley, and Penelope saw it was Maguire. A constable approached him and touched him on the arm briefly, and Maguire quickly followed him back into the narrow pathway between the two buildings.

Penelope finally reached the group and immediately joined Gladys and Brimble.

"What's going on?" she said. "Do you know?"

Gladys's eyes were nearly bugging out in her excitement. She pointed to the alley. "They've found a body down there."

Violet, who was huddled in a coat that looked two sizes too large for her, shivered.

"We'll all be murdered in our beds if things go on like this. I don't know what Chumley's coming to. My neighbor Sharon said it's all the fault of that social media. She said it will be the death of us."

Penelope opened her mouth but then decided it wasn't worth arguing. It was unlikely she would be able to persuade Violet that things weren't as bad as she imagined them to be. She craned her neck again but couldn't see much of anything over the heads of the constables clustered at the opening of the alley.

She looked at Violet. "You mentioned murder. How do you know it's murder? Have the police said anything?"

Violet sniffed. "What kind of an accident could it have been then? Suddenly dropping dead in the alley like that?"

Penelope stood on her tiptoes but, despite being quite a bit taller than average, she still couldn't see anything.

Someone across the street whistled and Gladys spun around. "There's Ralph standing in the doorway. I should get back to the shop." But she made no move to return to the Pig in a Poke.

"Who died? Do you know?" Pen said.

Gladys shook her head. "No. I asked Constable Cuthbert, but he wouldn't say."

Brimble stroked his mustache. "I tried to get a peek, but I couldn't get close enough to tell. All I saw was a bundle of what looked like rags."

"Maybe it wasn't murder," Pen said, shooting Violet a look, "but an accident of some sort?"

Brimble looked skeptical. "Doubt it. Hard to get into an accident in an alley." He pursed his lips. "Unless they took ill. Heart attack or something."

Penelope was about to leave when she saw Maguire making his way through the crowd. He looked like he needed a shave and was dressed in an old pair of jeans, a leather jacket, and a cable-knit scarf. The tips of his ears were red.

He took Penelope's arm and pulled her aside. He rubbed his chin and Penelope heard the rasp of his stubble. "I was supposed to have the morning off, but then this . . ." He sighed and waved a hand toward the alley.

"What happened?"

"A fellow who works at the hardware store across the

street was taking a shortcut through the alley when he came upon the body."

Maguire leaned back on his heels. "It looks like she was hit over the head with something—something heavy. We'll know more after the medical examiner examines the body."

"She? It's a woman?"

Maguire nodded and rubbed a hand over his face.

"Who is it? Someone from Chumley?"

Suddenly Penelope realized it could be someone she knew and her breath caught in her throat.

Maguire looked slightly pained. "Keep this under your hat." He looked around and lowered his voice. "It's Courtney Brown."

Penelope had to stifle a gasp. "Foster's daughter? Do you think this is related to his death in any way?"

Maguire shrugged. "It's too early to tell. Maybe. Maybe not. It could just be a terrible accident. She tripped and fell and hit her head. I'm no expert but that doesn't look like the case to me, though I've been surprised before."

A car screeched to a halt at the curb and a man jumped out. He was wearing a newsboy cap and had a camera slung over his shoulder.

Maguire groaned and scrubbed a hand over his face. "Looks like the press is here. Or what passes for the press in Chumley."

Penelope glanced at the fellow walking toward them. "Isn't he a bartender at the Book and Bottle?"

"Yes. George Taylor. He does double duty as the *Chumley Chronicle*'s reporter and photographer."

Taylor snapped photographs as he approached Maguire. "Is it murder?" he said, pulling a notebook from his pocket.

"No comment," Maguire said. "An official announcement

will be made in due course." He elbowed his way through the crowd and disappeared down the alley.

Penelope was turning to leave when she heard sirens and an ambulance come barreling around the corner.

Taylor put a hand on her arm. "Do they know who it is? Have you heard?"

Penelope shook her head. She wasn't about to tell him what Maguire had told her. Let him dig for the information himself.

Were Courtney's death and Foster's related? Penelope wondered. If not, there were two killers running around Upper Chumley-on-Stoke and that didn't seem very likely. And if they were related, then Courtney couldn't possibly have been responsible for Foster's death.

TWENTY-TWO

❧

Penelope heard the buzz of Mabel and Figgy's animated chatter as soon as she opened the door to the Open Book. They were leaning on either side of the counter, where India had joined them. Pen was pleased to note that although she was still leaning on her cane, India's cheeks were pink and her eyes bright.

All three women looked up at Penelope when she walked in, curiosity evident on their faces.

"Do you know what's going on down the street?" Mabel said, pushing her reading glasses up on top of her head. "We heard sirens and when I poked my head out the door, I noticed a crowd had gathered by the alley next to Pierre's. Something exciting seemed to be happening."

"Or something ghoulish," Figgy said. She looked at Penelope. "You should see the crowd that appears whenever there's an accident, no matter how minor, on the high street."

"They've found a body in the alley."

Penelope's words landed with a splash, like a rock being thrown into a lake.

"A body?" Figgy squeaked.

"Dear me," India said, the color leaving her face. "Who is it?"

Penelope hesitated. Maguire had asked her to keep the information under her hat, but she knew she could trust Mabel, Figgy, and India to be discreet. Still, she'd promised.

"They haven't identified the person yet," she said, her voice quavering with the lie—a white lie, she told herself.

Mabel gave Penelope a knowing look—as if she didn't believe her—but she didn't press.

"Was it an accident?" India said in horrified tones.

Pen took off her glasses and wiped them on the edge of her sweater. "They don't know yet. But the consensus seems to be that it's pretty hard to get into an accident walking down an alley."

"A medical emergency maybe?" Mabel picked some fuzz off the front of her sweater. "A heart attack or a stroke?"

Penelope wanted to believe that possibility as much as anyone. It was horrible to think of another murder disturbing the peace and tranquility of Chumley. Maguire had mentioned that Courtney had sustained a rather gruesome head wound. If she had fainted or had a stroke, it was possible she had hit her head when she collapsed, but the way Maguire had described it made that seem a rather unlikely possibility.

Penelope was afraid they had another murder on their hands.

Penelope spent some time chatting with India, who said that Charlotte had given her a lift into town and she was enjoying being out and about again. Pen then spent an hour reshelving books that had been left out around the bookstore before deciding it was time to get some writing done.

She powered up her laptop and stared at the blinking cursor. What was up next for Luna? She thought for a few minutes and then decided that Luna would be in her bedroom—a spartan space on the third floor of Raven's Castle, furnished with an iron cot, a desk, and an armoire—and when she decided to leave, she would discover someone had locked the door from the outside. Lord Hawthorne or his evil housekeeper? Penelope couldn't immediately decide.

No matter. She could decide later—after she got Luna out of the room. She thought about having her unscrew the doorknob but then she remembered she had done that with Eirene in her previous book.

Penelope nibbled on the edge of her thumb. There had to be a solution. Not for the first time, she wished she was the sort of writer who outlined everything in advance so they didn't end up plotting themselves into corners like she did.

Finally, inspiration hit. She would have the creepy illegitimate son, who skulked about the castle and who Luna suspected was actually the son of Lord Hawthorne and his housekeeper, rescue Luna by slipping the key to the bedroom under her door.

Why would he do that? Penelope tried to think of a logical reason, but the solution was eluding her, so she decided to shut down her computer and rejoin Mabel in the store. Answers to plot questions often came to her while she was doing something else.

Penelope was working with Mabel to plan the Open

Book's next newsletter when she looked out the window and noticed Gladys rushing across the street with a newspaper tucked under her arm. Moments later the door opened, and Gladys nearly catapulted into the shop in her excitement.

She waved the newspaper at them.

"Have you seen it?" she said breathlessly.

"What's that—the *Sun*?" Mabel said, reaching for her reading glasses. "I don't normally read that paper," she said, indicating the tabloid in Gladys's hand.

Gladys looked startled. "The stories are ever so good." She pointed to the front page. "There's one about Will and Kate moving into Adelaide Cottage in Windsor. That's where Princess Margaret's lover had lived with his wife. Now that was a scandal! My mum used to talk about it all the time, even long after the princess married that photographer fellow."

Gladys unfolded the paper and thumbed through the pages. She pointed at one headline with her index finger.

"Then there's this story about two blokes having a punch-up at a family resort. It says one of them was American." She looked at Penelope.

"Don't look at me," Penelope said, feeling the color rise to her face.

"Somehow I don't think that's what you came all the way over here to show us," Mabel said dryly.

Gladys shook her head and held up a finger. She turned some more pages, then stabbed one with her index finger.

"Look at that," she said triumphantly. "Chumley is in the *Sun*. Can you believe it? It's all about Foster's murder."

Mabel put on her reading glasses and adjusted them on her nose.

"Humph," she said, as she began reading.

"Did you see," Gladys said, tapping the paper again. "They've interviewed Clementine. I can't imagine why they picked her."

Mabel continued reading. She looked at Penelope and Gladys over her glasses.

"This is what Clementine had to say. 'I wasn't at the Guy Fawkes celebration that night myself. I kept my store, Icing on the Cake, open late in case anyone going to the celebration wanted to pick up something for dessert.'" Mabel put the paper down. "She managed to get in a plug for her shop, I see."

She picked up the paper again and continued reading. "When I moved to Upper Chumley-on-Stoke from London, I didn't expect to find it riddled with crime."

"It's hardly riddled!" Penelope exploded.

"The article goes on," Mabel said. "There's a lot about Foster, obviously, and how he started his chain of Epicurean Gourmet shops in London and then spread out to multiple locations." She sighed and took off her reading glasses. "It looks like our little town is gaining notoriety. But not necessarily in the way we'd like."

"Still, it's exciting, don't you think?" Gladys said, folding the paper in half and tucking it back under her arm. She turned to leave but suddenly stopped. "Blimey! Did you see that? A huge motor coach just went driving down the high street."

"Some tourists who are lost, perhaps?" Mabel said.

By now, Gladys had one foot out the door. She craned her neck and looked down the street.

"They're all getting off the coach and there's a fellow with a microphone leading them around."

Mabel pointed to the paper under Gladys's arm. "Maybe

they were headed to Worthington House for a tour but decided to take a ghoulish detour to see where the murder occurred."

"You're probably right," Pen said. "There hasn't been a busload of tourists here in town since I've been here."

"I haven't ever seen any either," said Gladys, her hand still on the door. "And I've been here a lot longer than you." She took one last look down the street. "I'd better get back to the shop. Maybe some of the tourists will stop in."

"Somehow I can't picture them carrying home fresh pork chops or a leg of lamb," Mabel said. "But you never know."

Gladys hadn't been gone for more than a few minutes when a customer entered the shop. She wasn't one of their regulars—Penelope had gotten to know them, and she'd never seen this woman before. She smiled encouragingly as the woman approached the counter.

She was wearing a plain black coat and clutching her purse in one hand and a bag from Icing on the Cake in the other.

"Can I help you?" Penelope said.

The woman smiled and her cheeks puffed out like a chipmunk's.

"I need something to read for the ride home."

"What sort of books do you like?"

Her face colored a bit. "I do love a good romance. Can you suggest something?"

"Have you read Charlotte Davenport's latest? *The Regency Rogue*?"

"No, I haven't." She leaned her elbows on the counter. "I understand she lives right here in Chumley."

"Yes. At Worthington House. She married the Duke of Upper Chumley-on-Stoke."

"I do remember that," the woman said. "There was

quite a to-do about it at the time. I don't see any reason why the duke couldn't marry whoever he wanted. Look at Prince Harry. He followed his heart." She clasped a hand to her chest. "It was so romantic."

"I'll fetch the book for you," Pen said. "Unless you want to look around first?"

"No. *The Regency Rogue* sounds positively delightful. Just the ticket to keep me occupied on the trip home." She smiled.

Pen plucked a copy of Charlotte's book from the display table up front. "Here you go." She handed the woman the book.

"Ooooh," she said, ogling the bare-chested man on the front cover, "this looks delicious." She giggled. "Almost as delicious as the slice of Bakewell tart I purchased at Clementine's shop. How I've missed her tarts and her banoffee pie. And her yummy jam roly-poly."

"So, you've been to Chumley before?" Penelope said, ringing up the book.

"Oh, no. This is my first time. But I used to visit Clementine's shop in London regularly." She smiled and dimples popped up in her cheeks. "I have to confess I have quite the sweet tooth."

"Clementine had a shop in London?" Pen said as she handed over the purchase.

"Yes. It was a tiny place but the smell when you walked in was heavenly. It was in Whitechapel, right on the corner of the Whitechapel high street and Goulston Street. Phillip—he's my husband—took a new job and got a pay rise so we moved to Hampstead, and I've missed Clementine's ever since. I can't tell you how thrilled I was to discover she had opened a shop here in Upper Chumley-on-Stoke."

"Are you on a tour?"

The woman bobbed her head. "Yes. We're on a day trip to see Worthington House, but when we heard about the murder—it was written up in the *Sun*—we persuaded the tour director to take a bit of a detour. He took us to the field where it happened. It was quite exciting—there was still a bit of crime scene tape left attached to some sticks." She clutched her bakery bag to her chest. "It was a bit morbid perhaps, but it will give us something to talk about when we get home."

Penelope couldn't help thinking, as she watched the woman leave the shop, that had they arrived a bit earlier, they would have been on the scene as Courtney Brown's body was removed from the alley. That certainly would have given them something to talk about.

Mabel had clearly thought of that as well. "Good thing those tourists don't know they missed the real show this morning. Our poor constables would have had quite a time holding them back."

"I can imagine them all whipping out their phones to take pictures." Penelope shivered.

Mabel clapped her hands. "Enough of that. It's too depressing to think about. Let's restock the display table." Mabel pointed to the front of the store. "Your customer bought the last copy of Charlotte Davenport's book that had been on display and there are several others that are getting low." She came out from behind the counter. "I'm pleased to see Charlotte's book is still selling quite well."

Pen pulled several copies of *The Regency Rogue* from the shelves and handed them to Mabel. "Did you know Clementine used to have a shop in London?" Pen said as she reached for some more books.

"I didn't. I've certainly never heard her mention it."

"It's rather odd, don't you think?"

Mabel paused with a book in her hand. "I don't know. Clementine is rather reserved. She doesn't ever talk much about herself."

A picture suddenly came into Penelope's mind—the photograph of a shop called Clementine's in the stockroom of the Icing on the Cake. Clementine had acted rather peculiarly when Penelope asked her about it. She had said that the picture had been taken in Paris and had nothing to do with her. But what if it actually was her own shop—the one that had been in London and, for all anyone knew, might still be there?

But why would Clementine lie about something like that? It didn't make any sense.

Penelope put the thought out of her mind and soon forgot about it as she helped Mabel open another carton of copies of *The Regency Rogue*.

Pen had just walked through the door of her cottage and was saying hello to Mrs. Danvers when her cell phone rang.

She was surprised to hear India's voice when she answered it.

"Hello, dear, I hope I'm not disturbing you." India's plummy tones came over the line.

"Not at all." Penelope wriggled out of her coat as she held the telephone to her ear. She dropped it on the sofa and plopped down next to it.

There was a pause. "I'm wondering if you could do me

a favor." India's voice trembled. "I do so hate to ask, but not that many people have a car."

"Do you need a ride somewhere?" Pen asked.

"Yes. It's hardly an emergency, so I feel terrible asking you to go to so much trouble."

"I'm sure it won't be any trouble," Penelope said, wondering what on earth India was getting at.

"I was hoping you wouldn't mind driving me to the Oxfam shop on the high street. They're open till eight o'clock tonight. Violet just phoned to say that she'd been there this afternoon and they just got in several good-quality wool coats that looked nearly brand-new. I'm afraid my dear old Gloverall has become quite worn and even though it's served me well, I fear I shall need to search out something new. If I wait until Violet can drive me, I'm afraid they will all be gone."

Penelope smiled. She knew how painful it was for India to ask for a favor. She prided herself on being independent and resourceful.

"I'd be more than happy to take you."

India's sigh of relief whispered down the phone line.

"I can pick you up in fifteen minutes. Would that work?"

"That would be excellent, dear. I shall be ready and waiting."

Penelope clicked off the call, drank a big glass of water, and slipped into her coat again.

As India had promised, she was ready and waiting and answered the door almost before Penelope knocked. She had progressed from her crutches to a sturdy hickory cane that she leaned on heavily as they made their way to Penelope's car. She kept a hand on India's elbow, but they made it to the MINI without incident.

"I do hope Oxfam has a suitable coat in my size and this won't be a wasted trip," India said as Penelope traversed the lane that led to the high street. "I fear I've waited too long to replace my old one. The collar is beginning to look quite frayed."

Penelope thanked her lucky stars when they found a parking space right in front of the shop so they didn't have far to walk. She helped India out of the car and through the door.

"I'm looking for a coat," India said to the clerk.

"We have some lovely choices over there." The clerk pointed to a rack in the women's department. "They've just come in."

India's face lit up when she saw the selection and that made Penelope's day. She felt a flow of satisfaction that she was able to help.

India picked out a black-and-white tweed A-line with large black buttons and a rounded collar. Penelope held her cane and steadied her arm while she tried it on, then led her over to the bank of mirrors along one of the walls.

"It's perfect," India said, regarding her reflection in the mirror. She examined the cuffs. "It appears to be in excellent condition."

"As a matter of fact," Penelope said, pulling a tag out of one of the sleeves, "It seems it's brand-new." She looked at the tag. "It's from Harvey Nichols."

India gave a small trill of excitement. "That's a lovely store," she whispered to Penelope.

"How splendid. This shall keep me delightfully warm this winter."

Penelope was helping India out of the coat when India gestured toward a nearby rack.

"Isn't that Terry Jones, who owns the Sweet Tooth?"

Penelope glanced over her shoulder. "Yes, I think you're right."

"He's looking at women's clothes. I know he isn't married. I suppose he must have a girlfriend."

Penelope looked in Terry's direction again. He was holding up a woman's bright fuchsia evening gown. It had a draped neckline with the top half covered in sequins. He held the gown up to himself.

"It's a beautiful dress, isn't it?" India said, glancing in Terry's direction. "Imagine giving away something so lovely." She handed Penelope the coat she'd been trying on.

"So, you've decided on this one?" Penelope said as she draped the tweed coat over her arm and handed India her cane.

"Certainly. It's perfect."

They were making their way toward the cashier when Terry suddenly rounded the end of the rack of women's dresses. Penelope didn't see him, and they bumped into each other.

"I'm so sorry," Penelope said.

Terry, meanwhile, appeared to be trying to hide the sequined dress he'd been carrying over his arm.

"Did you see the look on his face?" Penelope said to India after they'd left the store and were ensconced in Penelope's car.

"He looked positively horrified," India said as she reached for her seat belt. "No need for him to be embarrassed if he was buying the dress for himself. I understand there are men who are cross-dressers. There's no harm in it. It's been going on forever." She smiled at Penelope. "You young people didn't invent it, you know."

You never knew about people, Penelope thought as she pulled into the lane leading to India's cottage. She didn't know what was more surprising—the fact that Terry might be a cross-dresser or the fact that someone of India's background even knew what that was.

TWENTY-THREE

Penelope pulled into the parking lot of Tesco and walked toward the entrance. The bright red neon sign cast a wash of light over the front of the store. She stepped on the mat and the automatic door whooshed open. She needed to pick up a bottle of wine and perhaps some nibbles—Maguire was working late but had said he would stop by later that evening. Knowing him, his dinner probably would consist of a chip sandwich—or a chip butty, as he called it—from the vending machine and, no doubt, he'd still be hungry.

Penelope grabbed a basket from the stack by the entrance and began cruising the aisles. She found an inexpensive bottle of sauvignon blanc that the label claimed had been rated five stars by some obscure wine magazine. She was more interested in the price, which was quite reasonable.

She strolled down several more aisles and picked up

some crackers—which the British insisted on calling biscuits—something that still confused her even after all this time. She selected a wedge of Irish cheddar cheese, one of English stilton, some dry salami, and a crock of paté and would make what Brimble said was called a charcuterie board.

Penelope surveyed her basket. She thought she had enough. But perhaps something sweet as well? She chose half a loaf of lemon drizzle cake and added it to her purchases.

She was passing the meat counter, where two women were talking, when she thought she overheard her name. She stopped and pretended to be looking at the packages of kidneys in the case.

"I've just read her latest," the woman with the blue-tinged white hair said. "I positively adored it." She turned to her companion. "Have you read it—*The Woman in the Fog?*"

Penelope felt a glow of warmth despite the fact that she was getting cold standing over the refrigerated meat case. She rubbed her hands together.

The other woman was wearing a sparkly broach on the lapel of her coat. It reminded Penelope of the queen, who'd always worn a pin on her coat, although she supposed that the stones in this woman's broach were fake while the queen's were real. At least she assumed the jewels were real. She couldn't imagine that the queen, with her vast collection of gems, would've chosen to wear a piece of costume jewelry.

"I didn't care for *The Woman in the Fog*," the woman with the broach said. She sniffed. "I thought the book was overrated, if you ask me." Penelope tried not to react, but she felt her face flushing. She could never shake the feeling that she was responsible for a reader's dissatisfaction.

"Really?" the white-haired woman said. "I thoroughly enjoyed it. So did Clementine. She loaned me her copy."

"Speaking of Clementine," the other woman said. "I can't imagine what possessed her to change her vote on that man's proposal for one of his gourmet shops in Chumley." She picked up a package of chicken legs and tossed it into her cart. "I had lunch with Olive the other day at the Fox and Hound—such a darling place and they do a marvelous cottage pie—and she said that Clementine told her she was vehemently opposed to the idea. Then she found out from her husband—he's on the town council—that Clementine actually voted for the proposal."

"That is curious," the white-haired lady said. "I can't imagine what made her change her mind."

The conversation turned to Olive's daughter, who had become engaged to a barrister, and Penelope moved away.

So, Clementine had betrayed everyone by voting yes for Foster's proposal. Penelope was shocked. Clementine had been dead set against the idea. But something had obviously convinced her to change her mind.

Coercion? Had Foster threatened her in some way? Or blackmailed her?

Maybe it was time she learned a bit more about Clementine. And London might just be the place to start.

P enelope was up bright and early Sunday morning. Maguire hadn't stayed late—just long enough to devour the contents of Penelope's charcuterie board. She'd been right—he hadn't had time for dinner but had subsisted on a Cadbury Dairy Milk bar he'd wheedled out of the dispatcher. Unfortunately, a call had come in—a suspected break-in at a petrol station just outside of town—and they'd had to cut the evening short.

Pen twitched the curtain aside and looked out. It was clear and sunny—a perfect day for a trip to London. Rachel Friedman, an old friend from college, had called out of the blue—she was in town for an international convention of zoologists—and they'd planned to meet for lunch at the Scarsdale Tavern in Kensington. According to Rachel, their Sunday roast with Yorkshire pudding was not to be missed.

Penelope planned to spend the morning sightseeing and had settled on the Jack the Ripper tour in Whitechapel. What could be more perfect for a writer of Gothic novels? It also happened to be the location of Clementine's old shop. Perhaps there would still be someone around who remembered her.

She needed to dress with a bit more care than usual— London was the big city, after all—so she pulled her black pantsuit out of the closet. Dust had settled on the shoulders of the jacket and there was some lint clinging to the back of the pants. She poked around until she found her lint roller, then gave the suit a good going-over.

She had a quick breakfast of a few bits of leftover cheese, fed Mrs. Danvers and checked her water bowl, and in no time she was headed out the door.

The parking lot at the train station was nearly empty and she easily found a space for her MINI.

A couple of young girls were waiting on the platform, giggling and jostling each other and staring at a group of boys standing at the other end.

The train finally chugged down the tracks—looking at odds with the old Victorian station—as if they were in some sort of time-travel movie sequence.

The trip was swift. Penelope almost fell asleep as the train swayed around various curves, the wheels rattling rhythmically against the rails, and was surprised when the conductor announced that they had arrived at Whitechapel station.

Penelope rubbed her eyes, gathered together her tote bag and jacket, and followed the other passengers off the train and onto the platform. She felt a bit confused and paused for a moment to get her bearings.

A quick glance at her phone showed she had some time before the Jack the Ripper tour began, so she decided she would see if she could find the location of Clementine's previous bakery. She keyed the address into her cell phone and directions to the Whitechapel high street popped up.

She exited the train station onto Whitechapel Road and immediately the smell of coffee wafted toward her. She followed her nose to a tiny coffee bar and bought a cup. She wrapped her cold hands around the cup and sipped the coffee gratefully as she walked. The strong brew was invigorating her.

It was barely a ten-minute walk. She moved along briskly. The air was cold, but the sun felt warm on her face. The sidewalk wasn't crowded, although there were a few mothers pushing babies all bundled into their strollers and a couple of dog walkers who looked as if they had just tumbled out of bed on a sleepy Sunday morning.

The buildings here were older—most of them redbrick—which was a contrast to the modern skyscrapers visible in the distance. Penelope passed a stall where mounds of produce were piled high—purple rutabaga, bright orange carrots, and brown Jerusalem artichokes. Several women in hijabs were shopping, picking through the produce and weighing the vegetables in their hands.

Pen stopped to admire the White Hart, an old-fashioned pub where the front of the building was decorated with hanging baskets of fake flowers and greenery.

Finally, she came to the address the Open Book customer had mentioned—the corner of the Whitechapel high street and Goulston Street. She expected to see an older shop like the others on the street but was surprised by the newer building that stood on the site.

Next door to it was a small convenience store that looked as if it had been there at least since Jack the Ripper roamed the streets of Whitechapel at the end of the nineteenth century. The stripes on the ragged awning had faded nearly to oblivion and the name *Whitechapel Market* was barely visible. When Penelope went inside, she found an older woman behind the register. She looked as if years of hard work had worn off her color and was wearing an equally faded apron on which the floral print was barely visible. She was leaning on the counter, turning the pages of the *Sunday Mirror*.

Penelope prayed she'd been there when Clementine's shop had been next door.

She roamed the aisles of the tiny store, looking for something to buy that would give her an excuse to go up to the cashier. She was grateful that the shop was empty, which hopefully meant the woman would be more inclined to talk. She finally settled on a bottle of water and carried it up to the register, where she spied a rack of candy. Mabel was particularly fond of Cadbury's Double Decker bars, so Penelope grabbed two of those to take back to Chumley with her.

The woman pushed aside her newspaper and smiled at Penelope as she rang up the bottle of water and the candy bars.

"Is that all?" She slipped them into a white paper bag with *Whitechapel Market* written on the front in dark green script.

"Yes." Penelope dug in her tote for her wallet. "I was hoping Clementine's was still here," Penelope said as casually as possible. "I was thinking of picking up some scones."

The woman leaned on the counter as if settling in for a long chat. *Score,* Penelope thought to herself.

"I guess you didn't know. Clementine's burned down about ten years ago. There was nothing left but a pile of ash." She gestured with her thumb. "They built that new building next door in its place." She shook her head. "I fancied her Chelsea buns and bought myself one every morning before coming to work." She threw her hands in the air. "Harold—he's my better half—always asked why was I spending the money on something like that, but I told him to mind his own business. If I want to buy myself a Chelsea bun I will, and there's nothing he can do about it."

She laughed. "I imagine he was quite chuffed when Clementine's burned down."

"Were you here when the building caught fire?" Penelope said, dropping the paper bag into her tote.

"Yes, and it was really something. Smoke hovered over the whole block as far as Leman Street. And the flames! You wouldn't believe the heat. You could feel it even if you were standing across the street—like standing in front of the open door of an oven, it was. They made everyone in the buildings nearby evacuate because they were afraid the fire would spread. It was a miracle that it didn't."

Penelope was about to gather up her things and leave when the woman continued.

"You won't believe who used to work at Clementine's," she said.

Penelope was quite sure that at this point she'd believe almost anything.

The woman leaned over the counter, closer to Penelope.

"The fellow that owns that chain of Epicurean Gourmets. Odd name, if you ask me. What on earth does *epicurean* mean anyway?"

Penelope tried not to show her shock. "Simeon Foster? Is that who you're talking about?"

"The very one," she said with satisfaction. "I've got to say Simeon is an equally odd name. I don't know what drives some people. What's wrong with the old tried-and-true names, like Michael and John?"

"What did Foster do at Clementine's?" Penelope couldn't picture Foster baking lemon drizzle cakes or putting together a Victoria sponge.

"Oh, this and that. You know—sweeping the floors, stocking the shelves—things like that. That's a long way from owning a chain of shops."

"So, he knew Clementine before moving to Upper Chumley-on-Stoke."

It wasn't a question, but the cashier took it as such.

"Well, of course he did. He worked for her, didn't he?" Her expression turned somber. "I heard he was killed. Murdered. I swear, I never."

"Do you have any idea who might have killed him?"

She held up her hands and spread her fingers wide. "I dunno. I haven't even seen him in ten years, have I?"

"Did they ever find out how the fire started?"

"Not that I know of. I didn't take that much notice of it after it happened, I was that busy taking care of my youngest. He was two years old and a right handful at the time, I can tell you."

"I imagine it was written up in the papers," Pen said.

"Oh, yes, in all of them. If you're interested, you might ask old Mr. Fernsby. I know he was quite keen on following the story. He's across the street. He runs that little café. You can get yourself a cuppa and a bun while you're at it." She smiled.

Penelope thanked her and left. She stood on the sidewalk for a few minutes, shading her eyes against the sun with her hand and scanning the street. Catty-corner across the street she noticed a tiny shop with *Fernsby's* written on the plate-glass window in white paint.

She waited for the traffic to clear, then dashed across the street. A bell rang when she opened the door to the café. The interior looked as if it hadn't changed in decades, with a worn linoleum floor that had once been green but was now faded almost to gray. There were a half dozen Formica-topped tables with uncomfortable-looking wooden chairs arranged around them and a narrow wooden table at the back with packets of sugar and coffee creamer cups.

A man was behind the counter, swabbing it down with a damp rag. His hairline was receding and his wire-rimmed glasses were slipping down his nose.

Penelope ordered a coffee and a rather sad-looking bun. The fellow turned and reached for the coffeepot sitting on a warmer behind him.

As he filled a thick white mug with the streaming brew, Penelope asked him if he remembered Clementine's across the street.

"I certainly do," he said as he handed Pen the mug. He picked up a piece of glassine and reached for one of the buns. "My gran loved their Madeira cake. I would treat her to a slice whenever I could. I was quite partial to their biscuit cake myself." He put the bun on a plate and pushed it across the counter to Penelope. "It was a shame what happened."

"Oh?" Penelope feigned ignorance.

"There was quite the to-do when the place burned down." He scratched the top of his head. "My gran was that upset. She missed her Madeira cake. I tried several other bakeries, but she said it was never as good as Clementine's."

"The fire must have been very frightening."

"Sure was. The whole block was evacuated. Many of us fled without so much as a coat or scarf. It was a cold night with frost on the ground, so we appreciated the heat from the flames. It took hours for the fire brigade to put it out."

"Poor Clementine—losing her shop like that."

The fellow ran a hand through his hair. "I don't know. I heard that Clementine was complaining that the shop was losing money. If you ask me, she opened her bakery in the wrong part of London. Folks around here don't have money to spend on fancy cakes and pastries on a regular basis. She should have set up shop in Kensington or Mayfair."

"How did the fire start? Did they ever find out?"

He shook his head. "They never discovered the cause although there was talk that it started in a pile of oily rags in the storage room. But, frankly, most people found the whole thing to be a bit dodgy. The insurance company didn't want to pay up at first, but in the end it did."

He leaned closer over the counter and lowered his voice. "My gran used to live upstairs over the café. She couldn't get out much on account of her arthritis, so she spent a lot of time looking out the window. She claims she saw someone legging it away from Clementine's right before the fire started."

Penelope raised her eyebrows. "You think someone set the fire . . . on purpose?"

He shrugged. "Who knows?"

The door opened and another customer walked into the café. Penelope nodded at Mr. Fernsby and carried her mug of coffee and bun over to one of the tables by the window, where she could look across the street at the site Clementine's had occupied.

Had someone deliberately set the fire that burned the building down? If so, why did they do it? Could it have been a prank that started out innocently enough but had ended in tragedy? Or perhaps someone had borne a grudge against Clementine for some reason and wanted to cause her harm?

Pen took a bite of her bun and pushed her plate away. It was stale and no match for the fresh ones Figgy baked at the Open Book.

There was one other possibility, she thought, as she took a sip of her coffee, which had finally cooled enough to be drinkable.

Perhaps Clementine had arranged for someone to set that fire. Her shop was losing money, according to Mr. Fernsby. What better way to cut her losses than to burn the shop to the ground, collect the insurance money, and move elsewhere?

TWENTY-FOUR

❧

The Jack the Ripper tour ended in plenty of time for Penelope to get to her lunch date with Rachel at the Scarsdale Tavern in Kensington. She'd already plotted out the route—she'd take the underground to Edwardes Square.

The tour guide told her how to get to the nearest station and Penelope began to walk in that direction. Knowing that Jack the Ripper had stalked his victims on these very streets gave her a chill and she tightened the scarf around her neck.

The tour had started on Dorset Street, where the Ripper's first victim, Annie Chapman, had been staying in Crossingham's Lodging House. The tour group had traversed the same streets that had taken her to Hanbury Street, where she had been brutally murdered.

On the way, they passed Poppie's Fish-and-Chips and despite the gruesomeness of the tour, which would have put most people off their food, Penelope's stomach had rumbled as mouthwatering scents drifted from the doorway.

She had to admit, she was relieved when she reached Aldgate station, where the bright lights chased away some of the eerie chill of walking through the dark, cobbled alleyway where she could almost hear poor Annie Chapman's footsteps as, unbeknownst to her, she walked to her death.

Penelope didn't have to wait long before a train roared down the platform and shushed to a stop. She entered a carriage and found a seat, but the trip was brief and she was soon back on the street breathing in the fresh air. She began the walk to Edwardes Square and the Scarsdale Tavern, which opened in 1867 and was located on a charming street, facing Pembroke Square.

Penelope opened the door to the tavern and was greeted by Dre, the pub dog, who wandered freely behind the bar and throughout the restaurant. Rachel had not yet arrived, so Penelope took a moment to look around. The walls were adorned with gilt-framed antique paintings, the chairs around the tables were charmingly mismatched, a fire was roaring in the hearth, and the chef's specials were scrawled on a blackboard. The windows were made of stained glass and the lighting was dim, all of which added to the cozy atmosphere of the pub.

The door opened and Rachel Friedman rushed in.

"Penelope!" she exclaimed, taking her friend's hands in hers and air-kissing her on both cheeks. "It's been too long." Her strawberry blond hair was wound into a messy bun and her wide-open face was covered in freckles. She was wearing large tortoiseshell glasses and a bright blue pantsuit.

The hostess led them to a secluded table tucked into a snug corner and left them with menus.

"What do you think?" Rachel said, gesturing around the room. "It's charming, isn't it? Supposedly Lady Diana, Princess of Wales, came here frequently.

"Since it's Sunday," Rachel said, opening her menu, "you must have the Sunday roast. It's traditional in Britain. The home cook puts the roast in the oven in the morning and it's done by the time everyone returns from church. The custom dates back to Henry VII." She pointed at Penelope. "And you must have the Yorkshire pudding with it."

"I'm sold," Pen said, snapping her menu shut.

"How have you been?" Rachel said. "Aren't you living in some small town outside of the city?"

"Yes, Upper Chumley-on-Stoke," Pen said. "It's about an hour on the train."

The waitress stopped by their table to take down their order. She glanced at her notepad.

"Two sirloin roasts," she said. "That comes with Yorkshire pudding, cauliflower cheese, roast potatoes, and mushy peas. Also, two glasses of the pinot noir." She looked up. "Anything else?"

"That sounds like it will be more than enough," Pen said as she handed back her menu.

"I've read both *Lady of the Moors* and *The Woman in the Fog,*" Rachel said as the waitress made her way through the tables to the open kitchen. "Excellent reads. I'm very impressed."

Penelope ducked her head. She still felt shy about accepting compliments.

Rachel put her elbows on the table and leaned her chin on her hands. "Tell me what else you've been up to."

She told Rachel about the town of Chumley, the Open Book, the new friends she'd made.

They were quiet as the waitress placed their orders in

front of them. Penelope inhaled the delicious-smelling steam rising from the plate and her mouth began to water.

"Then there's the murder," she said, reaching for the salt.

Rachel paused with her fork in the air. "A murder?" She looked shocked.

"Two murders." Penelope explained about Foster and Courtney. "As a matter of fact, while I'm here in London, I was able to chase down a clue."

"How exciting." Rachel cut a roasted potato in half and dipped it in gravy. "What sort of clue?"

Penelope explained about Clementine, her shop, and the fire. "But I don't know if that has anything to do with Foster's murder or not. Besides, I can't think of a reason why Clementine would want to kill Courtney Brown, who was the other victim. I don't think they even knew each other."

Penelope forked up a piece of her roast. "Foster owned the Epicurean Gourmet—a chain of upscale food shops. He was quite well off. Courtney was the daughter he had never acknowledged. If it hadn't been for one of those DNA tests, she never would have known he was her father."

Penelope chewed carefully. "She and her mother had had to scrape to get by with no help from Foster. I thought that might have made Courtney mad enough to exact revenge by killing him, but then she turned up dead."

"What about the mother?" Rachel took a sip of her wine. "She must have been equally furious about the hand she'd been dealt."

"I thought of that," Pen said, "but then Courtney was killed. I can't imagine Karen Brown killing her own daughter." Penelope frowned. "Unless there really are two killers loose in Upper Chumley-on-Stoke."

"Are there any other suspects up your sleeve?" Rachel gave a sly smile.

"There's this fellow—Terry Jones." A picture of Terry Jones popped into Pen's mind and she shuddered. His strength was evident in the width of his shoulders and the muscles in his forearms. She could easily imagine him killing someone.

"Motive?" Rachel said as she forked up some cauliflower cheese. "That's what they always look for on those detective shows, isn't it?"

"Terry and Foster fought in the Falklands War together. Terry was injured and Foster left him behind to save himself."

Rachel whistled. "That's a motive all right."

"Terry also owns the Sweet Tooth—a candy store in town—and if Foster was really going to be flying in gourmet chocolates from Belgium like he said he planned to, it could have easily put Terry out of business. The locals would still visit the Sweet Tooth, of course, but all the la-di-da types who live in Birnam Wood would flock to Foster's Epicurean Gourmet. He stood to lose a lot of business."

"That's two good reasons why that Jones fellow might have wanted Foster dead. But what about the other victim? Courtney, I think you said."

Penelope made a face. "I can't think of any connection between her and Terry."

Rachel cut a piece of meat and skewered it on her fork. "Maybe the two murders aren't even connected then."

Penelope felt her shoulders droop. "True. But somehow I can't believe the two murders aren't related. There's got to be a connection. I just haven't found it yet."

Rachel dabbed at her lips with her napkin. Does this Terry have an alibi?"

"Not one that he's willing to admit to, according to the police."

Rachel cocked an eyebrow. "That sounds fishy to me."

Penelope put down her fork. "You're right. It does, doesn't it?"

That *was* fishy, Penelope thought after she'd said good-bye to Rachel and left the restaurant. What kind of alibi could Terry possibly have that he didn't want to own up to? She thought about it as she wandered the streets, admiring the charming housefronts with their brightly painted front doors and polished door knockers. What could be worse than being suspected of murder? Cheating on a spouse? Terry wasn't married, so that couldn't be it. Did it have anything to do with the fact that Terry was buying a woman's dress in Oxfam? That was hardly a crime. Doing something illegal, like selling drugs? But when it came to illegal doings, murder was at the top of the list. You'd think Terry would be willing to admit to anything rather than being suspected of killing someone.

Before Penelope knew it, she'd wandered down a street where the lovely houses had all but disappeared to be replaced by massage parlors with seedy signs out front and run-down shops.

A creeping sensation came over her as she turned around to retrace her steps. She couldn't help but think of Jack the Ripper lurking in the shadows, waiting for his next victim, and she quickened her steps. She imagined someone breathing down her neck and walked even faster.

A man came out of a door toward the end of the block. Penelope pushed her glasses up her nose and squinted into the distance. He looked familiar. Not for the first time, she wished she'd remembered to clean her glasses that morning—perhaps then she'd be able to get a better look at him.

He hesitated in the doorway, looked both ways, and then began to walk down the street toward Penelope. He had his head down and his hands stuffed into the pockets of his jacket. The closer he got, the more convinced Penelope became that she knew him.

As he passed her, still with his head bowed, she realized it was Terry Jones. He didn't appear to have recognized Penelope although he may not have even seen her, with his head lowered and his gaze on the sidewalk.

She'd noted the building he'd come out of and paused in front of it on her way back down the street. The sign above the door read *The Plaza Club* and plastered on the sidelight windows were black-and-white eight-by-ten photographs of what were obviously female impersonators. Penelope was about to turn away when one of the pictures caught her eye. The face looked familiar, and she had a shock when she realized it was Terry Jones. He was nearly unrecognizable in heavy makeup, false eyelashes, and with a feather boa draped around his neck. So, Terry must have been buying that dress at Oxfam for his show. It was possible he didn't want anyone to know about his alternate career. People of Terry's generation might not have been as open to this sort of thing as people were now. Could he have been in a show the night Foster was murdered? And was that why he'd refused to reveal his alibi?

There was one way to find out, Penelope thought. She tried the door handle and was pleased to find the door unlocked. She opened it and stepped inside. The interior was dim, with the only light coming from the bar that ran the length of the space.

Round tables were arranged around the room with a

small stage at the front. It was draped in a tired-looking red velvet curtain with gold braid trim. The air was stale and smelled like beer, sweat, and mold. A man in baggy gray pants and a white undershirt was pushing a sweeper across the worn red carpet.

He turned the vacuum off when he saw Penelope.

"I'm sorry, miss, but we're closed," he said as he approached her. "The next show is at seven o'clock." He smiled, showing stained, uneven teeth. "Why don't you come back then."

"I'm not here to see the show," Pen said, hoping her nervousness wasn't too obvious. "I just wanted some information."

A suspicious look wafted across the man's face. "What kind of information? If this is about the taxes, you'll have to speak to the boss." He jerked his thumb toward a door at the back of the club.

"No, it's nothing like that," Pen said quickly, shaking her head. "It's about one of the performers."

His look of wariness increased. "Most of our performers prefer to remain anonymous like." He rubbed his fingers together in a gesture Penelope couldn't miss.

She got the hint. She reached into her bag, pulled out her wallet, and handed him several bills.

He sucked air through his teeth as he stuffed the money into his pocket.

"You have a performer named Terry Jones, I believe."

The man frowned, drawing his unruly dark brows together.

"Terry Jones? That doesn't sound familiar." He tapped his chin with his index finger. "Oh, yeah, you must mean Miss Scarlet. That's his stage name," he added helpfully.

"Does he perform frequently?"

"Couple of times a week."

Penelope was beginning to feel as if she wasn't getting her money's worth.

"Does he perform on Fridays?"

"Sure. That's a big night. We get lots of customers on Fridays. He has a duet with Rosie L'Amour."

"Do you happen to know if he was performing on the night of the Guy Fawkes celebration? November fifth?"

He scratched his chin, running his finger over the stubble.

"So far's I know." He touched his pocket as if reminding himself that Penelope was paying handsomely for this information. "Want me to check?"

"If you wouldn't mind."

He shuffled to the door at the back of the club and disappeared. Penelope checked her phone while she waited for him to return. Fortunately, she still had plenty of time before her return train to Chumley.

After a couple of minutes, the fellow reappeared. "Malcolm, he's the owner of the club, said yeah, Terry was here performing that night."

Penelope was relieved that neither he nor Malcom seemed to possess an excess of curiosity and didn't ask her why she was asking so many questions.

She thanked him and, slightly poorer for the encounter, left the Plaza Club.

Penelope glanced at her watch. She still had a bit of time before her train was due to leave. She had yet to find a dress for Figgy's wedding—Figgy had said to wear whatever made her comfortable—and she certainly didn't have anything in her closet that was suitable.

The Kensington high street wasn't far. She'd take a stroll and look in the windows. Perhaps something would catch her eye.

It didn't take long for Penelope to reach the high street. She made her way down it, peering into boutique windows, until she came to Marks & Spencer. Surely, they would have something appropriate.

She glanced at their window display and was momentarily tempted by their enormous food hall, but she resisted and pushed open the door to the main store.

She slipped past the gleaming counters in the cosmetics department, where the air was heavy with perfume and the abundance of mirrors reflected shards of light across the area like lasers. After wandering around for a bit, distracted by all the displays, she asked a salesclerk where to find women's dresses.

Penelope strolled through the department, studying the outfits on the mannequins. She knew she wouldn't be comfortable in any of them. She began to go through the racks, pushing the hangers along one-by-one as she rejected the possibilities.

She was beginning to despair. As the maid of honor, she couldn't wear her pantsuit for Figgy's wedding. Figgy had given her carte blanche about the dress—long or short— she didn't care. For that matter, she'd told Penelope she could even wear pants if she wanted.

Figgy was going to be wearing a very colorful Pakistani bridal outfit, so Penelope decided she ought to opt for something neutral so they wouldn't clash. Her search through the racks wasn't turning up anything—pretty dresses for sure, but nothing she'd feel particularly comfortable in.

She was about to give up when something caught her eye. It was an ankle-length dress, fitted, with long sleeves in a pale dove gray. Beryl had once told her she looked good in gray. She only hoped it would be long enough, given her height.

She took it into the dressing room, hung it on the hook on the wall, and pulled the curtain closed.

She had a bit of trouble getting the garment over her head, but finally it fell into place. She reached behind her, did up the zipper, and smoothed the fabric over her hips. It was perfect. It fit perfectly and she could move comfortably in it. But was it right for the wedding? Was it too plain? Or not plain enough?

Assailed by doubts, she decided to phone Beryl. She didn't know why she hadn't asked for her sister's help in the first place, although Beryl could be a bit overbearing. She pulled out her cell phone and punched in Beryl's number.

Beryl answered on the last ring, sounding breathless.

"Am I disturbing you?"

"No," Beryl said, panting. "I was doing my Pilates routine. You should try it. It does wonders for your posture."

Did she slouch? Penelope wondered, glancing in the mirror.

"I thought you were going to London?"

"I have. I did. I'm looking at a dress for Figgy's wedding. I like it," she said decisively, "but I wondered what you thought of it."

"Oh." Beryl sounded pleased to be consulted. "Show me."

Penelope reversed the phone's camera and held it up so Beryl could see her reflection in the mirror.

"What do you think?" Pen said after Beryl had studied the view for several minutes.

She hesitated for so long that Penelope feared she was going to veto the dress.

"It's a bit plain," Beryl said slowly. "But in a good way.

I like it. I really do like it. It suits you. You'll look lovely but you won't be in danger of upstaging the bride."

Penelope thought of Figgy's bridal attire—there was very little danger anyone would be able to upstage that.

"So, I should buy it?"

"Definitely," Beryl said. "Next, we'll need to find you some shoes. Black suede heels would look lovely, don't you think?"

"Just so the heels aren't too high," Penelope grumbled.

"That's right. You and Maguire are almost the same height, aren't you?"

"I've got to go," Pen said, looking at her watch, "if I want to make my train."

"Okay. We'll talk accessories when you get back."

Accessories, Pen thought as she watched the salesclerk carefully fold the dress and slip it into a Marks & Spencer bag.

And here she thought finding a dress would be the end of it.

Penelope ran the last few blocks to the station and arrived panting and out of breath. The train was already idling on the platform, and she managed to jump on just as the doors were closing. The whistle blew as she collapsed into a seat and the train began to chug its way out of the station. She paused for a moment to catch her breath, then unwound her scarf and shrugged off her jacket. Heat was pouring into the compartment, and she was already warm from her sprint through the streets.

She hadn't had particularly high expectations of her trip to London, but she'd learned far more than she'd ever dreamed. The question was how to put it all together. It appeared as if Terry Jones had an alibi, so she could rule him out as the killer. Even if he had slipped out of the club early, he would never have made it back to Chumley in time. And she'd managed to find a connection between him and Courtney.

Then there was the issue of the fire at Clementine's bakery. What if that coffee shop owner's grandmother had been right and had actually seen a man fleeing from the shop right before it went up in flames? Clementine might or might not have been guilty of insurance fraud, but did that have anything to do with Foster and his murder? Or with Courtney's death, for that matter?

Foster was poisoned with sodium nitrite. Penelope had looked it up—it was a horrible death. The sodium nitrite inhibited the blood from transporting oxygen to the body, causing trouble breathing, a rapid heart rate and, ultimately, death. Where did anyone find sodium nitrite anyway? Gladys used it for curing bacon—could someone have stolen a bit of it from her shop? According to Penelope's research, it didn't take much to kill a person.

By the time the train pulled into Chumley's ancient Victorian station, she felt as if her head was spinning. She decided to push all of the information and speculation to the back of her mind and hoped that her subconscious would come up with something on its own. It sometimes worked when she was trying to solve a difficult plot problem, so maybe it would work for this as well.

Two women, their arms dripping with shopping bags, got off the train with Penelope. She fished her key fob out of her pocket as she walked through the parking lot and beeped open the locks on her MINI. The two women pulled out of the lot behind Penelope, leaving it empty until the following morning when it would fill up again with commuters heading back to work in the city.

Mrs. Danvers was ecstatic to see Penelope and wound in and out between her legs, flicking her tail back and forth as Penelope attempted to hang up her jacket.

Her plan was to pour herself a cold drink, kick off her shoes, collapse on the sofa, and read but, try as she might, she couldn't stop thinking about everything she'd learned that day. She sat on the edge of the sofa, rubbing the soles of her feet and going over the information she'd collected in her head.

Finally, she reached for her laptop, which was on the coffee table, and powered it up. She ought to be able to find at least one article on the fire that destroyed Clementine's original shop in London.

It didn't take her long to track something down—the *Daily Mirror* had devoted nearly a full page to the story, the article running alongside an ad for Sainsbury's frozen Jumbo King Prawns.

The article featured a picture of Clementine's shop as it had been before the fire and Penelope immediately recognized it as the same photograph that had been in the stockroom of the Icing on the Cake. Why on earth had Clementine tried to hide the truth about it?

There were several pictures of the rubble left behind by the fire. In some, you could still see smoke rising from the pile of charred wood.

Pen skimmed the article. There wasn't much she didn't already know—the facts were fairly straightforward. There was an interview with Mick Birdwhistle, who worked at the shop as a bakery bench hand and was bemoaning the fact that he'd now be unemployed.

Penelope clicked out of the story and closed the lid of

her laptop. She flopped back on the sofa and rested her tired feet on one of the throw pillows. What an odd name— Birdwhistle. He must have known Simeon Foster since they had both worked for Clementine at the same time. Could there have been anything in Foster's past that had led to his murder in the present?

Penelope decided to see if she could track down this Mick Birdwhistle. How many people in Britain could have a surname like that? It wouldn't be as pointless as trying to locate someone named Smith or Jones.

She sat up and reached for her laptop again and in no time was clicking on the BT Phone Book site.

In less than a minute, she'd located the address and phone number for Mick Birdwhistle. She was pleased to see he lived in Lower Chumley-on-Stoke. She reached for her cell phone, then changed her mind. It wouldn't be a far drive. She might get more information out of him if they met face-to-face.

It wasn't that late. Perhaps she'd pop over to see him now. Hopefully it wouldn't be a wasted trip.

TWENTY-FIVE

❧❧❧

Mick Birdwhistle lived in a redbrick semidetached house on the outskirts of Lower Chumley-on-Stoke. It had a tiny front yard with a small patch of grass and ragged-looking juniper bushes under the front window. Penelope pulled into the narrow driveway and got out of the car. The yard was decorated with numerous garden gnomes—she counted four of them as she approached the front door. Smoke was drifting from the chimney, and she hoped that meant Mick was at home.

She rang the bell and while she waited, she glanced at the house on the other side. Lace curtains hung in the front window and a birdbath with dead leaves in it was out on the lawn.

She heard footsteps and the door was flung open.

"Mick Birdwhistle?" she said.

"Yes."

He was short with small hands and feet, unruly white

eyebrows, and a white beard that made him look like one of the garden gnomes decorating his front yard.

"I wonder if I could talk to you for a minute?" Pen said. It wasn't the most brilliant opening line, but she couldn't think of anything else.

"Sure. Come on in. Are you taking a survey?"

"Not exactly."

Mick led her into a small sitting room furnished with a drab olive green sofa and a brown recliner with a hand-knitted afghan thrown over the back. A large-screen television sat on top of an old cabinet and a folded newspaper was next to it. A few embers from a dying fire in the fireplace still glowed red.

"Would you like some tea?" Mick said as Penelope took a seat on the sofa. "The missus always offered a nice cuppa to visitors. Sadly, she's been gone for three years now. It was her chest." He thumped his own with his fist. "We moved out of London because we thought maybe it was the smog that was doing it but, in the end, it turned out to be cancer." He bowed his head.

"I'm sorry," Penelope said.

She turned down the offer of tea and waited while Mick settled himself in the recliner. It appeared to swallow him, and only the tips of his toes reached the floor.

"I read an old article about the fire that happened at the bakery you used to work for in London—Clementine's."

"That's right." He nodded. "Burned to the ground, it was. A real tragedy. Put me and a lot of other people out of a job." He fingered his beard. "Of course, Miss Harrison—Clementine—got the insurance money, so you could say she landed on her feet."

Penelope had a sudden image of Clementine flying through the air like a character in *The Wizard of Oz* and coming to rest, with a slight jolt, on her feet. She shook her head. This was no time for silliness.

"Fortunately, I found a job at another bakery pretty sharpish. They're always in need of a good bench hand. The missus said I had certainly chosen the right trade. Not everyone has a feel for dough, but I was a dab hand at it. And of course, not everyone can shape the dough into the special forms that a bakery like Clementine's sells."

He looked quite pleased with himself, Penelope thought.

"I gather one of your fellow employees also landed on his feet," Pen said, leaning forward on the sofa. "Simeon Foster. He started that chain of Epicurean Gourmet shops."

Mick nodded energetically. "He certainly did. I was that surprised when I heard about it."

"Did you know he was planning something like that?"

Mick scratched behind his ear. "Well, he was always rabbiting on about how he was going to open his own place one day. And turn it into a chain of fancy shops for people who have the money for that sort of thing. I always said you can get everything you need at the local Tesco or Sainsbury's. No need to look any further."

He rubbed the back of his neck and shifted in the recliner.

"I always said to him, where are you going to get the money? He wasn't one for saving but was always splashing out on this new thing or that new thing." He grunted. "And he was a snitch—the first to notice if someone was a few minutes late or falling a bit behind in their work."

"It sounds like he wasn't very well-liked."

He snorted. "You could say that, yes."

"Did you hear the news? That Simeon Foster was murdered."

Mick's indrawn breath was the only answer Penelope needed. He barely blinked while she told him all about it.

"I won't say he got what was coming to him," Mick said, shaking his head. "Because no one deserves to be murdered. But I'm not going to shed any tears over it either."

It certainly sounded as if Simeon Foster had made his share of enemies, Penelope thought as she thanked Mick and said good-bye.

A thought struck her as she drove toward Upper Chumley-on-Stoke's high street. Mick had asked Simeon where he was going to get the money to open his shops. He might have borrowed it. But what if he'd made the money somehow?

The fellow in the café in London had said his gran saw someone fleeing right before the fire started at the bakery. What if that someone had been Foster? And what if Clementine had paid him to set the fire?

It's quite possible that's where he got the money to start his own store and ultimately grow it into the large chain it became.

Penelope's phone rang as she opened her front door. She was tempted to ignore it. She was tired and her feet hurt. In the end, she bumped the door closed with her hip and dug in her tote for her cell. She glanced at the number on the screen—the call was from Maguire. She was glad she'd decided to answer.

She was especially glad when he invited her for dinner at the Book and Bottle. She had just enough time to feed Mrs. Danvers and to freshen up slightly, which in Penelope's case meant running a hand through her hair and changing into more comfortable clothes.

Maguire arrived to pick her up right on schedule. Although there were lines of weariness creasing his forehead, he looked as if he, too, had freshened up. His hair was neatly combed and he smelled of newly applied aftershave.

He ushered Penelope out to his car and held the door open for her. Penelope always thought that the interior of a person's car could tell you a lot about them—whether it was neat and tidy or filled with discarded wrappers from fast-food restaurants, for instance.

As Penelope knew, Maguire's car was far from brand-new, but the interior was spick-and-span and the windows were clean. A small enamel four-leaf clover dangled from the rearview mirror.

The Book and Bottle wasn't crowded when they arrived, and the hostess immediately showed them to a table. Penelope decided on a glass of pinot noir and Maguire ordered a pint of stout. He rubbed a hand across his forehead.

"Tired?"

He gave a brief smile. "More like frustrated. I don't seem to be any closer to solving Simeon Foster's murder than I was the day he was killed." He squeezed the bridge of his nose. "Then there's the murder of Courtney Brown on top of it. I can't even find a reason for that. She didn't have much family and she didn't seem to have any friends, so who knew her enough to want her dead?" He ran a hand through his hair. "First the father is murdered and then his daughter. That's seems like too much of a coincidence to assume there isn't a connection between the two and that there are two separate killers."

They were quiet as the waitress placed their drinks in front of them and handed them menus. Maguire downed a quarter of his pint in one gulp, then swiped his napkin across his lips.

"Foster's murder is like the one in Agatha Christie's *Murder on the Orient Express*, where everyone on the train had a motive. No one I've talked to seemed particularly sorry that he's gone."

"Not even his own daughter," Penelope said.

Maguire ran a finger around the rim of his glass. "She had a good motive," he said, "but now she's dead, too. I honestly can't believe we have two murderers running around in Chumley. I don't *want* to believe it." He took another gulp of his stout. "But what's the connection between the two? Is there a connection? That's what has me stumped. They're threatening to bring in the big boys from the Met if we don't solve this soon." He laughed. "Although last time they sent a woman." He took another sip of his drink. "At least we solved the Secret Santa puzzle."

"Oh?" Penelope raised her eyebrows.

She hadn't wanted to get Grant in hot water, so she'd convinced him to stop leaving gifts on Rupert's doorstep and ringing the bell. For all she knew, there was some sort of nuisance law that could get Grant in trouble despite his intentions being completely innocent. She advised him to gather up his courage instead and find out if his affections were returned.

"Poor Grant." Maguire shook his head. "I told him to quit pestering Rupert and come clean about his intentions."

"I did, too," Pen said.

Maguire looked startled. "You did? You mean you knew?"

"I guessed." Pen hedged her words. She didn't want Maguire thinking she was withholding information from him. Which, in a way, she was.

"Do you have any guesses about Foster's murder?" Maguire said in a teasing tone. "You've helped me before." He held his hands out palms up. "I'm stumped. Perhaps we could make you an honorary member of the Chumley police force."

"No, thanks." Penelope told him about her visit to London and the information she'd uncovered about Clementine.

"That's certainly interesting," Maguire said, draining the last of his stout. "But that's all ancient history. And if Clementine was the killer, why would she decide to murder Foster now? And why murder him anyway?"

"I don't know," Penelope admitted.

But she felt as if the answer was on the tip of her tongue—as if all the clues were floating around in her head and all she needed to do was grasp them and piece them together.

Penelope was reaching for her jacket the next morning when her cell phone beeped with an incoming text. She debated waiting till she got to the Open Book to read it, but when her phone dinged a second time, she dug it out of her purse as she was opening the door.

The text was from Bettina. Penelope groaned as she read it.

Darling Pen,

I may have forgotten to tell you this (I'm moving apartments and my life is in utter turmoil as I am sure you can imagine) but we've had a request from Dark Stormy Night Magazine asking if you'd be willing to write a short article for them—subject of your choice—by this coming Wednesday. As you know, Dark Stormy Night Magazine is a favorite of

fans of Gothic novels so I told them yes. I was sure
you wouldn't want to miss this perfect opportunity
to plug *The Woman in the Fog*. Do forgive the short
notice—it couldn't be helped.

XXX Bettina

Penelope dropped the phone back into her tote bag and
pulled the door closed behind her.

What on earth was she going to write about? She
thought about it as she walked to the Open Book, but her
mind kept wandering back to Foster's murder.

"Good morning," Mabel called cheerfully from behind
the counter when Penelope arrived.

Clementine appeared from around the end of one of the
bookshelves. She smiled at Penelope. "Thank you again
for coming to my aid the other day."

If possible, Clementine appeared thinner than she had
the last time Penelope had seen her. Her wispy hair looked
as if it needed to be combed and there were dark crevasses
under her eyes. She put a copy of Penelope's *The Woman
in the Fog* on the counter.

"I read *Lady of the Moors* and loved it," she said shyly.
"I stayed up way too late to finish it."

"Thank you."

Penelope slapped a hand to her forehead. "I almost forgot." She reached into her tote and pulled out the bag from
the Whitechapel Market with the candy bars she'd bought
for Mabel. She put it on the counter.

She noticed Clementine staring at the bag, then at Penelope. Her mouth began to move but she clamped it shut.
She handed her money to Mabel, took her receipt and her
package, nodded good-bye, and left.

Had Pen given away the fact that she'd been investigating Clementine? She could kick herself for having pulled out that bag from Whitechapel Market when she did. Of course, Clementine would recognize the name. Too late to do anything about it now.

She leaned on the counter and filched a scone from the plate by Mabel's elbow.

"Thank you for the chocolates," Mabel said. "Very thoughtful of you." She looked away and swiped a finger under her eyes.

"Do you need me? I have an article to write. Last minute request from my editor."

Mabel waved a hand toward the back of the store. "Go on. Get some writing done." She smiled at Penelope. "I know you hoped that being here in England and at the Open Book would open up a new vein of creativity for you and get you over your writer's slump. I hope it's worked."

Penelope thought for a moment. "You know, it has. It's still not easy—I don't think it ever will be—but I don't feel as stuck and . . . helpless as I did in New York."

Mabel patted Penelope's hand. "I hope that means you're going to stay with us for a bit longer."

Penelope felt her face flush. "I hope to."

"Good," Mabel said decisively. "Now go write your article. We can manage without you for a bit."

Penelope snitched another scone and retreated to her writing room.

She opened her laptop and turned it on, then spent long minutes staring at the blinking cursor. Bettina was right—having an article in *Dark Stormy Night Magazine* would be a great boost for *The Woman in the Fog*. But the problem remained—what to write about?

The magazine was aimed at readers, not writers, so all

the usual topics were out—how to develop characters, to outline or not to outline, writing a synopsis.

None of those was right so Penelope forced herself to think more creatively.

Finally, she hit on a topic—the importance of setting in Gothic novels from Manderley in du Maurier's *Rebecca* to a Manhattan apartment house in *Rosemary's Baby*.

Now that she had the subject—one she was passionate about—the words began to flow, and an hour and a half later, Penelope triumphantly typed *the end*. The draft would need revision, of course, but she would do that later.

M abel was sealing a large manila envelope when Penelope emerged from her writing room.

She held up the envelope. "My lease for the next three years."

Penelope pointed to the envelope. "Do you want me to take that to the post office for you?"

"Would you? That would be grand. My arthritis is acting up today and I'm a bit stiff, I'm afraid."

"No problem," Penelope said as she reached for her jacket. She hesitated but then pulled on her hat as well. She decided she had better bundle up. She wasn't going far, but it had been quite cold that morning.

As soon as she opened the door to the Sweet Tooth, where the post office was located, she was surrounded by the enticing scents of vanilla, chocolate, and sugar, which just happened to be some of her favorite things.

A sign posted on a display case near the front door announced that the truffle flavor of the day was tiramisu. Each of the truffles sat in a frilled paper candy cup, which were arranged in tidy rows marching from the front of the case to the back. Penelope promised to buy herself one on her way out.

A woman in cranberry-colored slacks and a gray sweater but no coat was ahead of Penelope in line. The postmistress chatted with her while her mail was being weighed and stamped and Pen listened in.

"Do you have any treacle tart today? My Eric so loves a piece with his tea," the postmistress said.

"Yes. It was made fresh this morning. Shall I put one aside for you?"

"If you wouldn't mind. I'll pop round on my break."

The customer handed over some notes, took her change, and turned to go.

Penelope smiled at her. "You must be freezing without a coat." She gave an exaggerated shiver.

The woman laughed. She had a large gap between her two front teeth.

"I've only come from next door. I work part-time at the Icing on the Cake. But you're right—it's gotten right cold out. It almost feels like snow."

"Have you worked for Clementine long?"

The woman furrowed her brow. "It's going on three years now." She tapped Penelope's arm. "I get the pick of what didn't sell at the end of the day. Clementine insists on everything fresh each morning. It's such a treat."

Penelope nearly drooled at the thought, but she couldn't complain—Figgy certainly kept them well supplied with delicious baked goods.

"Anyway, I'm just running a quick errand for Clementine, so I didn't bother with a coat," the woman said.

"Oh?"

"I don't mind. It gets me out of the shop for a bit. Last

week she sent me over to the Sweet Tooth to fetch some chocolate red-wine truffles. It was the flavor of the day and she said they were his favorites." She looked at her watch and squealed. "I'd better be getting on. Nice to meet you. Ta."

Penelope was left standing with her mouth open, about to ask the woman what day she'd been to the Sweet Tooth buying truffles for Clementine. They were *his* favorites, the woman had said, so the candies weren't for Clementine herself. Had they been for Simeon Foster—the doctored truffles that had ended up killing him?

How could she prove it? Penelope mulled over the thought as she handed the manila envelope Mabel had asked her to mail to the postmistress. If only she knew what day chocolate red-wine truffles had been the daily special.

She was about to leave the shop when she thought of a solution so simple she couldn't believe she hadn't thought of it immediately. She would ask Terry Jones. With any luck he kept a record of the chocolates he featured each day in his shop.

She waited until the clerk had finished wrapping up a box of chocolate-covered cherries for a customer and then went up to the counter.

"Penelope. What can I get you? Your usual—peanut butter cookie dough truffles?"

Penelope was chagrined to realize that she'd bought so much candy from the Sweet Tooth that the clerk actually remembered her name and her favorite flavor. Peanut butter was a weakness of hers and she was known to scoop it straight from the jar and lick it off her finger.

"Nothing today, thanks, Ginny. I wanted to speak to Terry actually. Is he here?"

Ginny gave her a strange look but jerked a thumb in the

direction of the back of the shop. "He's in his office. Through that door, then make a left. You can't miss it."

Penelope found Terry's office easily enough. It was a small space with a battered oak desk, an old-fashioned wooden swivel chair, and a dusty standing floor fan in the corner.

Terry was bent over his laptop. There was a stack of papers by his elbow and the printer was humming with something that was in the process of printing.

Penelope cleared her throat and knocked on the door-jamb.

Terry jumped and swiveled his chair around. He frowned. "Can I help you? You're Penelope from the Open Book, right? The American?" His face relaxed and his chair creaked as he leaned back in it. "I've always had a hankering to see America myself—the wide-open spaces, cowboys rustling cattle." He took a deep breath. "Maybe someday."

Penelope thought of suburban Connecticut, where she grew up, which was far from the idyllic far-western picture he was envisioning. She was tempted to tell him America wasn't all Conestoga wagons and log cabins anymore, but she resisted.

Terry crossed his arms over his chest. "So, what can I do for you?"

"Do you keep a list of your flavors of the day?"

"You mean, like, which flavor is on which day?" He tapped a small notebook on his desk. "I certainly do. I want to make sure I don't repeat myself. Of course, at Christmas, everyone expects chocolate peppermint truffles and eggnog truffles, so I don't deviate from that."

"Do you have any idea what flavor you sold on November fifth?"

"Guy Fawkes Day?" Terry pulled the notebook toward him and opened it up. He licked his finger and thumbed through the page. "Here it is." He stabbed the page with his index finger. "The feature that day was chocolate red-wine truffles." He looked at Penelope. "Anything else?"

"No, that's perfect," Pen said. "Do you know when you plan on having them again?"

Terry flashed a grin. "So that's why you're asking." He scratched behind his neck, then thumbed through another section of his notebook. He squinted at the page. "It looks like I have them planned for December fifteenth." He tapped the page with his finger. "They're a hit at holiday parties."

Penelope thanked him and beat a hasty retreat.

TWENTY-SIX

❧

Pen left the Sweet Tooth and instead of turning left to go to the Open Book, she headed right toward home in order to get her car. As she walked, she pulled out her cell, dialed the Open Book, and told Mabel she'd be back in an hour.

Many of the things she'd learned so far were coming into focus, but she still couldn't imagine how Courtney Brown's death was related to it all.

She hoped Courtney's mother, Karen, would have a clue—possibly something she didn't even realize was important—that would tie everything together.

She retrieved her car and headed off in the direction of the Southfield Estate and Karen Brown's council flat.

As she parked her car, she prayed Karen would be home and was relieved when the door was opened promptly when she rang the bell. Karen was wearing an apron and a pair of bright yellow rubber gloves and was holding a broom in one hand and a dust cloth in the other.

"Oh," she said, her mouth rounded in surprise. "It's Penelope, isn't it?" She hesitated. "Won't you come in." She leaned the broom against the wall and stuffed the dust cloth into her apron pocket.

"Thank you."

"I'm afraid it's a bit of a mess. I'm in the midst of cleaning." She peeled off her rubber gloves as they walked down the hall.

Penelope followed her into the living room, where the tracks in the carpet indicated it had recently been vacuumed.

"Please have a seat."

Penelope sat on the sofa while Karen perched hesitantly on a chair.

"I'm terribly sorry for your loss," Pen said.

Karen ducked her head and was silent for a moment. When she looked up, Penelope could see there were tears glistening in her eyes.

"Thank you," Karen said, twisting the rubber gloves she was still holding in her hands.

"What can I do for you?" "I'm afraid I've told you everything I know."

"I'm sure you have," Pen said. "I thought there might be something you don't even realize is important."

Karen cocked her head and gave Penelope a quizzical look.

"Did Courtney know Clementine Harrison? She's the owner of Icing on the Cake. It's on Upper Chumley's high street, next to the Sweet Tooth."

Karen frowned. "I don't think so. I don't recall her ever

mentioning someone named Clementine. It's an unusual name, isn't it? Something you'd remember."

That settled that, Penelope thought. But then why did she see Courtney and Clementine quarreling that day? If they didn't know each other, why would they have gotten into such a heated argument?

"I do remember one thing now that you mention it," Karen said, perking up. "Courtney told me she saw something at the Guy Fawkes Day celebration that gave her an idea."

"An idea? Did she say what it was?" Pen leaned forward in her seat.

Karen shook her head. "No. But she did say it might bring us a bit of money."

Pen was so focused on her thoughts as she drove back to the Open Book that she forgot to keep to the left lane and there was a horrible moment when a Land Rover suddenly appeared around a bend, headed straight toward her. She jerked the wheel and managed to get out of the way in the nick of time. The woman driving the Land Rover gave Penelope a furious look as she shot past her.

Penelope's breathing didn't return to normal until she pulled into a parking space near the Open Book and turned off the engine. She was still a little wobbly when she got out of the car and was grateful when she reached the sanctuary of the bookstore.

She was even more grateful when Figgy suggested tea and wheeled a cart over with a steaming pot of Darjeeling and a plate of slices of Victoria sponge cake.

Mabel pushed her sleeves up and leaned her elbows on the counter. She raised an eyebrow at Penelope.

"Are you going to tell us what has you looking like the cat that swallowed the canary?"

Penelope feigned shock. "Me?" She put a hand on her chest.

Mabel laughed and gave a brisk nod.

Penelope hesitated. Her theory sounded solid to her, but what if it all fell apart when she said it out loud? Finally, she decided to just go for it. If Mabel and Figgy laughed, so what?

"I think I've figured out Foster's murder as well as Courtney Brown's."

Figgy dropped her teaspoon and it clattered against her saucer.

Mabel's eyes widened. "Do tell," she said somewhat breathlessly.

Penelope took a deep breath, licked her lips, and plunged.

"Do you remember when we saw Clementine arguing with Foster right before the town council meeting?"

Mabel's and Figgy's heads bobbed in unison.

"I couldn't help wondering what they could possibly be arguing about. Supposedly they barely knew each other." Penelope paused. "Then there was the vote. No one knew who had cast the vote to approve Foster's proposal, but I learned it was Clementine."

Mabel gasped. "But why would she do that? The Epicurean Gourmet could have put the Icing on the Cake out of business."

"Exactly," Penelope said. "She had to have had a really good reason. I think Foster blackmailed her."

"No!" Figgy exclaimed. "But how could that be? You just said they barely knew each other."

Penelope smiled. Now she knew how that cat must have felt when it swallowed the canary. "I discovered that Clementine and Foster did know each other. And quite well actually. Clementine once owned a bakery in London and Foster worked for her."

"Really?" Figgy squeaked.

"The shop burned down and that's when Clementine moved here to Chumley and opened Icing on the Cake." She took a bite of Victoria sponge. "And Foster went on to establish his chain of Epicurean Gourmet shops."

Penelope brushed some crumbs off her sweater. "The question is—was the fire really an accident and where did Foster get the money to start building his empire?"

Mabel and Figgy looked at each other and shrugged.

"I think the fire that burned down Clementine's business was set deliberately. There were questions about it even at the time but eventually the insurance company paid up. Also," she said, taking a deep breath, "I think Foster either knew she committed fraud or he actually lit the fire himself."

"But why would he do that?" Figgy refilled her teacup.

Penelope rubbed two fingers together. "Money. I think Clementine either paid him to set the fire or she paid him to keep quiet about it. Either way, Foster benefited. I think that was the nest egg he used to start his own business."

Penelope took a sip of her tea, but it was now lukewarm.

"The man who works in the café across the street from where Clementine's bakery had been located said his grandmother claimed to have seen someone fleeing the scene of the fire. I think it's quite possible that person was Foster."

Mabel was nodding. "So that's how he got Clementine to change her vote on his proposal. Blackmail."

Figgy screwed up her face. "But what about Courtney? What did Clementine have against her?"

"Courtney hinted to her mother that she saw something interesting at the Guy Fawkes Day celebration and that it was something that might bring them a bit of money. I think Courtney saw Clementine put that box of chocolates on Foster's blanket."

"So, Courtney was blackmailing Clementine—or threatening to."

"Yes. One day when I was passing the Icing on the Cake, I saw the two of them arguing. It seemed very heated. Again, it didn't make sense." Pen licked her finger and picked up the crumbs on her plate. "Courtney and Clementine didn't know each other. Why would they be fighting like that?"

Figgy frowned. "That must have been the first time Courtney tried to hit Clementine up for some money."

Pen agreed. "And Clementine wasn't about to be blackmailed a second time. She got rid of Foster, so there was no reason for her to hesitate to do the same to Courtney. Courtney was hit over the head. A woman could easily do that, don't you think?"

"Certainly, given a heavy enough object like a fireplace poker, a shovel, or possibly even a spanner," Mabel said.

Penelope had a sudden flashback to the night of the Guy Fawkes celebration. She remembered meeting Brimble outside of the Jolly Good Grub and then crossing the street in front of the Icing on the Cake.

"And there's something else," she said, her voice rising in excitement. "Remember the night of Guy Fawkes? We walked past the Icing on the Cake. I didn't think anything of it at the time, but Clementine claimed that she had stayed open late that night. But she lied. The store had been dark. I'm positive."

Mabel drew her brows together. "You're right. I remember glancing at the window and thinking how empty it looked without the usual display of pastries."

"She could have easily gone unnoticed at the celebration. It was dark and would have been easy for her to get lost in the crowd."

Mabel tapped her chin with her index finger. "I think you may be right. I'm sure the police have thought of all this as well, though, don't you think?"

"I don't know." Penelope put her empty plate on the tea cart. "I'm going to call Maguire and find out."

Penelope went into her writing room, punched in Maguire's number on her cell phone, and waited impatiently while it rang on the other end. She sighed and was about to hang up when Maguire finally answered, sounding slightly breathless.

"Maguire," he said curtly. His voice softened when he learned it was Penelope. "I was about to call you," he said. "Can you meet for a bite to eat at the Book and Bottle? I can't stomach another sandwich from the vending machine."

Perfect, Penelope thought to herself. She could lay out all the facts she'd collected about Clementine and have lunch at the same time. Despite Figgy's delicious Victoria sponge cake, she was famished.

Penelope was extra careful driving to the Book and Bottle, thanks to her earlier scare, and she was pleased when she pulled into the parking lot without incident.

Maguire was waiting by the door and his face, which sagged with weariness, lit up when he saw Penelope. He gave her a brief kiss.

The pub was fairly full, with all types of people dining companionably—from executives in suits and ties to men in work boots and mud-spattered jeans. Maguire found them a table in the back and went to the bar to order drinks as well as Welsh rarebit for Penelope and a steak and kidney pie for himself.

Penelope scrolled through her e-mails while she waited for him to return.

"Here are our drinks." Maguire appeared and put a glass in front of Penelope. "I'll be back in a tick with our food."

Penelope took a long sip of her lemon squash and sighed in satisfaction.

Maguire reappeared with a tray this time, and they settled down to eat.

"Did I tell you we figured out who ordered the spray-painting of Clementine's shop window?" Maguire said, cutting a piece of his steak and kidney pie.

Penelope had just taken a bite of her Welsh rarebit so she shook her head no.

"Martin Slade, who owns Brown's Hardware, called in a tip. He said Terry had recently bought two cans of spray paint from him. We interviewed Terry, and he confessed. He said he was convinced that it had been Clementine who had let everyone down by agreeing to Foster's proposal." Maguire forked up a bite of his pie. "He's in for a hefty fine and possible jail time. Although since his record is clean, the judge will probably be persuaded to suspend the sentence."

Maguire took a long pull on his drink, then swiped his napkin across his mouth.

"By the way, we looked into Karen Brown as a possible suspect and she has an alibi. Not that I ever really thought she would murder her own daughter, but the day Courtney was killed she was in London seeing her GP. And she has the train ticket to prove it. Besides, the fellow at the ticket counter remembered her. He's known her for years."

Penelope raised her eyebrows. "What about Foster's murder, though? She had a motive for that." Penelope bit her lip. "But that would mean there are two killers in Chum. Is that possible?"

Maguire pointed his fork at her. "She has an alibi for Foster's murder as well. She was babysitting her neighbor's daughter while her neighbor went to the Guy Fawkes fireworks. It all checks out."

Now was a good time to fill Maguire in on what she'd learned about Clementine. Penelope put down her fork and cleared her throat. Maguire listened quietly while she ticked off all the reasons that had convinced her Clementine was guilty of murdering Foster and Courtney.

Finally, she came to a stop. Maguire fiddled with the salt-and-pepper shakers for a moment, then finally spoke.

"You'd make a good detective," he said with a small smile. "We're looking into it. Unfortunately, I can't give you any particulars on that investigation or my governor would have my—" He colored slightly and ducked his head. "Sorry."

His expression turned serious as he reached out and put his hand over Penelope's.

"Please promise me you won't do any more snooping. It could get you in trouble. Remember the time—"

"Yes, yes," Penelope said. She didn't need to be reminded of any of her previous escapades.

"And promise me you won't confront Clementine or anyone else, for that matter."

Pen rolled her eyes. "I'm not stupid." She was momentarily miffed, but then she saw the concern in Maguire's eyes and softened. "Okay, I promise."

TWENTY-SEVEN

❧

Mabel called just as Penelope was struggling to get into her jacket.

"Could you possibly do me a favor?" she said, sounding apologetic.

"Of course. Shoot," Pen said as she slipped her second arm into her jacket sleeve.

"It's Laurence's birthday today and I ordered a cake for him from Icing on the Cake. But I completely forgot to pick it up on my way to work. I can't imagine what I was thinking, but by the time I'd realized it, I'd sailed straight past the store. I know you usually walk that way yourself. . . ."

"No problem." Pen bent down to give Mrs. Danvers a final pat before leaving. "I'd be glad to pick it up for you."

Penelope closed and locked the door to her cottage and began the trek down the high street. She was more than happy to pick up the cake for Mabel—it would give her an excuse to see if there was anything in Clementine's shop that she might have used to murder Courtney.

First, though, she'd have to think of a reason to sneak into the storeroom so she could take a look around. All she needed was a brief peek, and if she saw any likely objects she would tell Maguire and he could take care of the rest.

A cluster of women stood at the counter when Penelope opened the door to the Icing on the Cake. Hopefully they would keep Clementine distracted enough for her to risk a quick glance to see if the poker was missing.

Clementine herself was behind the counter, moving swiftly as she filled a large bakery bag with delectable-looking pastries. Her assistant, who Penelope had met in the Sweet Tooth, was nowhere in sight. Penelope supposed she had the day off.

The women waited patiently, chatting among themselves.

"I wonder if we'll get a glimpse of the duke?" one of them said and giggled. "He's quite handsome. I do love a man with red hair."

"I'd rather meet Charlotte—the duchess. I wonder if she's as pretty in person as she is in photographs. She's always so well-dressed."

She would have to remember to tell Beryl that, Penelope thought, since she was Charlotte's stylist and in charge of choosing her wardrobe.

"And their darling baby," another woman said with a faraway look in her eyes.

"I doubt we shall see any of them," the woman waiting at the counter said. She was dressed in a cashmere coat with an expensive-looking silk scarf knotted at her throat. "The tour is certainly not going to take us into their private rooms."

Penelope edged closer to the back of the shop and the door to the storeroom, keeping one eye on Clementine the entire time. Her palms were slick with sweat, and she wiped them surreptitiously on her coat.

She glanced at Clementine once more. She had moved to the register and was ringing up the sale. It was now or never. But before she could move any farther, the woman in the cashmere coat turned to the rest of the group, looked at her watch, and nodded briskly.

"It's time we got going. We don't want the coach to leave without us."

A murmur of assent rippled through the crowd, and they began to make their way toward the door. Penelope froze where she was.

"Penelope," Clementine called to her, and Penelope jumped. "What can I do for you? I have some freshly baked scones if you're interested." She gestured toward the tidy rows of sugar-sprinkled scones on the tray behind the counter.

Penelope eased away from the storeroom door. Clementine wasn't acting as if she suspected anything, and Penelope felt her shoulders relax and come down from near her ears where they'd been hovering.

"Thanks. They look delicious, but I came in for the birthday cake Mabel ordered."

"Ah, yes. It's Mr. Brimble's birthday, I gather. She wanted something special for him, so I've done a cake with a military history theme. Mabel said that's his passion. He's particularly fond of naval history so I chose the HMS *Furious* to decorate the top." She raised her eyebrows. "It proved to be quite tricky, but I think it turned out splendidly."

Penelope looked at Clementine's face. It was glowing

with pride. She was wearing a floral print dress that emphasized her slimness and Penelope had a hard time picturing her as a cold-blooded killer. Perhaps she'd been mistaken? Perhaps she'd read the clues all wrong?

"I'll just go get the cake. It's in the back." Clementine jerked a thumb toward the rear of the store.

She watched as Clementine walked through the storeroom and into the kitchen beyond. As soon as her footsteps died away, Pen stepped into the storeroom.

Her heart was pounding in her ears, nearly deafening her, and there was a mist swirling in front of her eyes, making it hard for her to see. She forced herself to take a deep breath and focus. She glanced around the storeroom, but nothing stood out immediately. Her gaze landed on the fireplace. The cobwebs that had draped its entrance the last time she was there were gone now. Penelope glanced at the fireplace tools in the hearth—the shovel, a brush, and a pair of tongs. Something was missing. Shouldn't there be a poker as well? She had a vision of her father standing in front of their fireplace poking at one of the logs. A chill made its way down her spine. Had Clementine used the missing poker to murder Courtney?

She was about to retreat back to the shop when Clementine appeared in the doorway of the kitchen. Penelope tried to say something, but her mouth had dried up and her tongue felt as if it was swollen to twice its size.

"I was coming to see if you needed any help," she finally managed to croak, sounding as if she'd been in the desert without water for days.

She couldn't read Clementine's expression. It hadn't changed, but was that a slight hardening in her eyes and a tightening of her mouth? Had she found it odd that Penelope had been standing in the storeroom instead of at the front counter?

"No, no. No worries. I'm coming," Clementine said briskly. She bustled toward Penelope holding a white bakery box out in front of her.

"How do you manage all by yourself?" Pen said as casually as she could. She hadn't heard anyone rattling about in the kitchen.

"Oh, I have help, but they work in shifts. Lou, who helps me with the scones, buns, and other breakfast goods, leaves by six in the morning, and Darlene will be in later in the afternoon to help with the cakes and pies. They each have their own specialties. Lou works magic with dough, and Darlene is an artist when it comes to decorating a cake."

Penelope trailed behind Clementine as she walked back into the store. Clementine put the cake on the counter but instead of going behind the counter herself, as Penelope had expected, she walked briskly toward the front door.

Before Penelope could take in what was happening, she heard the ominous click of the lock being turned and watched, horrified, as Clementine slipped the key into the pocket of her apron.

TWENTY-EIGHT

༒

Penelope was still standing at the counter, stunned, as Clementine approached. She didn't appear to be carrying a weapon, so perhaps Pen had misread her intentions. Maybe she was closing early, for some reason. But wouldn't she have said?

Her expression was unreadable. Penelope thought of bolting for the front door, but Clementine had locked it with a key, so there was no hope of her getting out.

Clementine still didn't say a word as she reached for the bakery box on the counter and slowly opened it. Penelope's eyes widened as she pulled out a long knife with a thick wooden handle.

Clementine stroked the handle lovingly. "This is a utility knife." She hefted it in her hand. "It's the workhorse of the kitchen." Her eyes gleamed. "And although it's smaller than a chef's knife, don't be fooled. It can do every bit as much damage as any other knife in the drawer."

She moved so swiftly Penelope barely had time to blink. Her eyes crossed as she stared down at the knife blade that was now inches from her nose. She began to retreat, but for every step she took backward, Clementine took one forward until Penelope found herself stumbling into the storeroom. She realized she could move faster if she turned and faced forward, but where would she go? She had no doubt the back door to the shop was as securely locked as the front door.

The hair on the nape of her neck stood up as she spun around and ran into the kitchen. She was expecting Clementine to launch the knife into her back at any moment, like the knife-throwing act in a circus—only this time she was the assistant up against the board acting as a target. And Clementine wouldn't miss.

Now what? Penelope thought as she looked around the kitchen frantically. The homey smell of bread baking seemed to mock the deadly situation she was in. She needed to find a weapon of her own but there were no other knives in sight. She spied a mallet sitting on the counter next to the sink. It just might do. It would have to. She lunged for the handle and nearly knocked it on the floor in her haste to grab it, but finally her fingers closed around it. It wasn't as deadly as Clementine's knife, but she might be able to do some damage with it.

Clementine was so close Penelope could hear her breathing. She whirled around, swinging the mallet, but unfortunately it contacted with nothing but air as it whirled in an arc, missing Clementine by at least a foot. Clementine had already taken the precaution of moving back several paces.

Penelope felt sweat beading on her forehead and trickling down her spine. She managed to maneuver behind the counter, putting it between herself and Clementine. By now she was panting from both fright and exertion. Clementine appeared positively mad—her eyes had a savage look in them and her mouth was curved into a smile—a sick, menacing one that made Penelope think of the Joker in the Batman movies.

Penelope struck out with the mallet again and missed Clementine's fingers by inches. She tried once more, and this time a blow glanced off Clementine's left arm. She winced but didn't lose her grip on the knife. Pen swung again and this time the mallet connected with Clementine's right arm. She roared in pain but her grip on the knife still didn't loosen.

How long was she going to be able to keep this up? Penelope wondered. She felt her energy flagging and her panic rising. Surely Clementine was losing steam by now as well.

They began to circle the counter. Penelope occasionally lashed out with the mallet, once again missing Clementine's fingers by inches. Clementine continued to grin as they chased each other around and around. She was enjoying this, Pen realized.

Suddenly, Clementine reversed direction. She moved so swiftly Penelope had no time to react. The next thing she knew, she felt the point of a knife pierce her clothing and prick the skin on her back.

"Give me the mallet," she said.

Penelope hesitated, but Clementine pressed the tip of the knife a bit harder into Penelope's back and Penelope handed it over.

Clementine prodded Penelope with the knife and Penelope hastily obliged, moving forward until they were standing in front of a baker's rack. An extension cord, coiled like a snake, was on the bottom shelf.

"You killed Foster, didn't you?" Pen managed to gasp.

"Yes. I had to or he would have ruined everything."

"He knew the fire that burned your bakery to the ground in London wasn't accidental."

Clementine cackled. "Of course, he knew. He set the fire. I rewarded him quite handsomely for it once the insurance company paid up. He used the cash as seed money to start his chain of gourmet shops."

Penelope held her breath as she tried to sidle away but when she felt the point of the knife at her throat, she changed her mind.

"I never expected to see Foster again, so you can imagine my surprise when he turned up here in Upper Chumley-on-Stoke. At first, I thought everything was going to be okay, but then one day he appeared on my doorstep demanding that I vote yes for his proposed gourmet shop."

"He blackmailed you?"

Clementine blew out a puff of air. "Not in so many words. He didn't have to. I knew right away that if I didn't do what he wanted, he would make trouble for me."

"But once you did as he asked—you voted to approve his proposal—why did you have to kill him?"

"Just changing my vote wasn't enough for him. He wanted his full pound of flesh. He demanded I close Icing on the Cake so there would be no competition with the fancy new pastries he was going to be importing from France. He was doing it to punish me."

"Why would he do that?"

"When he worked for me, he resented the fact that I had my own shop while he was sweeping my floors. He was one of those people who thought they were entitled to success. He had big plans even back then, but he didn't have the money to make them a reality and that made him bitter."

"Couldn't you have just as easily blackmailed him?" Pen said, her gaze never leaving the knife in Clementine's hand. If Clementine had been willing to resort to murder, certainly blackmail wasn't a bridge too far.

"There was no proof that he had set the fire. It would have been my word against his. He'd become so posh, owning all those stores, why wouldn't he be believed? And it would have raised suspicions about the fire. I was afraid that if the investigators reopened the case, they would discover that it had been set deliberately. I couldn't take any chances."

"So, you left the poisoned chocolates on Foster's blanket at the fireworks. Weren't you worried someone would see you?"

"It was a chance I had to take. It was dark, crowded and everyone was focused on the firework show. I was quite certain no one would notice me. I'm not the sort of person that gets noticed. Besides, it only took a second to drop the box on his blanket when he wasn't looking."

"How did you know he would eat them?"

Clementine gave a harsh laugh. "He never could resist sweets, especially chocolate. He used to snitch the little slivers of chocolate that were left on the cutting board after I'd made chocolate curls for one of my cakes." She shifted the knife in her hand. "Terry Jones told me that he was particularly fond of the Sweet Tooth's red-wine chocolate truffles and it was just my luck that they were the Sweet Tooth's truffle of the day."

Clementine narrowed her eyes. "Enough of that. This is

no time for a chin-wag. I know you would run to the police the minute you got out of here, so I'm going to have to make sure that doesn't happen."

She reached for the handle of a door next to the baker's rack. Penelope strained to get a look. It appeared to be a utility closet. Brooms and mops leaned against the wall and there was a large yellow bucket in the corner.

"In you go," Clementine said, giving Penelope a shove.

Penelope stumbled and nearly fell, but she grabbed for the doorjamb and caught herself in time. She held on while Clementine tried to force her into the darkened closet but eventually her fingers began to slip, her grip loosened, and when Clementine shoved her again, she catapulted into the closet. She barely had time to react before she felt the whoosh of air as the door was slammed shut behind her.

Once again, she heard the click of a lock being turned and, once again, it sent a shiver down her spine. What did Clementine intend to do with her?

It was dark inside the closet without so much as a glimmer of light. Before Clementine had shut the door, she thought she'd glimpsed a bulb in the ceiling with a string hanging from it. She waved her arm around and felt something brush against her hand. Two more tries and she had hold of the string. She pulled it and momentarily shut her eyes as light from the unshaded bulb flooded the closet.

She had the urge to bang on the door and demand to be let out, but she knew that was futile. She refused to give Clementine the satisfaction of hearing her panic. Besides, she might as well save her strength. The thought of what Clementine might do next made her mouth go dry.

If only she had her cell phone, but it was in her tote bag, which was still on the counter in the shop. She looked around for a spare key—running her fingers along the molding atop the door but she came away with nothing but dust that caused a sneezing fit.

A strange smell began to creep under the door. Penelope stopped for a moment and sniffed. At first, she couldn't place the scent but then the horrible realization struck her.

It was gas.

TWENTY-NINE

━◈━

Penelope tried to quell her panic. She had to think clearly or she'd never get out of this mess alive. The thought nearly made her heart stop. What would happen to Beryl, to Mabel and Figgy, to Maguire? She couldn't leave them.

She had to smash the lock with something. She rejected the mops and brooms—they were useless. A flash of red in the corner of the closet caught her eye. It was a fire extinguisher. She picked it up and weighed it in her hands. It ought to be heavy enough to do the job.

She raised it as high over her head as she could and brought it down on the doorknob. Unfortunately, that did little beyond sending a painful jolt up her arm and into her shoulder.

The smell of gas was stronger now, increasing Penelope's panic. How long before she'd lose consciousness?

A television show she'd recently seen flashed through

her mind. A gunman was holed up inside an apartment refusing to open the door to the police. One of the officers had used a battering ram and with one blow, the door had swung open.

Penelope shifted the fire extinguisher in her arms so that it was perpendicular to the door. It would have to do as a battering ram. She took a deep breath, said a quick prayer, swung her arm back, and hit the door as hard as she possibly could. The sound of wood splintering raised her spirits. One or two more tries ought to do it.

She counted to three, swung her arm back, and smashed the fire extinguisher into the door with as much force as she could muster. More wood splintering.

She stopped to catch her breath. She felt damp with sweat and quickly shrugged off her jacket. She put a hand to her head. Was she beginning to feel woozy from the gas or was it panic that was making her feel that way?

She bent to pick up the fire extinguisher again when a wave of dizziness came over her and she nearly fell. She had to get that door open immediately before she passed out.

She swung the extinguisher as hard as she could and was rewarded when the wooden door finally cracked and flew open, ricocheting off the wall and nearly slamming shut again.

Penelope rushed into the kitchen and looked around frantically. All the knobs on the large industrial stove were switched on but there was no blue flame flickering from the burners. Penelope hastily twisted each of them to the Off position.

The oven was turned on as well, but Clementine had obviously blown out the pilot light. The door was open and gas was hissing out. Penelope swayed slightly as she reached for the knob and turned it.

The gas was now off, but the room was still choked with it. She needed to get outside for some fresh air. She tried the back door of the shop but, as she had suspected, it was locked with a key. She already knew the front door was locked as well.

She ran into the shop and grabbed her tote bag off the counter. She rummaged around in it, nearly panicking until she finally touched her cell phone. She pulled it out and stared at the battery display in dismay. She'd forgotten to plug the phone in the night before and the battery was now dead.

She looked around the shop, but there didn't appear to be a landline. Clementine must take all calls on her cell phone.

There was nothing for it. She was going to have to break a window.

Unlike the Open Book's diamond-paned window, the window of Icing on the Cake was a single piece of glass. She was going to need something to break it with. She'd rejected several items when it occurred to her that the fire extinguisher she'd used to break down the closet door would do quite nicely. She ran into the kitchen, grabbed it, and ran back to the window. Her legs were beginning to feel rubbery and she hoped she had the strength to do the job.

Once again, she held the extinguisher like a battering ram, braced herself, and launched it at the window. Nothing. She tried again, and this time the glass shattered, scattering shards of glass onto the pastries displayed in the window.

Penelope took deep breaths as fresh air rushed into the shop. As the woozy feeling began to retreat, she contemplated climbing out the window. She'd have to be careful not to cut herself on the jagged edges of the bits of glass that remained.

First, she'd have to move all of the pastries out of the way. She gazed longingly at the slices of biscuit cake as she pulled the tray out of the window. What a shame they'd have to be thrown away—they smelled delicious.

She was pulling the tray of scones out when a car screeched to a halt in front of the store, followed by the wailing of sirens as two police cars barreled down the high street, also coming to a stop in front of Icing on the Cake.

Penelope felt her knees sag with relief when she saw Maguire getting out of one of the vehicles.

"Are you okay?" he shouted through the broken window.

Penelope couldn't find her voice, but she managed to nod her head.

Maguire tried the door and then, finding it locked, motioned to the two constables who had joined him on the sidewalk. One of them had a battering ram and he made short work of getting the front door to the shop open. He smiled at Penelope, took her by the elbow, and helped her out of the shop.

Relief flooded her and made her weak. She staggered across the sidewalk and straight into Maguire's arms.

THIRTY

❧

Penelope sighed with contentment and leaned back against Maguire's arm. They were seated on the sofa in her living room with a roaring fire crackling and spitting in the hearth. Mrs. Danvers, in an unusually good mood, was curled up next to Penelope.

"Would you like some more?" Maguire reached forward and picked up the champagne bottle on the coffee table. Next to it were the remains of a curry takeout from Kebabs and Curries.

He topped up Penelope's glass and handed it to her. She took a sip and giggled as the bubbles tickled her nose.

Maguire held his glass aloft. "Here's to another case solved. And a happy ending." His expression changed as his face clouded. "I can't help but shudder when I think of how things might have ended if not for your amazing resourcefulness."

Penelope pointed at her cat. "I have nine lives, I guess. Just like Mrs. Danvers." She stroked Mrs. Danvers's silky fur. "How did you know I was at the Icing on the Cake?"

Maguire took a gulp of his champagne. "I didn't. We were looking for Clementine. We wanted to question her in relation to Foster's death as well as Courtney's. We had enough evidence to charge her. A rambler found a fireplace poker discarded in the fields around Worthington House. He'd read about the murder in the *Chumley Chronicle* so he brought it to the police station thinking it might have been the weapon that killed Courtney Brown. We were able to lift Clementine's prints from it as well as traces of Courtney's blood."

"What about Clementine? She's not going to get away with it, is she?"

Maguire shook his head. "No, not at all. We picked her up at the train station. She was about to bolt for London. She's a scrappy little thing. She put up quite a fight, but she was no match for constable Cuthbert."

Penelope laughed. "I wish I could have seen that." She snuggled against Maguire's arm again.

"Once again you helped us crack the case." Maguire shifted on the sofa so he was looking at Penelope. "I'm going to have to unofficially deputize you Detective Constable Penelope Parish."

M y shoes," Figgy squealed, her hands on her head. She was standing in the middle of her tiny bedroom in her underwear.

Figgy, Penelope, and Mabel were helping her get ready

for her wedding to Derek Kahn and trying, somewhat unsuccessfully, to keep her from panicking.

"Here they are," Mabel said calmly, handing Figgy the red silk flats with gold embroidery on the toes. "They were in your closet."

Figgy laughed. "I guess I'm just a bit nervous."

"I'll say," Mabel said. "Too bad I didn't bring the bottle of Jameson. You could do with a sip or two."

An exquisite voluminous skirt in red silk decorated with sequins, beads, and gold embroidery was spread out on the bed.

"Can you help me with the lehenga?" Figgy said, pointing to the garment.

"I'd forgotten how beautiful that was," Mabel said. "It's very kind of your future mother-in-law to loan you the traditional Pakistani outfit she wore for her own wedding."

"My mother doesn't agree with you," Figgy said, frowning. "She was still hoping to talk me into a white wedding dress with a ball-gown skirt, a cathedral-length train, and a lace veil." She laughed and put her hands on her hips. "Can you even begin to imagine me in something like that?"

"Frankly, no," Mabel said.

"Me neither," Pen added. "But this," she said as she carefully lowered the skirt over Figgy's head, "suits you perfectly."

"And now the choli," Figgy said, picking up the matching blouse. It had short sleeves, a V-neck edged with gold embroidery, and came to a few inches above Figgy's waist.

Figgy slipped into it and Penelope helped her with the buttons. She stood back to look at her friend and both she and Mabel sighed.

"You look spectacular," Pen said.

Figgy's cheeks were tinged with pink and her hands were trembling slightly.

Mabel took her by the shoulders and led her over to the full-length mirror on the wall.

This time even Figgy gasped. There was no denying how lovely she looked.

"Here's the veil." Mabel gently draped the gossamer-like fabric over Figgy's head. "Now you're ready."

"Am I?" Figgy said, running her fingers down the folds of her skirt.

"You're not having second thoughts, are you?" Pen said.

"No. Of course not. I just have the about-to-be-married jitters."

"Off we go then," Mabel said.

"Do you want me to drive?" Pen said, reaching for her jacket, which she'd thrown across a chair.

"Good heavens, no," Mabel said firmly. "We want to get there in one piece. We'll go in my car. Besides, there's more room." She eyed Figgy's outfit. "That skirt is going to take up plenty of space all by itself."

Mabel pulled into a parking space in front of the chapel at Worthington House, where the wedding was being held courtesy of the Duke of Upper Chumley-on-Stoke. Penelope peeked into the chapel. The pews were already filled with guests eagerly awaiting the arrival of the bride. Together they accompanied Figgy to an anteroom, where her mother and father were waiting.

Lord Innes-Goldthorpe was quite rotund, with a fleshy face and a jovial countenance. He smelled of cigar smoke and Penelope thought he looked a bit like a penguin in his black morning coat and starched white shirt.

In spite of all her objections to Figgy's choice of wedding attire, Lady Innes-Goldthorpe couldn't completely hide the smile that lit her face when she saw her daughter. The feather on her fascinator bobbed as she reached out and twitched Figgy's veil into place.

"Now I think you're ready," she said, her voice choked with tears.

Mabel kissed Figgy on the cheek. "Best wishes, my dear."

"Is it time?" Figgy said.

"Let me check." Penelope peered into the chapel.

Sunlight came through the stained-glass window behind the altar and cast a kaleidoscope of colors on the walls and floor. Hats adorned with feathers, ribbons, flowers, and other fanciful touches were spread out like a colorful field of flowers among the black and white of the men's attire.

The rector from St. Andrews was officiating at the ceremony. He gave Penelope a sign that they were ready, and she ducked back into the anteroom.

"Looks like we can start." She picked up the bouquets of wildflowers that had been delivered to the church earlier that morning. She handed the larger one to Figgy.

She smoothed down the front of her dress. Beryl had talked her into black suede pumps, although they'd argued about the height of the heel. Penelope had finally gotten her to agree that a shorter, chunkier heel would look fine. She didn't want to be balancing on a pair of stilettos like someone on stilts. She'd kept the accessories simple—a pair of drop pearl earrings and a thin silver bracelet.

"You look quite splendid." Figgy's mother gave her one

last kiss, then made her way into the chapel, where an usher was waiting to escort her to her seat.

"My dear." Figgy's father held out his arm and gave her a broad smile. Figgy rested her hand on it and Penelope noticed it was shaking a bit.

She supposed every bride was a bit nervous on her wedding day. After all, she was about to make a lifetime commitment in front of all her friends and relatives. But Penelope was confident that Figgy and Derek would make a terrific go of it.

Penelope was to walk down the aisle first. Maguire looked up as she passed him. He was sitting in a pew toward the back. He gave her a broad smile and by the look on his face, Penelope knew she looked good.

Mabel had joined Beryl, India, and Gladys, who already had their handkerchiefs out in preparation for the ceremony. Brimble sat beside Mabel, his back ramrod straight as usual.

Penelope was glad to see Grant and Rupert sitting shoulder to shoulder in the same pew. Grant bent his head and whispered something in Rupert's ear. Rupert smiled and put his hand over Grant's.

The groom and his best man had come out of a side door and were standing at the end of the aisle to await the bride. In his nod to British custom, Derek, like his best man, was wearing a morning coat. He looked nervous and the best man patted him on the arm reassuringly.

Penelope smiled at Derek and took her place at the altar.

The music swelled and a rumble echoed to the rafters as everyone rose to their feet as Figgy and her father made their way toward the altar. She looked positively radiant, and Penelope sighed with satisfaction.

Derek's face lit up when he saw his bride. Figgy joined him at the altar and tucked her hand into his.

In no time at all, the couple was saying "I do" and recessing back down the aisle as husband and wife. Penelope dabbed at her eyes, which had become moist with emotion.

After the last person had made their way down the reception line, the photographer rounded everyone up for photographs in front of the altar. Penelope helped Figgy adjust her veil and fluffed her skirts before taking her place in the lineup. Her face was beginning to hurt from smiling when he herded them into the library for some more casual snaps.

Penelope was walking out of the library when Maguire motioned to her.

"Are you up for some champagne?" he said as he took Penelope's arm and they made their way into the great room where the reception was being held.

"Certainly," Penelope said, feeling a bit as if she'd already had champagne. Her happiness for Figgy was bubbling up inside of her.

Maguire signaled to a waiter circulating with a tray of champagne. He chose two flutes and handed one to Penelope.

The great room had been transformed with long tables set with rich, jewel-toned napery that echoed the colors of the heraldic banners hanging from the ceiling and china rimmed in gold. Dozens of lush bouquets of soft yellow Charlotte roses and silver dollar eucalyptus subtly perfumed the air. A space by the fireplace had been cleared for dancing and a quartet was playing, the music drifting down from the minstrel's gallery.

Mabel made her way through the crowd toward Penelope and Maguire. "Everything looks beautiful, doesn't it?"

She looked around the room. "It's all very elegant and yet it's still our Figgy." Mabel sniffed. "Something smells delicious. Must be our meal."

"Figgy said they will be serving something traditionally English, like roast lamb, as well as some Pakistani dishes."

Brimble caught up with Mabel and joined them. He touched her arm lightly.

"You must see the banner with the Worthington coat of arms. It's quite splendid."

Maguire looked at Penelope as Brimble led Mabel away. "Let's find a quiet spot," he said.

He appeared slightly nervous. His hand shook and a bit of champagne sloshed out of the glass.

"It is rather noisy in here," Pen said as the chatter of the guests echoed off the stone walls and floor.

Maguire took her by the hand and led her out of the great room, down the corridor, and to the library. He peeked into the room.

"It's empty," he said, leading Penelope inside and over to a damask-covered sofa.

Penelope sank into the sofa cushions, glad of a moment to relax. She kicked off her shoes and rubbed one foot with the other. She may not have been wearing stilettos, but she wasn't used to wearing shoes with anything but a flat heel.

Maguire held his glass in one hand as he fumbled in his pocket with the other. He pulled something out and concealed it in his palm.

"Penelope," he said earnestly, looking into her eyes. "I thought this might be a good time for us to . . . um . . . give some thought to our own future."

Penelope held her breath. What did he mean? Was he breaking up with her or was he . . . ?

Maguire put his glass down on the table beside him and opened his hand. Nestled in his palm was a tiny dark blue box with gold writing on top that was fading and starting to rub off.

He opened the box. Cushioned inside its velvet interior was a ring. He took it out and held it up. A gold band was set with a beautiful sapphire with tiny diamonds flanking it on either side. The stones winked in the light as Maguire held out the ring.

"This was my grandmother's," he said, with a catch in his voice. "I'm hoping you'll accept it and do me the honor of becoming my wife."

A million thoughts went through Penelope's mind. Was it too soon? Was she ready to settle down? And was she prepared to settle down in England? She looked at Maguire and her eyes filled with tears. "Yes, of course. Yes," she said again as he slipped the ring on her finger.

Penelope felt her head spin. She was engaged! She decided she wouldn't tell anyone until after Figgy's wedding. It was Figgy's day and Penelope didn't want to horn in on it. If anyone noticed that she suddenly had a sparkly sapphire ring on the third finger of her left hand, she'd say it had belonged to her grandmother. After all, it *had* belonged to a grandmother—just not hers.

Music drifted toward them from the great room. "Would you like to dance?" Maguire held out his hand and helped Penelope to her feet.

She was more than happy to hold on to him. Her knees were feeling decidedly weak. She felt as if she were in a daze or a dream, and she'd wake up at any moment. She glanced at the ring on her finger. But this was real. Really real.

They put their glasses down on a nearby table and made their way onto the dance floor. The quartet began to play a slow song and Penelope melted into Maguire's arms, feeling safe and warm and at home as they began to sway to the music.

She'd never expected to become a bestselling author, she thought, as they moved about the dance floor. And she'd never expected to find true love in England.

Occasionally, dreams really did come true.

Keep reading for an excerpt
from the first Open Book mystery

MURDER IN THE MARGINS

Available now from Berkley Prime Crime!

If Penelope "Pen" Parish had known how useless a master's degree in Gothic literature would turn out to be, she would have opted for something more practical instead—like accounting or mortuary science. After keeping herself somewhat afloat for several years with a hodgepodge of temporary jobs, like waitressing and data entry, she'd hit upon a solution.

Instead of studying other authors' Gothic novels, she would write one of her own.

She'd subsequently spent every bit of her spare time in her attic garret—okay, a fifth-floor walk-up with drafty windows—with her fingers on the keys of her used laptop, surrounded by empty takeout containers, channeling her favorite Gothic authors—Mary Shelley, the Brontës, and Ann Radcliffe. By adding a touch of horror à la Stephen King, she had managed to produce a book the critics called a "unique, fresh twist on the classic Gothic novel."

You could have knocked her over with a feather when *Lady of the Moors* became a bestseller.

And therein lies the rub, as Hamlet opined.

Publishers have a habit of expecting their authors to follow up one bestseller with another. And Penelope Parish was suffering from a terrible case of writer's block.

She thought of that old saying, "Be careful what you wish for." The truth of that old saw had certainly hit home. She'd done her share of wishing as she'd slogged through her first manuscript—and there were entire days, if not weeks, when it was definitely a slog. She'd dreamed of all the things every writer does—book signings, coast-to-coast book tours, hitting the bestseller lists, royalties pouring in to swell her dwindling bank account.

And while it hadn't been *exactly* like that—her publisher had nixed the idea of a coast-to-coast book tour—some of it had actually come true.

And it had given Penelope a terrible case of nerves. She'd been raised with the strict New England ethic of hard work and was quite accustomed to it—holding down two jobs while getting her degree hadn't exactly been a picnic—but sometimes hard work wasn't enough. Ever since her success, she'd forced herself to sit in her chair at her desk with her fingers on her laptop keys for hours on end, but the words had refused to come. She'd hit a writer's block the size of Rhode Island.

Salvation had come in the form of a writer-in-residence position at the Open Book bookstore in England. She'd seen the ad in the back of *The Writer* magazine and had impulsively applied.

The application had been curious, to say the least—filled with unusual and admittedly creative questions.

If you could be any character in fiction, who would you be? That had taken some thought on Penelope's part, but finally she had put down Bridget Jones. Because Bridget's friends and family liked her *just the way she was.*

Penelope's mother and sister were constantly trying to turn her into something she was not—a polished, put-together career woman balancing life and work as easily as a Cirque du Soleil performer juggled balls. Her friends were forever urging her to get it together and move on with her life. Yes, Bridget Jones it was.

If you were a type of food, what type of food would you be?

Penelope had thought long and hard about that one, too, and had finally come up with her answer—pizza. Everyone liked pizza. It was unpretentious. It was comfort food and always made you feel better. You could have it any way you wanted—with or without pepperoni; sausage; mushrooms; onion; green peppers; or even—if you insisted—pineapple.

Penelope had sent off the application without any great expectations. And for the second time in her life, you could have knocked her over with a feather when the letter came—the e-mail, actually, if you want to split hairs—announcing that she'd won.

It had seemed like a heaven-sent opportunity—the quiet of a charming English village where she could write in peace in exchange for running a book group and a writers group and anything else she could think up to enhance the bottom line of the Open Book.

And the chance to get away from everyone's expectations—her mother's, her sister's, and even her publisher's. It had crossed Penelope's mind that her decision might have looked to some as if she was running away, but she immediately dismissed the thought. She was having an adventure, and wasn't that what life was meant to be?

Penelope had thought of herself as well prepared for life in an English village. She was an avid reader of British authors—she knew her Miss Marple inside and out—and she never missed an episode of *The Crown* or *Victoria*.

She didn't expect to be homesick. Homesick for what? An unsatisfactory romantic relationship? Her overpriced Manhattan walk-up?

There'd been objections, of course. The road was never smooth sailing as far as Penelope was concerned. Her sister, Beryl, insisted that this "sabbatical," as she called it, wasn't going to get Penelope a career. Despite Penelope's publisher springing for a full-page ad in the *New York Times*, her sister didn't consider book writing a viable occupation. According to her, what Penelope ought to do was apply for an academic position at a prestigious university.

Penelope's mother had objected, too, telling Penelope that she'd never meet anyone in Britain, and, even if she did, all the men there had bad teeth and if she thought she was going to meet Prince Harry or any prince at all, she was sadly mistaken. And as far as breaking into British society was concerned, she could forget all about that. Besides, what about her boyfriend, Miles?

Miles had seemed mildly put out that she wouldn't be on hand to grace his arm at the annual Morgan Fund investor's dinner but, in the end, he'd been the only one who hadn't vigorously objected to Penelope's upping the stakes and moving overseas.

Fortunately Penelope was used to doing things that others objected to—she'd been doing them all her life—so that didn't stop her from accepting the Open Book's offer.

No, she was going to make a go of this opportunity, because really, she had no choice. And—she could hear her grandmother's voice in her head—*the Parishes aren't quitters.*

And thus it was that Penelope had arrived on the shores of Merrie Olde England with her laptop and her battered suitcases and how she now found herself driving down the wrong (wrong in her opinion, anyway) side of the high street in Upper Chumley-on-Stoke two weeks later.

Today Chum, as Upper Chumley-on-Stoke was affectionately known to its residents, was a beehive of activity. Tomorrow was the annual Worthington Fest.

Banners, adorned with the Worthington crest and announcing the fest, hung from every streetlamp along the high street and fluttered in the mild breeze. It was a brisk October day, but the sky was cloudless and the sun warmed the air enough so she could get about nicely with just a light coat or a heavy sweater.

Upper Chumley-on-Stoke was a charming village within commuting distance of London. It was the real deal—a well-preserved medieval town that even the bright, shiny new Tesco and the curry takeaway on the outskirts of the city couldn't spoil. The quaint cobblestoned streets were the delight of tourists even if they were a nuisance to the residents, who found them rough going in any footwear other than thick-soled walking shoes.

Buildings of brick, worn over the years to a rosy hue, followed a bend in the road until they petered out and gave way to a narrow road bordered by hedgerows that cut through the grassy green fields beyond and into the countryside.

Penelope found the town enchanting. She felt as if she had stepped into a storybook, and even the inconveniences didn't bother her—Wi-Fi that was spotty at best, narrow streets instead of wide modern roads, an absence of large chain stores and shopping malls, save the Tesco that had opened in recent years.

The Open Book was equally enchanting. It was fusty and musty in the best possible way, with books spilling willy-nilly from the shelves and arranged according to Mabel Morris, the proprietor's, unique shelving system, which Penelope soon discovered made finding a volume more of a treasure hunt than the usual cut-and-dried affair.

There was a low ceiling crisscrossed with wooden beams and a large diamond-paned front window where Penelope could imagine Charles Dickens's newly published *A Christmas Carol* might have been displayed while men in greatcoats and women in long dresses walked up and down the sidewalk outside, occasionally peering through the glass at the array of books.

Penelope negotiated the roundabout at the top of the high street and was admiring a red sweater in the window of the Knit Wit Shop when a horn blaring close by made her jump.

She returned her attention to the road and was horrified to see another car coming straight at her. She jerked the steering wheel, overcorrected, bumped up over the curb, slammed on her brakes, and came to a stop within an inch of a cement planter filled with bright orange and yellow mums.

Her heart was beating hard, her palms were sweaty, and there was a haze in front of her eyes.

The other car, a Ford, had stopped in the middle of the road and the driver was now standing next to it.

Penelope took a deep breath, opened her door, and got out.

"What do you mean driving down the wrong side of the street?" she said, still slightly breathless as she approached the other driver.

The driver looked amused. He wasn't handsome, but had a kind, open face that was very appealing. He was an inch or two shorter than Penelope's six feet. Penelope had sprouted up early and there had been hopes that she would follow in her mother's and sister's footsteps to model; but although she was attractive enough, the camera didn't love her the way it did them. Besides, Penelope had no interest in parading around having her picture taken.

The fellow still looked amused. She knew she needed to rein in her indignation but it was her default setting and not easy.

"You scared me half to death," she said, pushing her glasses back up her nose with her finger.

"You're American," the fellow said. He had a slight Irish lilt to his voice.

Penelope raised her chin slightly. "Yes." She was about to say *what of it* when a horn honking made her jump.

A line of cars had formed behind the driver's Ford Cortina and a red VW Golf was attempting to pull around it.

Penelope's hand flew to her mouth as the realization hit her. "*I* was on the wrong side of the road," she said in a horrified voice.

"Exactly."

"I'm so sorry. I forgot . . . I thought . . ." Penelope stuttered to a halt. "I'm so terribly sorry. You're not hurt . . . or anything . . . are you?" She swayed slightly.

"I'm fine," the fellow said, his face creasing in concern. "But I'm worried about you."

"I'll be okay." Penelope took a deep breath. "It's only that I think I forgot to eat lunch."

It used to drive Penelope's sister crazy that she had to constantly watch her diet to maintain a slim figure, while Penelope could go a whole day without even thinking about food, then devour a meal worthy of a linebacker and still never gain an ounce.

"As long as you're sure . . ."

Penelope waved at him. "I'll be fine." She gestured toward the cars lined up down the road. "You'd better get going. That mob looks ready to attack you."

He smiled. "I guess I'd better."

M abel Morris, whose Miss Marple–like appearance and demeanor belied her former career as an MI6 analyst, was behind the counter when Penelope pushed open the door to the bookstore.

She was all rounded curves and had fluffy white hair that tended to want to go every which way and pale powdery skin. Her blue eyes, however, had depths that suggested she wasn't unacquainted with tragedy and the seamier side of life.

"My sainted aunt," she said when she saw Penelope, "you look like you could use a good strong cup of tea."

"A shot of whiskey is more like it," Penelope said as she slumped against the counter. "Not that I'm in the habit of drinking in the middle of the day."

"This is strictly medicinal." Mabel pulled a bottle of Jameson and a glass from under the counter. She poured out a generous splash of whiskey and handed it to Penelope. "Drink up and then tell me what's having you look like Hamlet's father's ghost."

Penelope tossed back the whiskey and sighed as the warmth traced a path down her throat, to her stomach, and out to her limbs. She felt her shoulders and neck relax and her agitated breathing slow.

"I very nearly had an accident," she said, putting her glass down on the counter.

Mabel inclined her head toward the glass. "Another?"

Penelope shook her head. "Not on an empty stomach."

"You haven't eaten?" Mabel looked alarmed.

"I'll be fine," Penelope reassured her. "Thank goodness the other fellow was able to stop in time."

"What happened?"

Penelope sighed. "I'd like to say it was the other driver's fault, but I'm afraid I forgot where I was and ended up on the wrong side of the road." She felt her face color. She didn't like making mistakes.

"This is how many near misses now?" Mabel turned and put both hands palms down on the counter. "Maybe you should consider giving up the car. You can walk to the Open Book and if you need to go any farther than that, you can hire a taxi."

"That's very tempting," Penelope said, briefly reliving the horror of seeing another car headed straight at her. She raised her chin. "But I'm determined to nail this driving on the other side of the road if it's the last thing I do."

Mabel raised an eyebrow. "That's what has me worried— that it will one day *be* the last thing you do."

Gladys Watkins wandered up to the counter. She handed over a copy of romance novelist Charlotte Davenport's latest, *The Fire in My Bosom,* which featured a rather long-haired, bare-chested man on the cover and a damsel whose look of considerable distress seemed to match Gladys's own.

"I can't begin to imagine what the queen thinks of it," Gladys said as Mabel dropped some coins into her outstretched palm. "I imagine the poor thing is simply beside herself."

"One can't quite imagine the queen being beside herself," Mabel said as she turned toward the register and ripped off the receipt. "She's made of sterner stuff than that."

"That's certainly true," India Culpepper said. She'd casually sidled up to the counter in order to join the conversation. "What with all that nonsense about Charles and Camilla she's had to endure. You know, stiff upper lip and all, that's her majesty's motto."

"Yes, no doubt that's embroidered on the throw pillows in the drawing room at Buckingham Palace," Mabel said dryly.

"High time the Duke of Upper Chumley-on-Stoke settled down," Gladys said, her brow furrowed fiercely. "Driving up and down the high street in that sports car of his and getting drunk at the Book and Bottle, causing no end of embarrassment to the royal family. He's very nearly forty, after all."

"It's the red hair." India nodded sagely. "Everyone knows gingers are bound for trouble. Comes from his father's side. His great-grandfather was known to cheat at cards and"—she lowered her voice—"run around with loose women."

Penelope frowned. "Oh, pooh. That's an old wives' tale. Redheads aren't any more prone to getting into trouble than anyone else."

India looked far from convinced.

Penelope quashed the sudden desire to dye her brown hair red to prove them all wrong—although she was hardly the right person to challenge their assumption. Her father had often said that trouble was her middle name.

"But an American!" Gladys said, clutching her book even more tightly to her ample bosom and piercing Penelope with a laser-like stare.

Penelope stood up taller and straightened her shoulders. "Americans have become quite civilized, you know. We don't live in covered wagons anymore."

Gladys sniffed. She was as round as an apple with a ruddy complexion and large, guileless blue eyes.

"I agree with Gladys," India said, looking quite surprised that for once she and Gladys found themselves on the same page. "Most unsuitable. Of course, Arthur is barely in the line of succession, but *still.*" She said that last as if it was her final word on the subject and *that was that.*

India was *to the manor born* as the saying goes, and even though the family fortune had slipped through numerous fingers before reaching her in a significantly diminished amount, she comported herself as the aristocrat she considered herself to be.

"And not just an American," Gladys was continuing, "but Charlotte Davenport—an American romance novelist." She said that last as if it left a bad taste in her mouth.

India stared rather pointedly at the book in Gladys's hand, but the significance of India's glance was lost on Gladys.

"Charlotte Davenport is actually quite a lovely person," Pen said firmly.

Gladys's eyes goggled. "You've met her?"

"As a matter of fact, I have," Pen said. "It was at a writers' conference—my first. I was positively terrified and Charlotte very graciously took me under her wing. She was already a bestselling author and my book hadn't even come out yet. I was scheduled to appear on a panel she was moderating—I don't even remember what the topic was but

I do remember being horribly nervous." Penelope shuddered to think about it. "I developed a sudden case of stage fright when someone in the audience asked me a question and Charlotte managed to coax an answer out of me."

"Still . . ." India let the word hang in the air.

Mabel turned to Penelope and winked. "How is the book coming? Do tell us."

Penelope suddenly found three pairs of eyes trained on her. She was more than grateful for the change of subject, but she really wished it had been changed to something other than her nearly nonexistent book.

"It's coming," she said as firmly as possible. "I just need to find a reason to compel my main character, Annora, to go against all her best instincts and search this creepy castle basement alone in order to find a chest that's hidden down there."

Penelope thought of some of the pickles she'd gotten herself into growing up—climbing a tree and then not being able to get down, sneaking out her bedroom window the time she was grounded and falling off the roof and breaking her ankle, hitchhiking home her freshman year in college with a knife she'd taken from the cafeteria for protection—but even she knew better than to go into a basement alone with a killer on the loose.

"That's a tough one," Mabel said.

Penelope nodded. "Tell me about it! I can't have a heroine who is TSTL."

This time three sets of eyebrows were raised in unison.

"Too stupid to live," Penelope explained. "It's the sort of thing that makes a reader want to throw the book across the room."

"Quite." India fingered the yellowing pearls at her neck.

Penelope looked at her watch. "Ladies, it's almost time for our meeting of the Worthington Fest marketing committee. Shall we sit down?"

"Regina's not here yet." Gladys looked around as if expecting Regina to magically appear in a puff of smoke. "She's always late." She made a sour face.

"Let's get settled. I am sure Regina will be along shortly."

Penelope herded everyone to the table and chairs Mabel had set up in a cozy nook at the back of the store. Penelope used it for her writing group, although her book group tended to array themselves in the mismatched overstuffed chairs and sofa that Mabel had also furnished the nook with.

The Open Book was to have a stall at the fest, and Penelope had offered to head the marketing committee with the help of India and Gladys. Regina Bosworth was the chairwoman of the fest itself.

"Shall we start without Regina?" India said, looking around the table for confirmation.

"Let's give her a few more minutes," Penelope said decisively.

It was now nearly ten minutes past the hour. Penelope opened her mouth to begin the meeting, but just then a voice rang out from behind one of the stacks.

"I'm here. I'm coming."

Regina rounded the corner, flapping her hands furiously. "So sorry, ladies, couldn't be helped. I've had such a busy morning. There's masses to get through yet before the Worthington Fest opens tomorrow. The Duke of Upper Chumley-on-Stoke had me positively running off my feet."

Penelope noticed India roll her eyes. Hardly anyone

referred to the duke by his title—around the village he was *Arthur Worthington* or simply *Worthington* and was often greeted familiarly by the patrons of the Book and Bottle, where he was known to regularly pony up for a round or two, as *Worthington, old chap.*

He and India were vaguely related. Penelope couldn't remember how, but she thought it was through India's mother's line. Of course, while India lived in somewhat straitened circumstances in a cottage on the grounds of the estate, Worthington had inherited the castle itself along with a substantial amount of money.

Regina took her seat. She straightened the Hermès scarf at her neck—the queen had one just like it, she never failed to point out—opened her Louis Vuitton handbag, and spread out her things—an expensive notebook with an embossed leather cover and a blue lacquered Mont Blanc fountain pen.

"Now, Penelope," Regina said in an officious tone, "would you like to make your report?" She folded her hands on the table in front of her.

India and Gladys turned to Penelope expectantly.

"You've all seen the banners along the high street," Penelope began, and the others nodded. "We've placed posters in all the shops along the high street as well."

Gladys nodded. "We have one in our window."

Gladys's husband owned the Pig in a Poke, Upper Chumley-on-Stoke's butcher shop.

"And Regina was brave enough to volunteer to be on our local BBC radio station to talk up the fest," Penelope said. "Brava, Regina."

"As if she would have turned that opportunity down," India whispered to Penelope.

Regina looked around the table and beamed at them. "Thank you. Thank you." She cast her eyes down demurely. "And," she said, pausing dramatically, "our little fest has been written up in the *Sun*."

Gladys gasped and clasped her hands to her chest. India looked equally startled. Stories from their little corner of the world rarely made it into the national papers.

Regina preened. "Gordon—that's my husband," she said to Penelope, "places a lot of ads with the *Sun* for his business. He pulled some strings and, well . . ." Regina batted her eyelashes.

She reached into her purse, pulled out a copy of a newspaper, and placed it on the table. She thumbed it open to the fifth page and tapped a headline with a crimson-manicured fingernail.

"Here it is. 'Upper Chumley-on-Stoke to hold its annual Worthington Fest on Saturday. Hosted by the Duke of Upper Chumley-on-Stoke and his American fiancée, the fest is an annual event'—well, you can read the rest yourselves." She turned the paper around so the others could see it.

A stock photo of the duke and Charlotte Davenport taken at some other event was included with the article. Penelope had seen Worthington from a distance once or twice as he sped through the village in his vintage Aston Martin but had never gotten a close-up look at him.

He had a roguish air about him—in the photograph, at least—with blue eyes that twinkled beneath thick, straight brows and a mouth that looked to be curved in a perpetual half smile—as if he was privy to an especially delicious secret.

Charlotte looked every inch the duchess she was about to become in a pale pink dress with a full skirt and lace bodice. Her blond hair was in a sleek bun at the nape of her neck and she carried a tiny clutch bag in one hand. Her other hand—with its four-carat diamond solitaire—was laid lightly on the duke's arm.

"I still don't know why Worthington chose that woman," Gladys said, tapping Charlotte's picture.

"Well," Regina said, raising an eyebrow, "they're not married yet, are they? Anything could happen."

Regina folded the newspaper back up and tucked it in her handbag, and they went back to the business at hand, finishing up their meeting half an hour later. Regina gathered her things together and immediately took off at a trot, yelling over her shoulder that the duke was waiting for her and she simply mustn't be late. Everyone stood in a cluster as they listened for the sound of the door closing behind her.

"That woman becomes more insufferable by the day," India said. "Nouveau riche," she declared as if that explained it.

"I don't know why Worthington chose her to be the chairwoman of the fest," Gladys grumbled, her expression stormy.

"Quite," India said. "I understand that competition for the position was dreadfully fierce among the ladies of Chumley."

"She probably badgered him until he cried uncle," Penelope said.

India made a sound like a snort.

"I wonder what she meant about Worthington and Charlotte not being married yet," Penelope said. "It almost sounded like she was hinting at something. As if she knew something."

Gladys laughed. "What could Regina possibly know about it?"

"I don't know." India frowned. "But Regina collects secrets the way some people collect stamps. And she's not afraid to make use of them either."

Ready to find
your next great read?

Let us help.

Visit prh.com/nextread